My Story

CADOGAN SQUARE

Carol Drinkwater

■SCHOLASTIC

While the events described and some of the characters in this book may be based on actual historical events and real people, Flora Bonnington and Dollie Baxter are fictional characters, created by the author, and their diaries are works of fiction.

Scholastic Children's Books
Euston House, 24 Eversholt Street,
London, NW1 1DB, UK
A division of Scholastic Ltd
London ~ New York ~ Toronto ~ Sydney ~ Auckland
Mexico City ~ New Delhi ~ Hong Kong

First published in the UK in this edition by Scholastic Ltd, 2012

1900: A Brand-New Century
First published in the UK by Scholastic Ltd, 2001
(as *My Story: Twentieth-Century Girl*)
Published as *My Story: 1900: A Brand-New Century,* 2010
Text copyright © Carol Drinkwater, 2001

Suffragette
First published in the UK by Scholastic Ltd, 2003
Text copyright © Carol Drinkwater, 2003

Additional material © Carol Drinkwater, 2012

ISBN 978 1407 13476 5

Printed and bound by CPI Group (UK) Ltd, Croydon, CR0 4YY

2 4 6 8 10 9 7 5 3 1

The right of Carol Drinkwater to be identified as the author of this work has been asserted by her in accordance with the Copyright, Designs and Patents Act, 1988.

1900: A Brand-New Century

Cadogan Square, London, 18th December 1899

I shrieked and then shrieked again; each cry growing louder and more fearful. I covered my eyes. I couldn't bear to look and then I uncovered them again because I couldn't bear *not* to look! Lord, I was *so* afraid. I truly believed that the oncoming train was heading directly at me and that it was about to run me down and kill me! It was thrilling, and so lifelike. I swear that if I had been blindfolded, then transported by carriage, escorted to my seat and only allowed to open my eyes when I was in my place and the lights had gone to pitch darkness, I would never have guessed where I was. Pictures in motion! Who would ever have thought that such a thing could be dreamed of or that the created images could make you feel as though what you are watching is actually happening and that your life truly is in danger?

Afterwards, in the carriage home, reflecting on what I had seen and that all the images had been dark grey, I said to Miss Baker – she is my governess and it was she who took me to the moving picture house – "Strange that there's no colour. The trees in the background of the pictures, as well as the sky above, they were all varying shades of grey. And there was no sound. You don't *hear* the whistle of the approaching train, you cannot *hear* the hiss of its steam, or the locomotive's wheels rolling fast along the iron tracks."

"That's right, Flora, you cannot hear those things but you *see* them, see them moving, just as if they were real."

It is curious and I don't quite understand it yet, but it's such an exciting world to be caught up in. Altogether we saw ten different sequences, each lasting about a minute. Oh, I want everyone to go there and experience what I have experienced: moving pictures!

19th December 1899

"The only sound is the live pianist who accompanies each moving picture. He varies his tunes to suit the mood of each piece. I think he is there to create atmosphere. You know, a bit of drama and then lighter music for the comical bits."

I was recounting my outing of yesterday to my father, my sister, Henrietta, and also Grandmama during supper earlier this evening.

"Yes, I've heard about these flickering photographs," said Father. "I can't say that I really approve. I sincerely hope that

Miss Baker has not taken you to some amusement arcade to view this exhibition. Where was it held?"

"Oh, Thomas Bonnington! Do, for heaven's sake, stop being so stuffy! Miss Baker is a responsible young woman and a fine governess."

"Mmm, she's too 'modern', in my opinion. I don't want her teaching my two daughters bad habits."

"The event was held in a hall off Baker Street. It was perfectly respectable, Papa," I replied, with lessening enthusiasm. Why is it that Papa always manages to make me feel that what I have done is wrong? I am sure he doesn't intend to be so cold or indifferent.

"I would never have agreed to go," Henrietta chimed in, and I wanted to kick her under the table. She is such a perfectly well-behaved young lady and she always sides with Father. The fact is they always seem to side with each other.

"Tell us everything about it, Flora, my dear. I am dying to hear!" cried Grandmama, who is fascinated by any new idea.

"Well, it consists of photographic images," I began. "They are projected one after another, very, very fast on to a blank screen. The speed makes them flicker and creates the illusion of movement."

"How can it possibly do such a thing?" sneered Henry. (Henry's my nickname for my horrid older sister!)

"What is the subject of these pictures?"

"Well, they are about all different things, Grandmama. But the one which made me jump out of my skin was of a

5

locomotive train travelling right towards the camera. It was coming so fast I screamed, thinking that it would burst out of the screen and run me over!"

How my family laughed at me.

"Fancy being afraid of a photograph," scorned Henry, but I assured them that until you go and see it for yourself, sitting there in front of that giant screen, you cannot experience how *real* the motion of the pictures feels. According to Miss Baker, the idea was invented by two brothers in Paris who own the most successful factory in Europe for the manufacture of photographic plates and equipment. Their name is Lumière which is quite a curious coincidence because the translation from French of the word *lumière* is *light*, and you cannot make photographs without light! (Miss Baker teaches me French and she was very impressed that I remembered the word from my book of nouns!)

It is going to be the entertainment of the new century, she says. Oh, I hope so. It will be much more fun than going to a magic lantern show or the circus. There is something about the circus which rather upsets me. It's hard to say why exactly because I love the smell of sawdust and I don't mind all that pushing to get to one's seat through the great press of ordinary working people, who are as excited as I am at the prospect of a show. And I love all the bands playing lively tunes, the acrobats turning somersaults; those are great fun. But it's the animals. Yes, that's it. I cannot bear to see all those poor elephants trudging around in endless circles, with a ringmaster holding a whip to their backsides, bullying the poor creatures into standing on their hind legs like hungry dogs begging for titbits.

Dear Miss Baker, it was so kind of her to take me along with her to the house of moving pictures. I shall have to find something very special to buy her as a Christmas present in return.

21st December 1899

Preparations are afoot for the festive season. I have strict instructions to keep Bassett, our hound, well clear of the kitchens where there is a bustle of activity. Three plump geese have been purchased by Cook. Tomorrow, Harrods will deliver them and they will be plucked and then stuffed with onions and chestnuts and other divinely delicious things for our Christmas lunch. And then, for the last night of this dying nineteenth century into which both I and my sister have been born, Papa is preparing a very splendid and divinely swish party. Henrietta will be eighteen in January so Papa has decided to end this year with a houseful of guests. It is quite unlike him. Usually, he buries himself in his work and dedicates his spare time to his boring old accounts. He rarely has time for us, his two daughters.

Later the same day

Whichever room I pass through, the sweet tangy perfume of tangerines fills the air. It is one of my favourite smells because it always reminds me that Christmas is here once more. We are promised "a white one" this year. Or so Jenny, one of our maids, informed me as she built up the coal fire in my bedroom hearth. She pronounces the forecast, in that strong cockney accent of hers which I could not even begin to imitate, with such delightful certainty that I would never dare question how she could be so sure of such a thing.

Miss Baker left this afternoon with her suitcase, off to the station to take the train home to her family in Shrewsbury. I wished her a splendid Christmas and gave her the small bottle of scent from Worth which I bought for her this morning.

22nd December 1899

"Rise and shine, Lady Flora Bonnington!" Jenny's plump cheeks were flushed with pride this morning when she came in to wake me. She pulled up the blinds, called me to the window and, when I peered out, I discovered that it was snowing! What a beautiful sight! And to complete the picture, a robin was perched on the outer sill, tilting his head and fluffing his feathers and strutting to and fro in a very self-important way, as though he had been there for ages, impatiently waiting for lazy old me to "rise and shine"! His were the sole prints in a deliciously crisp, white world.

"I told you, didn't I?" Jenny yelled, as she began to prepare my bath.

Our tree is being delivered before lunch and Papa has promised that it will be tremendously tall.

Grandmama, Henry and I are going to Harrods this afternoon to shop for presents and crackers and coloured-glass decorations to hang on our tree. After, Grandmama has promised us tall mugs of hot chocolate and cream puffs at the coffee shop across the street from the store. What a divine day!

I bought a journal and have begun to transfer all my scribblings of the last few days into it. It will record my journey into the new century. I shall call it "Twentieth-Century Girl", for that is what I intend to be!

23rd December 1899

There were secret comings and goings today as a large box arrived at the tradesmen's entrance and was instantly vanished away out of sight. I was in the kitchen at the time, starving and in search of a delicious snack, or I wouldn't have known a thing about it. Judging by the expressions on the faces of both Cook and Jones (he is our butler and a simply divine sport), and the general carry on, I am guessing it was a Christmas present for *ME*. What on earth could it be, I wonder? It looked heavy and was sort of squarish and large and, due to the manner in which it was being handled, I think rather fragile. When I asked Jonesy to give me a clue, he simply winked and trotted away.

I can't wait, I love surprises!

24th December 1899

Bassett is dozing on the rug in front of the fire. He is making funny snuffling noises and seems to be dreaming happily. It is late and I am completely exhausted, but I cannot sleep. Instead, I have been occupying myself with the joyfully secret business of wrapping my Christmas gifts: a leather journal for Henry (far more stylish than the one I bought for myself), a brooch for Grandmama, boxes of chocolates for Jenny and Anna and Cook, a hairbrush for Jones and a silver photograph frame for Papa. When all that was accomplished I curled up lazily in my nightgown on to this cushioned sill. Except to note these few lines in my journal, I have not moved from here these last two hours. I have no motivation to read and so have been staring out of my bedroom window on to the crisp tranquillity of Cadogan Square. Nose pressed against the cold steamy glass, I have been watching the comings and goings of strangers and neighbours and cherishing these hectic days and navy, starry nights because they are the very last I shall ever see of this century.

The clip-clop of the horses' hooves drawing late-night carriages filled with exhausted partygoers is muffled by the deeply lying snow. Passing pedestrians, tightly wrapped in extravagantly flowing fur overcoats, move swiftly towards their destinations while their breath rises like clouds of smoked tobacco towards the brightly burning, gas street lamps. How I love London in winter! And how excited I am feeling.

Time is marching forward, carrying us over the threshold and pitching us, willy-nilly, into a new century. The prospect of growing up in that unexplored territory is so thrilling that I fancy, if I close my eyes tight, I can almost see the process taking place! The clock ticks, its hands turn, chimes ring out the hours, servants change linen, meals are prepared, footsteps creak on the landing, calls of "Goodnight" from the carpeted stairs: Christmas approaches like a cheery friend. A day slips away like sand in a sandglass and then another day dawns and so we are caught up in this inevitable passage towards 1900. And here I am, Flora Bonnington, being drawn helplessly along with it, whether I wish it or no. Oh, but yes, I do wish it, fervently. All my life, save for these first fourteen-and-a-half years, will be lived out there, in the twentieth century. Exit 1899, enter 1900. How it makes me question my future. What will become of me in this soon-to-be-born century? Will I look back on these days as happy ones, remembering *me* before I grew up into a young aristocratic lady? Or will my life be snatched from me, tragically and without warning, like my darling mother who is and always will remain a stranger to me? Might I achieve great things and be applauded for my wisdom, energy and grace, like dearest Grandmama? Or will I follow in my father's footsteps and take the city by storm? I think I can safely predict that I shan't be going into business and making millions like Papa for I have no real head for figures and such matters are tedious to me. In any case, such opportunities are not available to women. We live in a world ruled and governed by men.

My father is Thomas Bonnington. He has his offices in the Square Mile of London which is the city's prosperous financial quarter. His company is named after him: Bonningtons. It is a well-known and highly esteemed import and export business, transporting merchandise from the British colonies worldwide into London's Docklands.

As you might imagine, Papa is a very wealthy man. He is also a good and fair father and I love him deeply, but we do not think alike. It is not that we quarrel, it is simply that I feel I would have been better understood by my mother. In any case, he is so rarely available to us. He is too busy with his work as a merchant and a businessman. (Grandmama calls him a "gentleman capitalist"!) His ambitions for my future are not my own. He wants nothing more than to see me and my older sister, Henrietta, happily married, living in fine London homes, the toast of respectable society with upright husbands and families of our own. Henry dreams those dreams, too. But I am restless. I have longings within me. I want to do something special with my life though I have no idea what that *something* is. Just so long as it is exciting and I do not have to live a run-of-the-mill type of existence.

To be an artist or a bohemian or a campaigner, any of those would be marvellous, but the thought of simply being someone's wife fills me with a kind of horror. People tell me that I talk nonsense and that it is because I am too young to understand. When I meet the right man for me, they say, I will know it and be happy. Even Miss Baker says such things, yet she's not married and she's already past 28.

Grandmama doesn't talk like the others. She listens to what I have to say and encourages me. I tell her that I would like to go to university and read languages or literature and she approves of that idea. In fact, she spurs me on. My mother went to university. She was part of the first wave of British women to go on to higher education. That was thanks to the vision and encouragement of my dear grandmother, Lady Violet Campbell, who lives with us in our five-storey home in Cadogan Square and about whom I shall write reams later. It is getting cold sitting on this windowsill, my toes are tingling and I am falling asleep. Tomorrow is Christmas! Hooray!

25th December 1899

Well, what a magnificent surprise! The box I accidentally witnessed being delivered the other morning turns out to be our present from Papa. It is to be shared by Henry and me, but will be for the pleasure of us all. What a moment when Father unwrapped it. He insisted on doing it. "In case we damaged it," he said. Then, he play-acted and staged the whole thing, just like a conjuror. At the very instant, the box-machine was revealed, Father called, "Hey, jingo!" and *orchestra music came out of it.* The gift wrapping fell to the floor, Bassett began tearing at the ribbons and papers and we stood in awe and amazement.

"I believe it's a phonograph, dears!" said Grandmama.

"Quite right, Violet, that is exactly what it is," said Father, smiling.

It really is a most remarkable invention. I had heard about them but had never actually heard one playing before. It is quite extraordinary to cluster around it in the drawing room and listen to sounds coming out of it. Music from a box! What a world I am growing up into! Here, in our very own home, we have a machine that plays tunes and only one week ago, I saw moving pictures without any sound. What a step it would be if, in this new century which awaits us, a method could be found to somehow gel these two discoveries together and create moving pictures with sound! But I fantasize! Perhaps I should grow up to be an inventor, then I could create these ideas myself. Think how splendid that would be!

Grandmama has given me a most beautiful, leather-bound book of plays by a Russian playwright who I do not know but who is becoming highly regarded, she tells me. His name is Anton Chekhov. Henry gave me a very elegant tortoiseshell hair slide which should keep my wretched hair from always falling all over my face. Lovely presents, all of them. I feel deliciously spoilt. After lunch, Papa took Henry and me for a drive round Hyde Park in his new horseless carriage. Bassett came with us and barked and howled at everything and everyone, and made us laugh merrily. We saw several others with similar vehicles; they seem to be becoming quite the rage, and Papa hooted and we waved. It was rather like another boat passing by when you are punting on the river. Everybody honks and cheers and waves. It's quite curious really, but thoroughly enjoyable.

There were crowds of people about because, in spite of the snow these last few days, the sun was shining a gentle lukewarm. We were driving through a perfect, pure white world. There was snow on the grass and branches of the tall, spreading trees and the sky was streaky with milky-white clouds. Fortunately, we had wrapped up warm with dozens of scarves, mink mittens and rugs because this new vehicle is less protected than our old carriage. It catches the wind and is a blustery adventure, but also a thrilling one.

Hyde Park was wintry, but magical. There were many parties skating on the frozen water. Nannies sat nattering together on park benches, watching out for the skaters or wheeling small children in prams, young boys were throwing snowballs or building snowmen and I saw dozens of couples wrapped and muffled in woolly scarves to protect against the cold. How comical they looked, like tortoises standing on their hind legs, holding hands. Tranquil holiday pastimes. I felt exquisitely happy.

As I watched everyone and took in the passing sights, I was trying to imagine how it would be to make moving pictures of some of the scenes I was witnessing. A skater turning and falling on the ice, for example. But would that image be as dramatic and scary as the train driving into the camera? Or might it be a sight to make the audience roar with laughter? What does it depend on, I asked myself? The position of the camera? I long to learn more and wish I knew someone who could teach me.

Later, before tea, at Grandmama's insistence, Henry and I accompanied her on a brisk walk through the gas-lit streets to Brompton oratory to hear organ music by the French composer, Saint-Saëns. It was heavenly, but quite complex.

I am stuffed with good food, but not too much so. It has been a truly memorable Christmas Day.

26th December 1899

Curled up in the warmth of the drawing room, a fire crackling in front of me, I glance up from my book, out towards the tree-lined streets and crescents of London where snow is falling again and settling softly. I am reading my Chekhov. Marvellous scenes crammed with snowstorms and passionate emotions. Those Russian lives and their country *dachas* seem all the more real to me today because by looking on to that expanse of untouched whiteness beyond my windows, I can very easily picture all those Russian characters living out their hopes and despairs.

Grandmama tells me that, before too long, Russia will most likely fall into the hands of the working class. She predicts that the farmworkers and servants will revolt and may grow violent – not unlike France towards the end of the last century, during the time of their Revolution. "Why?" I asked her.

"Because there is so much poverty and inequality between the landowners and the working people."

"Will they chop off the heads of the Tsar and his Tsarina," I asked her, "in the same way the French chopped off the royal heads?"

"It wouldn't surprise me, dear."

My grandmother was once a landowner of some standing but now she is a socialist, as my mother might have been had she lived. Grandmama hoots with laughter and accuses me of being preposterous sometimes because I describe her as a *revolutionary*. "You have such an air of the dramatic, Flora. I am a socialist, young lady, as I hope you will be when you begin to put your mind to such matters." She brought my mother up to believe in and fight for the rights of women, but Mama died five days after I was born, so I never knew her. I was never given the opportunity to discuss with her what she thought about Grandmama's ideals. And I never discuss such matters with Papa because I suspect he doesn't approve. He always grows silent and serious when the conversation turns to such subjects, though to be fair to Papa, he never openly criticizes Grandmama or her ideas.

It was after the death of my mother that Grandmama sold her estates and came south to live with us, keeping only one large country house in Gloucestershire which is where we go for weekends from time to time.

28th December 1899

How I long for Miss Baker to return from her family holiday so that we can make another visit to the moving pictures.

I cannot stop thinking of the experience and must learn more about it. Today, in Paris, four years ago, was the first public showing of the moving images.

Preparations for our end-of-year house party leave me no time to write more. I have a new dress. It is silk aquamarine. I am anxious about it because it feels horribly formal which is most unsuitable for me. I feel as though I must not move when I am wearing it, in case it tears, but Jenny reassures me by saying, I look a "right royal treat"!

31st December 1899

Grandmother has gone to the Embankment, where the down-and-outs sleep, to dish out cups of steaming Bovril. I offered to accompany her but she would not hear of it.

"Why?" I protested. "Are you concerned that I would be upset by such squalor?"

"I do not feel a need to protect you from life, Flora, but your father requires your presence here. You must assist with the reception of guests. I shall be back well before midnight and not a soul apart from you and I will have noticed my absence."

Which, of course, is entirely untrue. Everyone will ask after her and Father will smile politely and tell the truth and our society friends will coo and judge Grandmama terrifically lively but eccentric, which she is. Still, few recognize her for her real worth except Papa who, though he does not agree with her politics at all, respects the mould my mother was cast from. In any case, no one could deny that Grandmama is intellectually brilliant and a force in her own right. She is a brave and independent woman. I often think that the loss of her only child must have caused her immense grief and much to reflect on. She never discusses these matters with me. I like to imagine that if my mother had not died she would have been like my grandmother. I can see from the photographs I have of her and the two portraits that Papa keeps in his bedroom that she was as elegant and handsome as my grandmother is.

I must stop writing and hurry downstairs for I hear Bassett barking, the chatter of arriving guests and Jones taking coats and greeting folk at the front door.

1st January 1900

Father invited a jolly group of people to our supper party last evening. Well, there were one or two old fuddy bores, like Sir Vincent Andersen, but not many. Amongst them all was a journalist whose name is Winston Churchill. I think

Henry was rather smitten with him; she didn't take her eyes off him all evening. I thought at first that if I were going to fall in love, which I'd really rather not, I might pick such a type. Not for his stature or looks, but because he's a writer, well-travelled, and because he has an individual, thinking mind. Although, on reflection, Mr Churchill is rather fond of the sound of his own voice. Once he got going he talked unstintingly and did not seem to have a mind to stop. I think he has been a soldier but now he's a correspondent in South Africa, writing for the *Morning Post*. He referred on several occasions to his experiences in the Boer War. Father asked him his opinion of the young back-bencher Lloyd George who vehemently opposes that war in Africa. Mr Churchill replied, "I believe it will not be long before he is a major player in mainstream politics. Yes, in my humble opinion, Mr Lloyd George will go far, sir." He went on to describe Lloyd George as a jolly good orator and said that you can't get far in politics these days without such an asset. The way he talked, I began to think he was practising for office himself!

Both he and Father discussed politics – for too long, in my opinion – and the mighty power and prosperity of the British Empire. My poor ears were ringing with it all. I was growing weary and drowsy, but then Grandmama returned and brightened up the evening. She was looking flushed from the cold, but full of beans.

"I believe you are all acquainted with my mother-in-law, Lady Violet Campbell?" said Father, rising as Gran approached.

"Forgive my tardy arrival," she cried with gleaming eyes and open arms. She came straight to the table, gave both Henry and me a big hug, sat herself down and asked Jones to bring her a whisky. "Be a dear, Jonesy," she said to him, *sotto voce*, "and bring the old girl a large double."

Jones smiled and withdrew.

Her behaviour usually causes a flurry of interest – sometimes, shock – for some of her good works have been written about and certainly her politics are talked of.

"Do you not fear for your safety, Madam, alone on the Embankment late at night in the midst of so many cut-throats and ruffians? Surely, you will agree that it is no place for a woman and most certainly not an unaccompanied lady?" Sir Vincent Andersen, one of Father's business colleagues or competitors, whichever he is, quizzed her – rather too sharply, I thought. Gran sipped her drink and warmed her hands by the fire. Lord, she was excellent. Then, she leant across the table, elegantly caressing her fine pearl necklace with her long fingers, smiled disarmingly and enquired: "Pray, what, in your opinion, *is* the place for women in this mighty empire of ours?"

"Women, Madam?" he asked in a rather confused manner. I fear he is used to conferring only with gentlemen and Gran's forthright approach can be alarming.

"Do you not feel that as we sally forth into a new century,

a new brand of woman is called for? Or would you feel safer if we all stayed home, checking our laundry lists?"

That stopped old whiskery Andersen in his tracks. His pink cheeks were flushed with temper. "Women belong at home, Madam. Every well-bred woman knows that her contribution is as a mother and a wife and that public office should be left to the gentlemen. My good wife certainly knows it," was his response. Meanwhile his plump wife blushed, nodded obediently and stuffed a hefty morsel of cherry pie into her mouth.

Grandmother smiled and said no more.

Then young Winston piped up, "What brand of new woman are you speaking of, Lady Campbell?"

"The pioneering woman who is fighting for our rights. One who is filled with the energy and enthusiasm necessary to create national awareness."

"I fear it is going to take a great deal more, Lady Campbell, than vociferous idealism, to make every girl and housewife reconsider her place in society."

"Well, I, for one, am not daunted by the work needed to achieve our goals. A new century is dawning, in 25 minutes it will have dawned, and I want every female, no, every citizen, to question and reject the world we are living in. Such pioneers of this new, twentieth century must needs be as brave as the soldiers you so loudly applaud, Mr Churchill. But we need something more."

"And what is that, pray, Lady Campbell?"

"We need to be angry and determined, at all costs, to shake up the fusty attitudes of this male-dominated society in which we women are kept down like lesser beings. Times are changing, Mr Churchill. Women are not objects put on this earth for the amusement and convenience of men. We never were. The difference is that now women everywhere are waking up to their potential and they are no longer willing to tolerate the situation."

Mr Churchill went pale with shock. As did several other guests. There was a certain amount of coughing and shuffling of chairs. I feared she had gone too far, but Grandmama was not to be deterred. Clearly, she was as impatient with the masculine chatter of wars and fighting and imperialism as I had been.

Smiling broadly, eyes twinkling, she sailed on. "Still, when my Twentieth-Century Woman has won the day, as she no doubt will during the early years of this approaching decade, I pray that she will enjoy the very same levels of freedom as you gentlemen cherish."

"I can envisage no such female," Sir Vincent cut in curtly.

"But of course, you can't, Sir Vincent, because you do not want to. Our Twentieth-Century Woman will be an inconvenience to you," said Gran with a smile. It was tremendous to listen to her argue her case without ever losing her cool or her grace or good manners.

Father rang for Jones and ordered the champagne. It

was twenty minutes to midnight and I sensed that he was desperate for the diversion. Moments later, two of the maids came through carrying silver trays of crystal champagne flutes. These were distributed in silence.

"Thank you dears, Anna and Jenny. In this new century, what I wish for my two granddaughters here, as well as for those two young women who have just left the room, is that they will be able to hold their heads high, having won the right to vote for the government of the country in which they live, Mr Churchill. And once they have the right to a voice in politics, then they can begin to take part in the governing of this country…"

"Grandmama, you talk as though every woman wanted the vote. Not all of us care for such a tedious responsibility!" It was Henrietta interrupting, in a very impatient manner. We have always been brought up to respect one another's opinions, never to cut them short, but Henry cannot abide it when Grandmama gets going on suffrage or social matters.

"Let your grandmother complete her thought, Henrietta," said Father without rancour.

"Thank you, Thomas. To me it is an unpalatable fact that Britain maintains the greatest empire this planet has ever known – we govern islands in every ocean of the world, have staked our Union Jack in distant outposts, somewhere in the region of 400 million people of every caste and colour are ruled by our Queen and her parliament, we build colonies and instruct on a world scale – and yet we do not regard women as equals."

"You exaggerate, Lady Campbell." This was Robert Booth talking. He writes for the *Daily Telegraph* newspaper. "In the last 40 years we have conceded the right to higher education for women and given several financial benefits. What more can women seriously desire?"

"The vote, Mr Booth. Women do not have the right to vote, and we cannot claim sexual equality. A delicate issue which I will not address in the company of young girls, but where is the enlightenment in such thinking, Mr Booth?"

"Pah! The vote is a dream, Lady Campbell. What do women know of politics and governments?"

Before this argument went any further, Mr Churchill tactfully intervened. "And you, Miss Henrietta, what are your thoughts on the subject, what do you wish for yourself in this new approaching century?"

"My interests and hopes are simple, Mr Churchill, and befit a young lady of breeding, though neither my grandmother or sister would agree with my sentiments. I dream of an honourable marriage and countless children but, before having children, I hope for a life of modish balls and weekends spent at the grandest of country houses with weekly visits to play golf at the links or promenades to the seaside."

"You have a daughter of sound mind, Thomas," declared Sir Vincent, rubbing his greying mutton chop whiskers. His wife nodded her agreement again but she did not speak for she was engaged in another slice of tart.

For my part, I felt ashamed for Henry. I caught the look in Mr Churchill's eyes and I felt sure that the picture she had painted would bore him to tears.

"And so I wish it for you," was his response. "For if your beauty is the mark of your power, then you will be free to command whatever your heart desires."

Henry grinned, melting at his words.

"And what of you, Miss Flora?"

"I should like to be involved in the making of moving pictures," I replied without hesitation. Mr Churchill looked most amazed. "Really, well that's a most unusual response. I believe they are all the rage in Paris though I have not seen any myself."

"Oh you must, sir, they will be the entertainment of the new century," which sent everyone around the table into gales of laughter. I have no idea why.

"You mustn't pay any attention to my young Flora, she is young yet and still a dreamer," said Father. Then the clock struck midnight and he asked Jones to put out the oil lamps and, when that was achieved, he rose to his feet in the candlelight, to propose a toast. What an impressive figure he was in his starched white evening shirt and bow-tie, his black coat and evening tails, standing in the dusky glow at the head of our dining table. Behind him, his shadow loomed tall and imposing and I suddenly felt sick in my stomach, believing that the day would come when I could not help but disappoint him.

"To my two daughters," he began. "May this twentieth century bring them both good fortune and the fine husbands and loving obedient children they both deserve. To all of us here, health and prosperity. And to our Queen, Victoria and her glorious British Empire."

Everyone rose. "The Queen," they roared.

I bowed my head. Into this new century I was about to pour my life. "Please, let me make good of it," I muttered to myself.

Outside, in Cadogan Square, a crowd of neighbours began to let off fireworks in the private gardens. They whizzed and whooshed past our windows lighting up each of the faces within the room with a rosy glow. All over London, fireworks were cracking, people were shouting and calling. I closed my eyes an instant. Flora Bonnington, I said to myself, may you grow up to be a fine Twentieth-Century Woman. When I opened my eyes, everybody in the room was moving between chairs, shaking hands and expressing goodwill.

"Come, Flora, let us offer our good wishes to the heart of the house," said Gran and she led me by the arm to the kitchen where Cook and Jonesy and Anna and Jenny were toasting one another with glasses of sherry. Cook's cheeks were as red as beetroots from all the roasting and basting and, no doubt, from the sherry. Gran stepped forward and gave each of them an embrace.

"Thank you for a very splendid evening," she said. "I wish peace and dignity and prosperity to each of you."

I think the tippling had loosened them up a little for they joked with her and told her what a fine but eccentric mistress she was and then we left them to their partying and returned to the guests.

Later, while Jenny unpinned Henrietta's hair, Henry sighed in a most lovesick manner and then asked me, "Do you think you could fall in love with that young writer, Flo?"

"Mr Churchill! He's far too old. He must be at least twenty-SIX. It is true that he is intellectually quite brilliant but he never stops talking. And besides what does he know of women apart from charming them senseless, which is probably the goal of every man?"

"Why must you always talk like Grandmama?" she cried and stormed from the dressing room in her corset and petticoats, leaving me alone with poor bemused Jenny who was helpless with a handful of pins and her work half accomplished.

2nd January 1900

I talked to a fascinating young man on New Year's Eve. I had no time to mention him in yesterday's entry. His name was Leonard something or other. He was very gangly and tall with sandy hair and a freckled complexion. I believe he said that he is reading Classics at Cambridge though I am not too sure because there were so many guests to talk to and remember. At first I did not pay him a great deal of attention, but then he returned to my remark about the moving pictures and claimed to have an interest in the subject himself. When I asked him if he had seen the Lumière brothers' exhibition, he told me that he had and has seen several others from their displays in Paris. It was Louis Lumière himself, Leonard informed me, who photographed the moving pictures I saw.

"The travelling train sequence is entitled: *Arrivée d'un train à la Ciotat*. Or in English, *Arrival of a train at Ciotat*. Louis Lumière is the driving force behind the whole enterprise. It was very realistic, don't you agree?"

"I do! I screamed loudly and felt quite afraid."

"Lumière used a special new camera which he has constructed at the Lumière factory."

I learnt from Leonard that they showed their moving pictures to a paying audience for the very first time at the Grand Café in the Boulevard des Capucines in Paris. It is proving to be an enormous success. Not only are there viewings in London now, but also in many other major European capitals. Even places as exotic and far afield as Mexico City and Alexandria in Egypt.

"Thomas Edison, I am sure you have heard of that man, Flora?"

"You mean, the American who invented the light bulb?"

"Yes, he did, as well as the splendid phonograph your father has been playing to us this evening. That's the fellow. He has been marketing a contrivance called the kinetoscope, more commonly known as the peep show. Well, he's very interested in this new type of camera. He wants to take it to America. In fact, this new apparatus is very similar to his kinetoscope but working at a higher stage of development," explained Leonard who spoke with as much passion and interest as I had been exhibiting. "Edison has built a small studio in the grounds where his laboratories are based in New Jersey, America. He calls the studio 'Black Maria'. There, he has been making moving pictures, each of which lasts about twenty seconds. Oh, I believe this moving picture business has far-reaching possibilities."

"So do I," I cried.

"It is already highly international. Exhibitions in Osaka, Japan and Melbourne in Australia, even Maracaibo in Venezuela. I can think of no finer way to work and see the world."

"I have been thinking the very same thing!"

Just at that moment Father approached us from amongst the chattering guests.

"Has our young Flora got you going on this moving picture craze of hers? She really is quite a fan of it. No lasting harm in it, I suppose, as long as it does not interfere with her education and she doesn't take it too seriously. It's important for young ladies to be able to amuse themselves, just so long as it is in a decent fashion."

And that put an end to our conversation because, once Papa left us, Leonard looked a bit awkward and moved on to talk to someone else, and soon after it was time for everyone to go home.

How I would love to own one of those cameras! I could never persuade Papa to buy me one for my birthday. They are surely exorbitantly expensive, and he does not consider it anything but an amusement. Anyway, perhaps there is only the one in the world and Louis Lumière must guard it jealously, which is precisely what I would do. But, oh, a moving pictures camera!

4th January 1900

I managed to catch Gran on her own this afternoon. She was in the drawing room and I invited myself to sit with her. I had been thinking about the debate at the table on New Year's Eve and I wanted her to tell me all about her experiences. "Gladly," she cried, squeezing my hand, and then rang for tea and scones.

Gran is a follower of the women's suffrage movement. Actually, she is one of the founding members of the London Society for Women's Suffrage which was created in 1867.

"I would like to be a Twentieth-Century Woman, Grandmama," I declared nervously. "I don't want to end up like Sir Vincent Andersen's wife. I want to achieve something special and wonderful with my life."

Grandmama placed her book on the arm of the sofa alongside her and looked at me intently. "I believe you will, Flora," she smiled softly. "You are a brave and courageous girl and that counts for a great deal. You remind me so much of…"

Tea arrived, brought in by Anna. Grandmama thanked her warmly and asked her if Cook would be kind enough to send us through some of her delicious biscuits.

I waited eagerly, bursting with curiosity. And when Anna had left us, I did not give Gran one second to pour our tea. "Of what, Gran?"

"Of Millicent. Your mother, dear."

"Was she brave?"

Gran nodded. "Brave and very beautiful. But let us talk of you. What would you like me to talk to you about?"

"First tell me, what does it mean exactly, the word *suffrage*?"

"Well, the actual definition of the word is to give support to, to vote for or side with. In our case, in this instance, women's suffrage is about females supporting one another.

A suffragette is a female who is fighting for the right of women to vote. Some suffragettes go further – they want women to have the same rights as men; we call this equal rights."

"How did it get started in the first place?" I asked her.

"It is almost impossible to pinpoint these matters to one single date. I suppose, the movement began up north, in Sheffield, in 1851 when the Sheffield Women's Political Association was formed. While in the late '50s, here in London, I was involved with a very dynamic group of women who called themselves the Langham Place group. But suffrage really got going in the '60s."

"Why? Why did it happen then?"

"Women were – still are – dissatisfied with, and brought down by, the role forced upon them by a society which is ruled by men. As things stand now women are ruled by men. Men are the privileged class and women are cast as the lesser, the weaker of the two sexes, which is utter nonsense."

"Do you hate men, Grandmama?"

My question made her laugh loudly and she paused, stroked my head and buttered herself a scone. "Of course not, dear! There are many men I respect and admire. But there are, equally, many women who deserve to be respected and admired. Unfortunately, they are so rarely given the opportunities to achieve the goals they dream of in life, or of reaching their full potential, because the laws – laid down by men – do not allow them certain rights."

I chewed for a while thinking about what she was telling me. I dolloped a second helping of jam on my scone and tried to think it through.

"How did you get involved in the London Society?"

"Well, there we were, my dear Flora, in the year of 1867, awaiting an amendment to a parliamentary bill which was known as the Reform Act. If the amendment was accepted, it promised to give equal voting rights to women. But unfortunately the bill – voted upon exclusively by men, I hasten to add – was passed but without the change we so passionately had hoped for. A wider selection of men had been given voting rights but not a single woman. Lord, we were furious with Benjamin Disraeli, Chancellor at the time, and the government. It was so frustrating and upsetting because the matter was out of our control. So, we decided that it was time to go to work and create awareness amongst the female sex throughout the capital. Take power into our own hands."

"Was that the real beginning of suffrage?"

"It was not the very beginning but it was a turning point for us. Things began to change in the '60s. There were some marvellous women working with us; Florence Nightingale, Josephine Butler, Emily Davis to name but a few. I was living in London at the time. As I say, we were frustrated and felt betrayed by what had happened – or rather had *not* happened with the Reform Act, so a group of us founded the London Society. I suggested that we start writing pamphlets and hand them out wherever we could. You see, half the trouble is that so many women have never questioned their roles as subordinates of men. They are asleep, dear! Look at your sister, what a remark to make: Some women don't want the 'tedious responsibility'! If only she could understand that it is about so much more than simply being given the vote. Why, when I was a girl, and that is not as long ago as you might think, Flora, we were forced to stand up and fight for rights which you young things already take for granted."

"What sort of rights?"

"Property rights, higher education, admission to the medical profession, as well as sole custody of our own children."

"What does that mean, 'sole custody'?" I asked her.

"Up until fourteen years ago, the year after you were born, dear, if a man died and left children behind, his wife was not allowed to be the legal parent of her sons and daughters. Consider it a moment. A mother was obliged to continue her role as a parent alongside a nominated male who, in the eyes of the law, was the child's guardian."

"Why?"

"Women were not judged sufficiently wise to make the necessary decisions regarding the upbringing or education of their children."

Anna came through with the plate of biscuits. I was puzzling about why we are not thought wise. And when Anna had left, I said to Gran, "It seems a bit unfair and skew-whiff to me to refuse women the chance of further education and then tell them that they are not wise enough to look after their own children."

"My dear, you are a suffragette in the making!" she hooted. "How right you are. You see, it's a vicious circle."

I had finished my scone and jam so I helped myself to one of Cook's ginger biscuits. She makes them herself and they are utterly delicious; chewy and not too hard or crumbly: just how I like them.

"And when you begin to look at the world from that point of view, Flora, you will see that the inequality does not rest only with women."

"What do you mean?"

"It applies to poverty and the poor, as well as to many of the colonial peoples who are ruled by our empire."

"I don't understand."

At that very moment Papa walked in. He was handing his cane and top hat to Jones and was looking harassed as he often does when he first arrives home from work.

"Good evening, Violet," he muttered solemnly.

I thought I should leave them alone, but I didn't really want to. I wanted to linger and talk, spend time with Papa. Still, in readiness, I placed my cup back on the table.

"Hello, Flora, are you leaving?" Papa kissed me on the top of my head but his mind was elsewhere and I felt as though he were telling me to go, so I rose obediently. Feeling a bit downhearted about being sent away, I glanced back at Gran and at Father who barely seemed to register my departure. "Can we finish our talk another time, please?" I asked her softly.

She smiled and nodded. "Most definitely, dear."

Alone in my room, I tried to figure out what Grandmama had meant about the colonial peoples, but I failed to find an answer so I lay on my bed staring at the photograph of my mother that I keep on my dresser. I felt proud and happy that Gran should judge me brave like my mother. If she were alive, I was thinking, I would want to make her so proud of me.

10th January 1900

My days are filled with lessons again. Christmas already seems so long ago. Grandmama runs around buzzing like a fly. Henry and Papa went to Gloucestershire for the weekend but I did not want to go. They took Bassett with them. Well, he is a hunting hound and it seems only fair to let the poor fellow run wild from time to time though I can't bear to think of him charging about with dead foxes or rabbits in his mouth. I was hoping Gran and I would have a wonderful time together chit-chatting and discussing all the things we fancied but she has been attending meetings and luncheons all over town. Twice this week, she has been at the Royal Geographical Society of which she is one of the very few women members. So, I have barely seen her. I hung about the house, and read. Felt a bit lonely.

20th January 1900

Miss Baker and I visited the Royal Academy this afternoon, and then we went for ices at Fortnum and Mason. That is the kind of schooling I enjoy the most!

25th January 1900

Henry's birthday. She is eighteen today. Gosh, eighteen; it seems so grown-up! She received a bouquet of red roses from an admirer and seemed thrilled by them. I teased her about having a beau which made her blush and giggle but she was irritatingly secretive about who the flowers had come from.

As a treat, Father took us both to a new play which

opened just a few days ago at the Princess's Theatre. It is entitled *The Absent-Minded Beggar* and is the story of an African Boer who falls in love with the wife of a British soldier. There was an awful lot of shooting and battle carry-on as the British soldiers defended the woman and fought the war. The audience stood and cheered at the end. It was a great success. I found there were rather too many gunshots for my taste and not enough ideas.

Everyone chatted loudly and merrily while they waited outside the theatre for their carriages. The Earl of Londonderry and his wife, who is very regal both in her bearing and her clothes which were all furs and satin, were amongst the audience. Father introduced us.

"Ah, yes Lady Henrietta Bonnington! You're coming out this year, I understand?"

Henrietta, who was a little daunted, I think, by such a very grand and haughty lady, only nodded. It is true though, she will be coming out this year, which means that she, like other young ladies of our class, will attend society balls and be presented to Queen Victoria.

"Then we must send you an invitation to our ball. Thomas, you have attended one or two of our little *soirées* in the past so you know the mix of people. Well, it will be a rather fine affair. At our address in Park Lane. Goodnight." And they swept off in one of the grandest carriages I have ever set eyes on. After, Father took Henry and me for supper at Claridges where several rather fusty-looking politicians were dining. I did not know who they were. To me they were just a table of ageing men in dark suits. Father went over and shook hands and shared a few exchanges with them, but he did not introduce us.

Later, as we undressed for bed, Henry declared that it had been a perfect day. As I was closing my door, Jenny hurried by carrying a vase. It was filled with the red roses. She was delivering them to Henry's room, no doubt destined for Henry's dresser. How silly of Henry not to tell me who they are from!

30th January 1900

I think I have discovered the identity of the flower-sender. His name is the Honourable Viscount Archibald Marsh. He is the dreariest of fellows, wet as a fish, and sports a *very unattractive* waxed moustache which sticks upwards like a pair of opened scissors. Henry met him at Grandmama's country estate in Gloucestershire a couple of weeks ago. Since her birthday, he seems to have popped up wherever we have been visiting. It's very irritating. He's like a retriever all set for the hunt. Actually, that's unkind because I really like retrievers!

"She's smitten, dear," whispered Gran after the three of us

had returned from riding in the park where – guess what?! – we bumped into him again, or rather, he bumped into us. "Oh, haw, haw, I say, fancy seeing you here!" he chortled. It was SO PATHETIC.

Henry must be keen on him because she acts so silly in his presence – coy and girlish – and then giggles senselessly at every jest he makes. It's quite embarrassing because, truthfully, his jokes are neither witty nor ingenious. Then she becomes awfully cross and flies into one of her temper tantrums with me when I speak frankly about how ugly I find him and what a frightful experience it would be to be kissed by someone with such a stiff, pointed moustache.

"Won't it get stuck up your nostrils and give you a nosebleed?" I asked her, but she threw a book at me and told me to get out of her room. Love seems to be depriving her of her sense of humour. Gosh, I hope she isn't *really* falling for such a daft sort.

10th February 1900

Father had been expecting a rather valuable cargo – ivory, I believe – to arrive at the docks but due to rough seas the steamer was delayed. This morning he received a telegram to say that there has been another delay and the ship will not be berthing in London before the end of the month, at the very earliest. He looked very disturbed by the news. I wasn't quite sure why and did not like to intrude upon his thoughts to ask him.

11th February 1900

Yesterday, Henry snapped at me, twice, for calling her by her nickname.

"Why must you try to belittle me like that?" she cried.

"Like what?" said I.

"Calling me 'Henry' in front of Archie. Whatever must he think of me?"

I was taken by surprise because she has never objected before, but there she stood erect as a soldier, shoulders back, eyes staring like a barn owl, announcing in a very high and mighty fashion, "It does not become a young lady, Flora, to be thought of by such a boyish name. I am Lady Henrietta Bonnington and that is what you must call me, particularly in front of others." At first, I was hurt by her anger towards me but then I had to fight hard not to smile for I believe her change of attitude, these airs and graces, are the fault of this dreadful fellow, Archie Marsh. It's too silly for words. After all, she is only eighteen and will not even come out until the spring. I hope I shan't be so daft when I reach her age.

Grandmama says I shouldn't mind so. "It's natural, my dear Flora, to have one's head turned by a young man or two at Henrietta's time of life, though it's most important to bear in mind that we have not been put on this earth for the pleasure of men. We should not come alive like clockwork when any man looks upon us. There is far more to us than that." By "we" and "us" Grandmama is speaking, of course, of women.

13th February 1900

Henrietta's talk – I dare not think of her as Henry! – is all of dresses and the trip she will be making to Paris next week to be measured for her wardrobe. And balls. Her season of coming-out balls is already being drawn up, for Father is quite determined that she be presented to the very best of society. He probably hopes that new company will take her mind off Archie Marsh. I certainly do.

She tells me that she intends to return from Paris

accompanied by trunks laden with dresses which will make her "the very epitome of high society fashion". It seems to have entirely escaped her overexcited brain that every other young lady will also have been shipped off to Paris to shop!

Still, I have to admit that I am jealous not to have the opportunity to visit Paris with her. While she was being fitted and dressed by Worth, I would go in search of the moving picture houses. Oh, think how divine that would be.

15th February 1900

I hate this role of chaperone! If Henrietta is not allowed to go out with Archie on her own, why must it always be me who is dragged along for the sake of social decorum? I have spent a most disagreeable afternoon. Archie took us and his beastly younger sister, Lydia, to the famous Earl's Court Exhibition Grounds. It is perfectly enormous and covers some two dozen acres of land. Archie tried his hand in a shooting gallery called Boerland. There, with a gun, you could "take a snipe at the enemy", which is what he did.

I was heartily amused because most of his shots were way off the mark.

In another part of the grounds, in a huge theatre known

as the Empress Theatre, we witnessed hundreds of savages from the African colonies presented in dramatic spectacles. Among them was a prince, a warrior chieftain, who – in real life – was taken prisoner in the war and brought over to England as a captive. The performance is intended to show to great effect Britain's triumphs in Africa. Amongst the other captives were quite a few female savages.

"I thoroughly enjoyed that," said Archie as we were leaving the show. "It seems to be a splendid way to show Londoners the importance of Britain's domination of those unschooled, dark-skinned savages. It certainly shows who's master and that's no bad thing."

"Oh, I so agree!" gushed Henrietta, almost before he had finished spouting his opinions.

"What ugly people they are, those savages," said Lydia. "I feel afraid to look upon them. They should be sent back to the jungle."

I could not bring myself to say anything for I found the very idea of exhibiting those people rather disgusting. After all, they are human beings. I felt sorry for those tribes men and women and I am not quite sure why it seems necessary for us to prove our strength by humiliating them. If I had my way, I would not allow such horrid, cruel exhibitions.

Yes, I know that I am bad-tempered but it is not for nothing. I cannot bear to see what is happening to my sister. She dotes on Archie. Well, that is her business, I suppose, but why must she deny her own personality in the doing of it? Whatever opinion he voices, she instantly agrees with him. It is as though she has absolutely no opinions of her own. Even when he talks nonsense, which, frankly, is frequently, she nods and swoons. He is so irritating and bossy!

Tonight, she came and sat on my bed and confided to me that she has fallen in love with him and she hopes that he will propose to her. I was open-mouthed. I cannot believe such a thing. The thought of becoming the sister-in-law of Archie Marsh! Oh, it would be a most awful business. I should be hauled off to social gatherings where I would prefer never to show my face and where I should be expected to smile, be friends with nasty Lydia and play the obedient young lady. I think I would rather run away. I should escape to Paris. I *wish* I could.

17th February 1900

And when you begin to look at the world from that point of view, you will see that the inequality does not rest only with women. It applies to poverty and the poor, as well as to many of the colonial peoples who are ruled by our empire.

This is a quote of Grandmama's which I wrote in my journal in January. We have had no opportunity to discuss it since then, but I have thought about it and I wonder now about all that I saw at the theatre with Archie and Lydia and Henry. Could those shows be what she was talking about? I must ask her.

I feel bloated and tired as though I had been eating too much. My back is aching, too. It's curious. I hope that I am not ill.

18th February 1900

When I woke this morning, my thighs felt sticky and I found that I was bleeding. I was very alarmed until I recalled, ages ago, that Henry had experienced the same thing and she had been angry and weepy when I'd asked her about it. I wanted to speak to Gran about it. She was preparing to go out when I caught up with her.

"You look as though you have something very serious to tell me," she smiled as Jones helped her with her coat. "Thank you, Jonesy."

"I have no lessons today and was wondering whether I could spend some time with you."

"I thought you and Henry were going to Regent's Park Zoo with Archie and Lydia?"

I shrugged. "I'd really rather not."

"Yes, all those caged animals on show for a shilling a visit. I wouldn't want to either."

I stared at her. I hadn't been thinking about the animals, caged or not. I had been thinking about the thought of Archie and Lydia's company and how miserable and worried I was feeling. "Where are you off to?" I asked her, hoping she would invite me along. She took me by the hand and led me through from the hall into the drawing room. Once inside, she closed the door. "What is it?" she asked softly.

Tears welled in my eyes. They surprised me as much as Gran, I think. A lump stuck in my throat and I couldn't speak so I just shook my head. "Nothing," I murmured eventually.

"Must be something, dear," said Gran, pulling me to her and hugging me tight, which somehow made me want to weep all the more.

"I don't know. I can't explain. It's just… I…"

"Feel lost, confused, at sixes and sevens? Those sort of things?"

I nodded. "It's as though I don't belong here." I wept.

"Of course, you do. But I understand your heavy heart."

And then eventually, I braved it. "I'm not very well," I whispered, feeling ashamed about what was happening to me. "There's something wrong. I fear it may run in the family because Henry has suffered from it, too."

"Good Lord, child, what is it?" Grandmama exclaimed.

When I finally managed to speak of what had happened, she stroked my head and said to me, "It's nothing to be afraid of. On the contrary, you can be proud. Now, you are a fully fledged young woman." She called to Jones and requested that he cancel her carriage and ask Anna to bring us some hot chocolate and a plate of Cook's fudge. She took off her coat, flung it carelessly across one of Father's prized French armchairs and said, "It's time for us to have a nice long chat."

20th February 1900

Henrietta and Grandmama left for Paris this morning. I was in a blue funk all day. But my stomach pains have gone, which is a relief. The bleeding continues but I don't mind it now. It seems rather fantastical to me, the notion that I could give birth to a baby. I had been intending to mention it to Henry yesterday evening, I so wanted to tell her that I am a grown-up lady too, but she was flushed with talk of Archie and the zoo and Paris, so I will tell her another time. I am no longer such a LITTLE sister.

Miss Baker cheered me with exciting news. She has heard about a woman working over in Paris for one of the moving picture companies; her name is Alice Guy. She is the secretary of a man called Gaumont and is the *only* woman in the *world* directing moving pictures. How I wish I could be her! How frustrated I feel about not being able to visit Paris with the others, especially now that I am GROWN UP!

22nd February 1900

Weather vile: cold, damp and horribly foggy.

My day was cheered up by a really splendid woman who came looking for Grandmama and stayed to dinner. Her name is Mary Kingsley. She is the niece of the novelist, Charles Kingsley, and she is also a writer as well as a friend of Gran's. She is in London but bound for Simonstown in South Africa where she is intending to nurse Boer prisoners of war. What a brave and energetic person, I thought her. I could not help calculating as I watched her across the table, attired from head to foot in black, that my mother would probably have been about her age. Did they know one another? Might they have become friends? I feel sure my mother would have been as lively and high-minded; it is certainly how I picture her. Miss Kingsley published a book recently entitled *Travels in West Africa* which has made her rather famous and she has promised to send me a signed copy which I can keep as my very own. I told her that I would like to be involved with the directing of moving pictures.

"The directing of moving pictures?" she repeated in amazement.

"Yes." I assured her that the idea was not too fantastical. "I take my inspiration from and would rather like to follow in the footsteps of a woman called Alice Guy, who is working in Paris."

"Alice Guy. Her name is not familiar to me. I must find out about her."

"Perhaps, one day you would allow me to visit you in Africa, Miss Kingsley, and we could take moving pictures of everything you have seen and written about," I suggested to her. "I have learnt that the beginnings of this moving picture business was originally invented by a Frenchman, a scientist named Étienne Jules Marey. He intended the photographs to be used as a study for science. The idea was that by looking at the photographs displayed together in quick succession, the differing styles of movement in animals could be more easily understood. The word *cinematic* comes from the French and means the geometry of motion. It was his work, his research, that first inspired the Lumière Brothers."

"My word, you really have taken an interest in this!"

"Come now, Flora…" said Papa, but so carried away was I with my subject that I barely registered his warning.

"Oh, yes, Miss Kingsley, and I really believe that it would be possible to make moving pictures of animals and tribes in the jungle and, surely, these would be of interest to people who may never have the opportunity to go to Africa and see these sights for themselves."

"What a simply fascinating concept!" she cried. "To take moving pictures and document the lives and customs of the African tribes. Mr Bonnington, you have a very brilliant daughter!"

"Thank you," he said. "I fear that you may be right."

"Oh, do not fear it, sir. Intelligence and sensitivity in a woman are to be applauded and encouraged, not feared. And Flora seems to be richly gifted in both these qualities."

I was speechless and felt so proud I wanted to yell and shout. If only Gran had been there. Or my mother.

"Oh, dear," said Father, "I seem to be surrounded by what my mother-in-law, your friend Lady Campbell, describes as the 'Twentieth-Century Woman', and I am afraid that I do fear it. I fear that you will all be the undoing of me." He spoke politely – in fact, he was very charming to Miss Kingsley – but I worried that I had said too much. As she was leaving, Miss Kingsley expressed again how disappointed she was to have missed Grandmama but has promised to come and have dinner with us upon her return from Africa.

Father was not too distant this evening, but after Miss Kingsley had gone he told me that a young lady who talks too much is considered unattractive. "It is not polite, Flora, to hog all the attention when there are guests at the table. You really must learn your place if you are to do well in society."

I was wounded by his words but, on reflection, I am sure that he is right. I do get carried away with my ideas. Still, I feel hurt that he felt the need to chastise me so. I had thought that Miss Kingsley had been genuinely interested in what I was telling her.

23rd February 1900

All is not lost! Yesterday evening, Papa received a telegram to say that his long-awaited ship will be docking the day after tomorrow. During our dinner this evening, I begged him to take me with him to the port which he readily agreed to do. I think he knows how I love visiting the docks with all its bustle and busyness and mixture of faces and languages. I am only sad that I cannot take photographs and show them as moving pictures. I would like, as Miss Kingsley described it, to document the life of London's extraordinary port; our link with the rest of the world.

There are really only four companies, including Father's, who, between them, own the entire East End docklands. Father and two other companies have the north side of the Thames. Their lands stretch from Tower Hill, just beyond the city, right along as far as Tilbury. This area is known as the Docklands and is entirely situated on the banks of the River Thames. There is one other important dock site on the south bank of the river which is known as the Surrey Commercial Docks, but Father's company has no shares in it, nor does he own any land or warehouses over there. Everything Father owns is on the north bank.

I love to go and watch the cargo from Father's ships being unloaded on to the quays alongside where the ships have berthed. Papa owns literally miles of three- and four-storeyed warehouses behind the docks of Limehouse, Albert and St Katherine's. These are where he stores his valuable cargoes. If you have never been inside a warehouse you would be amazed. They are huge cavernous storage spaces set back from the river. It is like visiting Aladdin's cave because you walk in and you are instantly hit by the various scents of dozens and dozens of unfamiliar, exotic produce. There is nowhere else I have ever been in London that has such a curious mixture of smells and perfumes. Once you begin to look round you find yourself surrounded by treasures of every imaginable kind; chests of fine-leaved Indian tea, for example, or gold coins from Australia or gold bars brought over from the mines worked by the natives in South Africa, sugar from the plantations belonging to British island colonies in the Caribbean, bales of cotton, crates of Jamaican rum, spices, peppers, wood and many, many other delights; all waiting to be sold or collected. Standing in one of the warehouses with your eyes closed and breathing in those scents or opening your eyes and staring at the weird-looking fruits with names like pineapple, even though they don't even vaguely resemble pines or apples, is like being transported to somewhere you will probably never visit in your whole life.

Back out on the quays, once Father's ship has been unloaded and has been left empty it is ready to be cleaned and prepared for its next departure. Then the vessel will be restocked by the stevedores. Stevedores are dockers specially skilled in the business of shiploading. Many of Father's ships carry silver bars and silver coins bound for the colonies of Hong Kong and Bombay, India. These are heavy and valuable cargoes. A vessel which is unevenly loaded runs the serious risk of capsizing out at sea in stormy weather, so being a stevedore is a job of enormous responsibility. Father transports an assortment of British goods out of England, as well as in to it. They are destined for dozens of exotic ports as far-flung as India or China. Father's main business is importation but he exports produce for two reasons. The first is that if the ships travel across the seas empty – en route to collect cargo – it costs money, so it is better to load them and make money in both directions. Secondly, the import business in London is not quite as healthy as it was fifteen or so years ago. Father says that all the major traders are aware that their profits are not as handsome as they were ten years ago.

Although there is competition between Bonningtons and the three other major import companies, Father's main adversaries have become the small wharf businesses. Also, the ports in the cities of Liverpool and Bristol are expanding rapidly. Both of these dock sites have been modernized which means they are now able to accept the latest steamers and ocean-going vessels. Even those ships which are so substantial and cumbersome that, until recently, there was no British port other than London that was wide enough and mechanically sound enough to berth them, can now be berthed in Liverpool or Bristol. These modern advances taking place outside of the capital are unfortunate for Father because it means that London is losing some of its share of the import trade.

Still, I don't think he is really concerned about it. He has a whole fleet of ships of his own, acres and acres of four-storey yellow brick warehouses and the land on which they stand so, whatever happens, he will always have a thriving business.

25th February 1900

Papa and I set off directly we had finished breakfast, which was my favourite: kippers and scrambled eggs and lashings of hot buttered toast laden with home-made marmalade. Cook said we needed a good hearty meal, to keep the chill off us. "It comes in on those winds down by the waterside. You'll catch your death, if you don't eat right." I begged Father to allow me to take Bassett with us but he wouldn't agree to it because, he said, the dog would cause chaos on the docksides, which is probably true. So, the dear hound stayed in my room, looking very glum. He probably felt as miserable about seeing us go out as I did, watching the others depart for Paris, full of *joie de vivre*, without me.

Papa and I motored together, laughing like carefree chums, in his automobile. I felt so happy that his upset towards me of the other evening seems to have been forgiven. It was a fine morning, not too blustery. We took the route along the Strand passing the Gaiety Theatre. As we neared the Aldwych, Father slowed and pointed out to me where the proposed new north-south avenue is to be constructed. It is intended to link Waterloo with King's Cross, if our Lord Mayor and the London County Council ever agree on the architect and designs, that is. Father said that there is a great deal of indecision on the matter.

We passed along through to the city where Father's offices are, passing by Mansion House, the lord mayor's residence, towards Tower Hill and made for the docks from there.

When we arrived at the port, there were dozens and dozens of labourers, many of them bare-torsoed, dark-skinned men, unloading chests from the holds of five other steamers belonging to one or other of the rival import companies. There was coffee and sugar, from Java, I believe, and massive trunks of ivory – African elephants I would guess judging by the size of the pieces – wooden chests of Indian tea bearing the lettering *Darjeeling,* a heavily guarded shipment of gold from South Africa and another of spices from Ceylon and the South Sea islands of Fiji.

One shipment, which must have come in from Africa, was disembarking live, wild animals. Such cries the creatures were letting out. Roarings and screechings (just as well I didn't bring Bassett!). I found it distressing to see monumental jungle beasts such as elephants being pulleyed helplessly off the decks while folk stood around oohing and aahing and gawping. It was worse than the circus. There were cages with lions in them, too. And though, on the one hand, it was extremely exciting to see creatures in the flesh that I recognized only from drawings in books, it was a horrid sight to see them with their power and majesty all trussed up. It brought to mind a line of Rudyard Kipling's which quite touched me when I first read it, "that packet of assorted miseries which we call a ship". Perhaps Kipling's words affected me because my own father owns so many seafaring crafts though, thank the Lord, I have never heard Papa speak of transporting live creatures.

"See there, Flora, there's our vessel." Father had moved away from my side and was calling to me and waving from further along the quay. I ran to where he was standing and there at a distance riding the muddy Thames water was the looming silhouette of the steamer, SS *Victoria*.

It is such an impressive affair when a huge ship approaches the docks. It always makes me feel so small – Alice in Wonderland-like – and unschooled in the secrets of the world. My heart never fails to flutter at the thought of all the seas the watercraft has crossed and all the different peoples it has carried. I so long to be one of those passengers or sailors standing on the upper decks, leaning against iron railings, watching the sight of land grow closer. Dreaming thus, suddenly I thought of the moving pictures again. What would it be like to have a camera up there with me, to document our arrival!

At the ship's side, small tugboats were spinning and turning like harassed insects engineering those final moments of safe passage. Then the dock gates opened, as if by magic, and the ship glided majestically and surely to its berth. What an achievement! After all those months at sea, all those storms and rocky passages, all those dangerous capes, all the scary moments of wondering whether the cargo will ever safely reach its destination and then the anchor is lowered, sinking to rest in the thick slimes of mud on the bed of the Thames, and the vessel rocks imperceptibly to a standstill, mission completed! Hoorah! Bravo! I longed to cry out, but no one else seemed to think the moment particularly special so I kept silent.

Perhaps, I should decide to earn my livelihood as a ship's captain but, alas, that is not a profession for a woman. *And why ever not, I ask myself?*

The sailors, of course, were disembarking as swiftly as they could. They are always desperate to stretch their land legs after so many months at sea and in many cases to hurry home to wives and families, but the craft was not deserted for more than a few minutes because almost as soon as it was moored, swarms of impatient stevedores began to climb aboard, beginning the process of unloading the precious cargo.

Within no time, the quay was laden with produce which was being sorted and listed before being trucked along the jetties to our warehouses where the merchandise is catalogued and then stored.

I have never before stopped to consider the labour force

involved in such an enormous enterprise as Father's. Where do all these men come from? I noticed that not a few of them were negroes as well as several other types of colonial peoples, many of whom are not Christians for I have heard tell that they practise strange religious rituals on the docksides. I would have dearly liked to have engaged a few of them in conversation and learnt from them how they came to be in England in the first place and from which corners of our empire they have originally hailed. But it would not be considered ladylike or dignified for a young woman of my background to speak to such men, and my behaviour would certainly anger my father.

Still, I sincerely hope that their working conditions are not as the Kipling quotation describes, "a packet of assorted miseries".

While I was musing on all these matters, and as we were making our way from the dockside back to where Father had parked his automobile, my attention was drawn by a cry of distress coming from somewhere distant from where we were.

"What was that?" I called to Papa who continued to move towards the gates. I paused and looked back and caught sight of a policeman engaged in what looked like a scuffle with a scruffy, bearded man who I took to be a docker. Two more policemen were running to join the first and back him up. I ran and grabbed Father by the sleeve. "What's happening?" I asked him. He barely glanced back.

"Life on the docks, Flora. Nothing to concern yourself about." But as he said these words the three bobbies grabbed and held fast the man who had been shouting. By this point he had been rendered helpless as they pressed him hard and beat him on his back. His knees began to buckle and he fell forwards, hitting the cobbles with a thud and a groan. Driven to the ground, balanced on all fours like an animal, the policemen continued to hit him and kick him in the ribs.

"They're hurting that man!" I cried, without thinking. "We have to do something. Papa!" My father continued on towards the exit to the dockside.

I stood my ground. "Please wait, Papa," I cried again at which my father stopped and retraced his steps until he reached my side.

"What is it, Flora?"

I was fighting to catch my breath.

I think Father was most amazed and shocked to see how upset I was about the incident taking place. The man was now being forcibly dragged by the bobbies away from the dockside. He was not going peaceably and I noticed another blow or two fall upon the back of his head. He yowled with pain.

"Stop!" I yelled, but they were now beyond hearing me.

"Come, Flora, don't upset yourself. The man is a low thief and probably a drunk into the bargain. We must go." Papa took me gently by the arm and led me away. "You really mustn't be so sensitive. It will be the undoing of you. Men who have done wrong must be punished."

"But what could he have done that is so bad to warrant such a beating?" I entreated, but Father was no longer listening.

When I glanced backwards, there was no further sighting of the quartet of men. Still, I was left feeling troubled and upset by the cruelty I had witnessed. All the way home, I remained silent, which suited Father who was miles away in his own thoughts. I stared out of the automobile at the passing streets fighting back tears, feeling so miserable at the prospect of returning to a house which did not contain Grandmama to whom I would have rushed in search of an explanation or, at the least, a huge hug and companionship.

26th February 1900

Grandmama and Henry are back from Paris, full of beans and stories. I was so OVERJOYED to see them. This evening at dinner, Henry talked of nothing but the grand stores and the designer houses and the splendours of the Seine river lit by gaslight. She said the train station, the Gare du Nord, was the most magnificent she had ever set eyes on. I refrained from pointing out to her that she hasn't seen all that many but she would have accused me of being jealous, which I was and, in any case, I did not want upsets. I wanted us all to be happy and to be like a real family.

Grandmama brought me delightful presents including lavender toilet water and a choker-necklace and then, with eyes beaming, she gave me the prize. The present that she knew I would treasure above all others. Leaflets about the moving pictures. She had taken the time to visit the Society for the Encouragement of National Industry to find out more information for me. I hugged her so tight for the trouble she had taken and for thinking of me when she could have been having a wonderful time.

"We did have a wonderful time, dear, but it doesn't mean we have to forget you."

Henry told us that they had lunched at a brasserie which, she explained, is a very informal eating house on the south side of the river, known as the left bank in a district called Montparnasse. "It was filled with starving artists wearing funny flat hats and clothes stained with paint. All bohemians, and I thought it simply horrid, but Grandmama loved it and she felt sure that you would too, Flora. Father, you wouldn't have liked it one little bit."

"No, you are right, Henrietta, and I rather disapprove of your grandmother taking you to such an establishment. But nothing I say will discourage you, eh, Violet?"

"It's important to know how other folk live. In any case, it is a perfectly respectable establishment, Thomas, dear."

"Oh, when can I go, Papa?"

I caught a conspiratorial look exchanged between my father and my grandmother and I knew instantly that they must have discussed the matter.

"Can I go?" I cried.

"We have to return in a fortnight to collect the dresses that are being made for Henrietta. Of course, we won't need to stay so long. A day or two at the most…"

"Unless, of course, they don't fit me."

"And why wouldn't they?" laughed Grandmama. "They are being made by the finest couture houses in the world."

"Yes, but I was measured before we ate so many French meals," wailed Henry. "I must not eat another thing before the Court Ball is over! Queen Victoria is going to take one look at me and judge me the plumpest of partridges."

"Don't be ridiculous, dear."

I waited, bursting with impatience for this exchange to end, forcing myself not to butt in or push my luck until eventually, I could wait no longer. "And may I accompany you, then? May I, Father? Oh, please, I beg you, let me go with them!"

"I don't see why not. Actually, I think it might do you the world of good. It seems to me that you spend too much time alone and thinking," he smiled. "But no artists' cafés on the left bank, do you understand, Violet?"

I threw my napkin into the air which produced tuts all round, but I didn't care, and I rushed from my seat and hugged my father so tightly, in a way I rarely ever do. "Thank you, thank you so much."

Alone, in my room, Bassett snoring soundly on the bed at my feet, I simply cannot sleep. I am bursting to tell Miss Baker my news. "I AM GOING TO PARIS AND I WILL VISIT ALL THE MOVING PICTURE SHOWS!!!"

27th February 1900

Reading, I discover that the camera used to photograph the moving pictures was patented by Louis Lumière in 1895 and he has named it the cinematograph.

28th February 1900

This is fascinating! Two years ago, according to an extract from an American science journal, a Monsieur Camille Flammarion undertook to cinematograph the sky. On a clear night, he takes up to 3,000 photographs. Does that mean that you can see the sunset happening all at once? The stars coming out? See the moon rising and waning? My mind is shooting like fireworks with the possibilities of cinematographing moving objects. Then, why not people, too? Think how it would be if I had my very own camera. I could cinematograph our trip to Paris and then show it to Father. Of course, it would not be quite so simple because I would need to have another apparatus, a form of magic lantern, to show the pictures and a dark room so that the flickering images could be seen to best effect. But, IF I had all those things, I could reproduce the trip and show it to Father, or to anyone else. The point I think I am trying to get at is that these cameras could show images of objects, scenes and events to people who would not otherwise be able to see them. Rather like writing in this journal and then sending it to someone to read but, instead of words, I would use moving pictures.

I could become a journalist, like Miss Kingsley, but with photographs. But who would want such a person? Certainly not the newspapers who use drawings rather than photographs.

1st March 1900

In all the excitement of my presents from Paris, I had forgotten to mention to Grandmama that Mary Kingsley had dined here with us. Gran was most upset to have missed her and described her as "a rare and extraordinary woman".

"Her uncle, Charles Kingsley the novelist, was one of the original supporters of our suffrage movement, did she tell you that?"

I shook my head.

"He was among those who were instrumental in the bringing about of the Married Women's Property Act of 1870. This was the first of three acts which eventually gave women the right to their own property and possessions instead of everything being held in the name of the husband."

"How did you first meet her?"

"Goodness, our paths have crossed all over the place. I don't remember, but when the Royal Geographical Society agreed, finally, to open its doors to women and allow them to become members – a decision, I hasten to add, which was debated and fought over by all those silly men who then changed their minds and withdrew the right to female membership. Anyway, before the decision was revoked, I was invited to be among that first handful of women who were given membership. Not so long ago, Mary came along and gave us a fascinating talk about her travels in Africa and about the effects of British rule on that continent. Although to be quite fair, she has never approved of women accepting membership to long established men's clubs, even those with a particular purpose such as the Royal Geographical Society. Still, she and I immediately saw eye to eye. She, like me, I am happy to say, is not a hundred per cent in favour of all this tedious flag waving by 'the world's greatest empire'. Certainly, we British have done good but it seems to me and to Mary, who has travelled a great deal more than I have, that a certain amount of damage is being done as well…"

"What sort of damage?" I interrupted, feeling quite shocked by Gran's remark, for everyone I know agrees that Britain is the saving force of the world. Papa certainly believes it and *The Times* newspaper always boasts about it.

"You know that there is much about our British society that I do not approve of, Flora. The lack of women's rights first and foremost. It is as I have tried to explain to you once before. Any form of domination, whether it be male over female or rich over poor is, in my opinion, against the basic rights of human beings, Flora. So, the fight for the vote, for women's equality with men has become a political issue."

I thought about the man at the dockside. That image of

71

him being kicked like a dog came back to me but I decided not to mention it. I felt that to tell Grandmama was, in a way that I cannot quite explain even to myself, a betrayal of Father.

14th March 1900

PARIS. Finally, at last! We have arrived after a tempestuous boat journey and then a train ride from the port of Calais which was quite rocky but great fun. We are staying at the Hôtel Ritz. Lord, I have never seen such sumptuous luxury! I feel most out of place and want to whisper all the time. Everyone we pass in the lobby must be a king or potentate, I am sure of it. It is rather like being in a fairy story and I am quite swept away by it all, being not quite certain whether it makes me uncomfortable or not, but Grandmama promises that there are many places to visit in this city and they will be of a very different complexion. From the little I have seen out on the streets, it is a very pretty place. It seems to be smaller than London, more compact. There is a river, called the Seine, which runs right through the centre of it and divides the city into two; the left bank of the river which is south and the right bank which is north. I wonder if they have mighty docksides here, like Papa's. I wonder if he misses us; all his "young ladies" gone. He is probably too busy to notice.

Gran took us to dinner at Maxims restaurant which opened last year and has become very fashionable. Everyone was very chic.

15th March 1900

Yesterday evening, at dusk, when all the shops were closed and there was simply nothing left for Henrietta to buy, we took a fiacre – these are four-wheeled box-shaped coaches which are for hire everywhere. They are named after the Hôtel Saint-Fiacre in Paris where they were first used. Anyway, we took a fiacre to the Musée Grévin. There, they are giving shows using this new style of film exhibition. It was rather basic and, I felt, disappointing. It did not excite and open my mind in the way that I dream is possible with these moving pictures, but it was worth a visit none the less.

We learnt that these cameras, the cinematographs, are not available for sale, which was why what we saw at the Musée was not of the same quality. The Lumières guard the cinematographs for their exclusive use. The moving pictures they have photographed are not for sale either.

They are rented out all over the world along with an operator who works the apparatus which shows them. This machine is called a projector and the man who operates it, a projectionist.

Other people who are interested in pursuing the moving pictures are building their own cameras or commissioning someone to build them on their behalf because they are impossible to buy. For example, there is a very famous French illusionist whose name is Georges Méliès. He owns the Robert-Houdin Theatre in Paris and, in order that he can record performances of his shows, he has ordered one of these cameras to be built for his exclusive use. He has also constructed a big glass house in his garden which he calls a studio. In this glass house he creates his moving pictures. Last year, he photographed a moving picture which lasted for THIRTEEN minutes and was a newsreel of a real event. It was titled *The Dreyfus Affair*. Also, Monsieur Méliès *works with women.* I must remember this and IMPROVE MY FRENCH!

16th March 1900

Where to begin to recount the joys and adventures we have enjoyed during these two crammed but too short days in

Paris? Now we are in the train on our return journey to the coast of France and, very soon, it will all be over, but it will NEVER be forgotten. There was shopping, of course, which did not greatly excite me but I am pleased with the new winter coat Grandmama bought for me. Henrietta, quite rightly, is laden with outfits and necklaces and gloves and perfumes and feathers and hats; all for her coming out which is to begin in a few weeks.

Watching her now across the carriage, she has flushed excited cheeks and a very glamorous new curly style of hair. She has barely mentioned the name of Archie Marsh, so I feel sure that Papa's decision to give her a very splendid coming out is the perfect plan and will introduce her to many other far more interesting people. And then I won't need to be the sister-in-law of such a buffoon! Lord, she would hit me if she read these words, but I mean her no ill. She is my big sister and I love her. It's her foolishness that makes me impatient. But enough of all this, I want to write about Paris and our splendidly exciting expeditions.

Yesterday morning, after breakfast, one of the concierges working in the reception of the Hôtel Ritz told Gran about a man named Pathé who has made a great deal of money out of selling phonographs, but also has an interest in the moving pictures. Because he was unable to buy any cinematographs from Lumière, he commissioned a man named Joly to build him a model of his own. So, while Henry was busy with the dressmaker who was putting the final touches to her ball gowns, Gran and I went all the way to Vincennes where we were told this Monsieur Pathé has his business but we were unable to find him. I was very disappointed. So, then we took a fiacre to another location where there are studios owned by a man named Monsieur Léon Gaumont. Gaumont's studio is where the woman director, Alice Guy, directs pictures but, alas, we were not able to meet with her nor see any of the material she has photographed. For some reason, it was a day off. Still, it was very exciting to be shown around. The studios were surprisingly basic. They have an open-air stage area about the size of our drawing room and another, covered area where they store items known as "props". The word "props" is an abbreviation of the word "properties". Properties are the articles used in the pictures. Chairs, for example, or swords and feathers and a few old battered helmets. It was a curious collection of items. The very notion of props struck me as curious. I had simply never considered that someone making moving pictures needs to collect things to create the world of the moving picture but, now that I have learnt that fact, it seems rather obvious.

I suppose I had simply assumed that every moving picture was a true reproduction of what was actually happening in front of the camera. It had not occurred to me that the director or camera operator is capable of *creating* the world that they cinematograph. This must mean that stories can be invented and filmed. So, it must be rather like storytelling in books except that photographs are used instead of words. It is not necessarily a form of journalism.

The most breathlessly exciting moment came when we were shown the famous cinematograph camera. It was all wrapped up in black velvet cloth as though it would be damaged by the daylight. I was very taken aback when the gentleman showing us around unveiled it because it appeared to be a frightfully complicated contraption. I asked the monsieur – with the help of Gran's French – to explain it to us but he shrugged and said that he did not understand it at all. He was only the caretaker of the studio.

If Father ever did agree to buy me one, I am not sure that I would know what on earth to do with it. Still, I do long to find a place for myself in this world of cinematographs. The more I learn, the more exciting the scope of it becomes. I just cannot see how it could ever happen. I fear it will always remain a dream.

Later in the day, while Henrietta was *still* occupied with her dress fittings and matching her accessories – Lord, I shall never agree to all this coming out – Grandmama and I took a stroll to the quays where wonderful men in berets were sitting on stools making sketches of the water and the bridges and the tall, leaning buildings. As well as the artists, there were dozens of bookstalls. All of them were situated along the length of the riverside with the cathedral of

Notre-Dame as a backdrop. It was a beautiful sight. There, they were selling parchment-yellow posters of Parisian theatre shows and antique books, several with very ornate gilt covers. It was too magnificent for words. I wished that my French had been good enough to investigate the books but I was a stranger to all their secrets. Miss Baker will be delighted to know that I have finally understood the point of reciting all those infernal French and German verbs. Languages are the tools for communication! Grandmama, of course, nattered away with all the stallholders just as though she were a French native. While she talked, I browsed and, suddenly, at one of the farther stalls, I caught sight of a poster. It was pegged to a line, which reached across the stall like washing hanging out to dry. Written across the poster in large letters were the words: CINÉMATOGRAPHE LUMIÈRE. Even with my hopelessly basic understanding of the French language I could not fail to comprehend the meaning of those two words! I moved up close to study what it was about and, lo and behold, what a wonderful discovery I had made. There, on the poster, was a sketched reproduction of six people seated in a theatre in front of an open curtained screen. They are animated and falling about laughing, staring at an image which is being projected on to the screen. Alongside these audience figures stands a boy in a uniform, rather similar to that of a bellboy. He is laughing, too. The moving picture they are so amused by is entitled

L'Arroseur Arrosé, which, when I shouted to Grandmama to come and look, she translated for me. Literally, it means, "The Waterer Watered."

"I saw this picture," I cried, "with Miss Baker in London!"

The image on the screen is of a gardener holding a hosepipe which is spraying water all over his face and, in the background, a mischievous-looking boy is running away, triumphant.

The stallholder explained to Grandmama that this little story was one of the original examples screened at that first public exhibition in the basement room of the Grand Café in the Boulevard des Capucines in 1895.

"The audience are laughing," I jumped in to explain, "because the boy has deliberately trodden on the hosepipe and blocked its flow of water. When the gardener lifts up the nozzle to examine what is wrong with it, the boy steps off the pipe and runs away, leaving the poor man soaked in water. It is very funny."

"This poster is a memento which will be worth keeping," added the salesman.

"Really?" I cried. "Have you seen the film, too?"

"Me, *hélas*, no, but on that very first evening at the Grand Café when each member of the audience paid a franc, a programme of ten different films, lasting a total running time of 25 minutes, was shown. This moving picture was among that ten. How the audience laughed! And what a success! Within no time, the brothers were giving twenty screenings a day with long queues winding along the streets of Paris. Now they show their moving pictures everywhere in Europe. Ah, they are magnificent these brothers, Lumières."

"Actually, forgive me for disagreeing, but there are screenings all over the world now. Pictures in motion have become a very international affair." I was almost hopping with excitement and begging Grandmama to translate for me. Grandmama laughed and told the rheumy-eyed man what I had said. He nodded, looking impressed that I should know so much.

"Would you like this as a souvenir of our time in Paris, Flora?" Grandmama whispered to me.

"Oh, yes, please!" I cried.

So, after Grandmama had agreed a price with the whiskery stallholder, the precious poster was very carefully unpegged from where it had been hanging, rolled in paper as soft as a handkerchief, and handed over to me. I was speechless with joy.

17th March 1900

I forgot to mention that before leaving for the train station yesterday Gran took Henry and me on a short sight-seeing tour. She wanted us to take a look at a very strange and unusual new tower. It is known as the Eiffel Tower and juts high into the sky on the south side of the river. I am not quite sure what its purpose is because no one can live in it – it has no walls and is very narrow at the top – but it is quite splendid to behold.

I have clipped my poster to the mirror in my bedroom. It will inspire me.

6th April 1900

Henrietta's invitation arrived this morning to the Earl and Lady Londonderry's ball. It is to be held on 24th May, 1900 at their home, Londonderry House, Park Lane, Mayfair. She ran up and down the stairs with it clasped to her bosom as though she had just received the greatest of news.

"I will meet every titled person and politician in England," she cried with joy. Well, that's better than swooning over Archie Marsh I wanted to say but I was careful not to make any comment which might spoil her good mood.

Grandmama was less thrilled. "Undoubtedly, Lady Londonderry is the queen of British society and it is perfectly right that Henrietta should go. However, although she wishes so dearly to be present at such a gathering, she must not be blinded by all this pomp and circumstance. The Marchioness is extremely powerful. She charms and manipulates almost every gentleman in office as well as those who aspire to be in the government, which is all very well – each of us to our own battle – but it is not that kind of power I wish to see you young girls, or indeed any woman, aspire to." Here, Gran paused and sighed and took hold of my hand, holding it tight and seemed to be considering matters so deeply that she began to frown. "I wish that Thomas, your father, was more … less… He's very conservative, dear."

"Is that bad?" I asked her.

"What? No, no of course not. It's that … if Millicent, your mother, were here… She was less of a conformist… Still, better to see Henrietta out there in society than sitting at home like Sir Vincent Andersen's dull wife who does nothing but eat cakes all day long. We women cannot deaden our sensibilities, Flora. We have much to do in the world, dear and… Oh, I had wished more for Henrietta!"

I wasn't entirely certain what Grandmama was worrying about, but her remark about Papa troubled me. And her mention of my mother surprised me because it is so unusual for her to be mentioned by either Papa or Gran.

22nd April 1900

My birthday. Fifteen today. Nothing special has been planned. Still, Father had said that the trip to Paris was my present given to me early, and it was unforgettable. I would simply adore to be in Paris now. A rather splendid exhibition has just opened. It is everywhere on the streets as well as the exhibition houses such as the Grand Palais. It is known as the *Exposition Universelle* and there are paintings by modern artists from all over the world. There is also a moving pavement – can you imagine such a thing? – a monumental fair and a giant Ferris wheel. Oh, it would be too divine to return there now.

10th May 1900

Horrid guests to dinner this evening. Lord Duncan from the Colonial Office and his wife, Lady Duncan. Grandmama and Henrietta were both out for the evening, so there was only

Father and me. I wish now that I had stayed in my room.

Lord Duncan said of Mary Kingsley that she keeps company with black people and, "it is whispered, even allows some of that kind to visit her."

"How could one respect such a creature?" sniped Lady Duncan. "She is a disgrace to the British. She even sets herself against the Colonial Office thinking that she knows better than they how to run West Africa."

"Yes, what my wife says is true. Miss Kingsley actually wants the place to be governed by the traders. Really, she is quite ludicrous."

"It is hardly surprising," Lady Duncan, who seemed to be relishing this gossip, added. "After all, she is the illegitimate child of a serving maid who her father married only days before she was born. Her blood lacks class and breeding, that is obvious. Why else would she entertain the notion that Blacks have anything to say that is worth hearing? Anyone can see that they are of a lower caste and intellect than us."

"She came here for dinner," said Father. "Shortly before she left on her last trip to Africa. I supposed that she must be a supporter of the vote for women, but I had no idea that she keeps company with negroes. If I had known, I probably would not have invited her to eat with us."

When Father said that, I rose from the table and asked to be excused. I have never spoken to a dark person but what Father said made me feel sick. It is true what Grandmama told me, there are horrid things about Britain. Miss Kingsley is a kind and brave person. I hate to hear people speak so ill of her and those she befriends when she is not here to defend herself.

12th May 1900

I related to Grandmama what Lord and Lady Duncan had been discussing at dinner with Father. In return, Gran explained to me that it is true that Mary Kingsley has been battling with the Colonial Office because she does not approve of the way they want to run West Africa. Then she quoted something that Mary had written a few years ago, after one of her trips to Africa. "I feel certain," she had said, "that a black man is no more an undeveloped white man than a woman is an undeveloped man."

"You see how important our battle for the vote is, Flora. A world ruled exclusively by white men who believe themselves to be superior beings is a dangerous one. It is a world built on prejudice and lack of respect."

"But it was not only the men saying those things. Lady Duncan was equally nasty."

"I suppose we should not judge her too harshly. She is not

thinking for herself. She is simply mouthing what she has heard voiced by others. A woman like that is not interested in discovering life or finding out for herself what the world has to teach and offer her. Hers is a mindless existence. Of course she and her husband oppose Mary; she is courageous. She is too honest for them and she is not afraid to recognize that everyone, whether they be black or white, male or female, has something to offer the rest of us."

"Even Lady Duncan?"

Grandmama laughed. "Yes, even Lady Duncan. You have learnt a lesson from her narrow-mindedness, have you not?"

I nodded.

"And, no doubt, if she allowed herself to be more open to life, she would discover qualities about herself that might surprise her."

I would love to travel in Africa and make cinematograph pictures there. I want to be open to life and make new discoveries every day!

20th May 1900

The newspapers speak of nothing but victory in the South African Boer War. The British garrison in the town of

86

Mafeking has been saved. It seems that all of England is celebrating. In the East End of London, people are hanging out bunting and banners. Even Father's warehouses are flying flags. Britain is proving yet again to the world just what a powerful nation it is. As I passed the kitchen this morning, I overheard Cook say to Jonesy: "Makes yer proud to be British, don't it?"

22nd May 1900

Last night, Henrietta attended her first society ball. She arrived home in a carriage in the small hours of this morning, she told me later, exhausted but "still spinning with pleasure". Her gown, which was the palest of pinks and was decorated with fresh roses, was a huge success. I think she must have been complimented greatly for she has been rushing about the house as lively as a cricket all afternoon. I must admit that she did look breathtakingly beautiful. Grandmama gave her the most elegant diamond earrings as her coming-out gift.

I will agree to come out *only* if my gift is a cinematograph which, of course, I couldn't wear to a ball! But I could take pictures of the ball and of all those who attended it…!

3rd June 1900

Henrietta has been to five balls in almost as many days. She sleeps in till the afternoon because she is so tired and then, after a brief canter through Hyde Park for fresh air and exercise, returns home to prepare for that evening's entertainment. Last night, she danced four times with Archie, she announced at luncheon today. So, he's still hanging around then!

4th June 1900

Our home was worse than a train station today with all the comings and goings and preparations for Henrietta's presentation to Queen Victoria at Buckingham Palace this evening. Grandmama has accompanied her and they spent *hours* discussing how to walk and then curtsey. Henrietta was practising her curtseys to Bassett who howled and barked and ran to hide beneath one of the chairs in the dining room. The sight of him, glowering from between chair legs, and then Henry shouting and getting cross with the poor thing sent Jenny and me into gales of laughter. It all seems extremely silly.

Before Henrietta left for the Palace this evening she came in to my room.

"Wish me luck," she said in a very nervous voice. She was dressed up in a glorious white satin gown and a flowing train that goes with it, clutching a bouquet of flowers. "I'm terrified."

"No need to be," I said. "You look divine." Which she did. "Will you still be able to curtsey with all those clothes on?"

"Don't, Flora, why must you be so horrid!" she cried. "You make me twice as nervous." And with that she was gone. I expect I shall get into trouble for upsetting her which I hadn't meant to do. It's just that I find it hard to take it as seriously as she does. Still, my sister is wondrously beautiful.

5th June 1900

Well, it all went off swimmingly at the Palace. Thank heavens! According to Henry, there were more than 300 young ladies being presented and she was number two hundred and something or other! What an absolute bore it must be for Queen Victoria to sit there while a procession of young ladies files past. Each one pauses in front of her while their names are announced, then curtseys to her twice before moving along. I don't quite see the point. I think I must be what is known as the "black sheep of the family"! I am amazed that all this stuff interests Grandmama. What has it got to do with winning the vote for women? It does not seem like equal rights to me. Do young men go through the same rigmarole? No, they go into the army instead!

This evening at dinner, Henry was describing the interior of the Palace. She claims that the nicest part is the entrance. All the entertaining salons are enormous, she said, and filled with brightly glowing chandeliers. Well, they would need to be spacious to receive so many debutantes.

Still, there is only the Court Ball this coming Friday and then the important dates will all be over. And life will be back to normal. Henry's coming out into society will have been achieved.

6th June 1900

I saw in this morning's copy of *The Times*, which Papa had been reading at breakfast, that a dock strike began yesterday morning. It seems that it has been caused by a contracting firm who have refused to hire labour from outside the dock gates. Angry dockers walked off the jetties shouting about weakening the power of the unions.

I wondered why Father had been so sullen at dinner last night. I have no idea what effect this will have on his company but judging by the frown on his forehead when he set off for work today, I feel sure he must be troubled. Poor Papa, he seems to be having a rather difficult time of it. I do wish that there was some way in which I could help, but he so rarely shares his concerns and I feel unable to offer my love and compassion because I fear he will reject me. Would it be different if my mother was still alive? Would he talk to her?

How different people's worlds are. Henry is flustered at the prospect of the Court Ball, Papa is worrying about who will unload his ships and how he will protect his merchandise and the dockers are angry because they fear their jobs are at risk.

7th June 1900

If the newspapers are to be believed, the contracting firm who refused to hire the labour force is working *for Father*. Yesterday, the situation worsened when the contractors locked out the strikers of the day before, who then broke into the docks and called to the men who were still working to put down their tools. They wanted every single docker to stop work and to strike with them. Most of the dockers followed the call, but a few didn't. This caused disagreements. A couple of fights broke out and the police were called again. I asked Father this evening about what was happening and he said that the strikers were troublemakers and they would be punished.

"How?" I asked him.

"We are bringing in workers from elsewhere. The strikers will lose their jobs."

Suddenly, I recalled the image of that bearded docker I saw on the quay all those months ago who was being knocked about by the police. I suppose he must have been a troublemaker too.

8th June 1900

"Well, the band strikes up its opening notes and the ball commences with a dance known as Royal Quadrilles. Queen Victoria led it, of course, but she didn't dance for very long because she is fearfully old and rather dumpy. Still, once she was on the floor, every other member of royalty, including all guests from foreign royal families, were allowed to dance. Lord, it was splendid. All those great dignitaries swirling and turning while the rest of us looked on. Then, only when that dance had been concluded, were we all entitled to take a turn. It was the most enormous fun. Of course, when you take the floor, if any members of royalty are dancing, you must respect a certain distance. I was danced off my feet. Whirling and turning in the arms of so many young men! In fact, I barely remember the names of some of those who requested my hand on the floor..."

While Henrietta was recounting the itinerary of her evening at the Court Ball, I could not help noticing the expression on Father's face. Although he was listening, or trying very hard to affect an air of interest, I felt that his thoughts were elsewhere.

I know that he would do anything in the world for Henry. She is his very special girl, I am aware of that, and he encourages and believes in these society affairs, but he was troubled, I am sure of it. It must be to do with this wretched strike. Now that Grandmama is less occupied with Henry's social calendar, I shall try to talk to her and find out what is going on.

I am glad it's Saturday tomorrow. Father can stay home and rest.

9th June 1900

Saturday or not, Papa went off at the crack of dawn this morning. I don't know where to and he didn't say anything about when he'd be back.

Gran, Henry and I breakfasted together. Then, after breakfast, Henry set off to stay with friends of Gran's outside Oxford who are holding a grand ball at their country estate this evening.

I was glad to have some time alone with Grandmama. It seems ages since we talked and I needed an opportunity to ask her about Father. We had luncheon together and then went horse riding in Hyde Park.

No wonder Father has been depressed. The union workers stopped work in support of the strikers on Thursday. In retaliation, the contracting company working for Father has started to employ outside labour. Now, the situation is very serious. Grandmama says that under these conditions, the struggle will not get resolved. She thinks that it will most likely spread to all the other docks.

"Your father's company are bringing in strikebreakers from all over England. Some are even being shipped in from

Ireland and Holland. They are housing them all on ships and in sheds at the ports, paying them handsomely and feeding them three full meals a day, which is a great deal more than the regular dockers ever received."

"Lord, it must be very hard for Father," I said as we rode beneath the flowering chestnuts in the park. I was feeling terribly concerned.

"Why do you say that, Flora?"

"Because it will be very expensive for him to employ so many labourers who are not part of the strike."

"It is one way of looking at the situation."

"Why? What other way is there?" I asked in surprise.

"One might also consider how those strikers' families are going to survive without money to buy food."

I fell silent. I had not considered such a thing, at all.

When we returned to the house, Father was home, supping a whisky in the drawing room. He seemed to be in a rather good mood, greeting us with the news that Pretoria, in South Africa, has surrendered to British troops. He talked of the celebrations that were taking place down at the docksides. They began at eight this morning, he said, "At our docks. I ordered every vessel of the fleet we had in port to hoist flags from stem to stern and from foremast to mizzen. During the course of the day other ships followed suit so that, by the time I left at five this evening, the entire dockside was covered in bunting and looked like a party event."

"Such outstanding patriotism, Thomas! Well, you have certainly given the strikers something to worry about. Excuse me, I'm going to get out of these riding clothes," declared Gran who then strode from the room.

I followed up the stairs moments after her, confused by this exchange between her and my father. He had been happy by his news of the day, it seemed, and for a reason that I did not understand, his recounting of it had made her cross. Might it be that Gran feels the celebrations are out of place because the strikers' families have no money for food? I am not quite sure.

10th June 1900

Terrible, terrible news. Gran received a telegram this morning to say that Mary Kingsley died of enteric fever in Africa on the third of this month. Grandmama is awfully shocked and very upset. I also feel quietly saddened and I could not help remembering her promise to me of a signed copy of her book which I never received. Such a selfish thought on my part!

20th June 1900

According to the newspapers, there are celebratory processions everywhere through the East End of London. Apparently, they are sponsored by the *Daily Telegraph*. The newspaper has arranged for collecting boxes to be handed out everywhere. Money is being collected for the widows of soldiers who have died in the war in South Africa. These collections seem to have done far better than the boxes which are to help feed and support the strikers' families. Many of the people collecting for the striking dockers have been charged with breach of the peace and taken to court.

In the East End, the pubs and the local inhabitants have given generously to the war and the war widows but not to the strikers or their families. Gran says that the dockers will find it difficult to hold out much longer. These demonstrations and the lack of support for their cause will force them back to work.

22nd June 1900

It's peculiar to be a part of a country at war when the war is so far away. Still, people argue all the time in the press and at the dinner table about it. It seems that there are many who oppose it. For my part, I don't really know what to think. Except that I hate the idea of people killing people and when I remember how horribly those savages were treated at the Great Exhibition, I cannot see that power over anyone is such a good thing.

24th June 1900

A most extraordinary and wonderful thing happened this morning! I received a small parcel which had been stamped in South Africa. I tore open the brown paper wrapping and discovered that it was from Mary Kingsley; the book she promised me all those months ago. In it she has inscribed in ink:

Dear Flora,

Thank you for your interest in my little book. I hope that it may inspire you to set off along the route of your own travels, your own path and destiny.

May I be so bold as to advise? Well, my advice is: create opportunities for yourself. Make those moving pictures you spoke to me so passionately of. They will be a lasting document of a time which will pass all too soon.

I wish you success and look forward to the next opportunity we have to talk together.

Yours,

Mary Kingsley

My heart beat so fast when I read her words to me. The idea that she had taken my dreams seriously made me flush with pride. She must have posted the packet just before she fell sick. I look forward to reading her book and shall cherish it deeply.

25th June 1900

A month's stay in Suffolk has been arranged for our holidays in August. Father has rented an estate near a small town called Yoxford, which is not too far from the sea. Grandmama is not going to come with us. "Too busy, dear," she says, "to go gallivanting about the countryside in the heat."

For my part, I do not greatly look forward to going because there is not a great deal to do there, aside from reading which I can do here and riding which I can enjoy in Hyde Park. I am not attached to nature, having decided that hunting and shooting are not my favourite pastimes. I prefer the city. Still, we will travel there in Father's automobile so that will be fun. I can't quite see the point of summer holidays. Does that mean that I shall end up obsessed with work like Father? We have hardly seen him in weeks. I suppose we must blame the strike for his continual absence.

26th June 1900

A woman turned up here today. When Jones answered the door, she requested to speak with Father who, he informed her, was not at home. "I won't go, till I speak with 'im," she insisted in a very loud and rather bad-tempered voice.

Miss Baker and I were descending the stairs when we heard this exchange. We had just finished a horrid German verbs class, at which I had fared rather badly, and were on our way to the dining room for lunch. I hung back to find out what was going on and who the rather scruffily dressed woman was.

"I wanna see Bonninton. My 'usband works for 'im at the docks."

"Is Grandmama at home?" I asked of Jones who shook his head.

Miss Baker pulled at my sleeve, saying, "Flora, this is none of your affair."

But I would have none of it and stepped up to the door. "Can I help you?" I enquired of the woman who, when we stood face to face, I realized was a great deal younger than I had originally supposed.

She was a little taken aback and I don't think she fancied discussing her concerns with the likes of me, a person so young and ill-equipped. So, I tried to reassure her by telling her that I was Mr Bonnington's daughter and would be happy to pass on any message she wanted me to give to him.

"You're just a bleedin' kid," she scoffed.

"I am fifteen," I asserted, a little hurt by her dismissal of me after I had thought to be considerate and caring.

"Fifteen, blimey! I got boys your age out working. When they can get the work, that is, and get paid for it. Shows what class does, eh? And an easy life."

"I think you should come and eat your lunch, Flora," chided Miss Baker.

"If you would like me to pass on a message to my father, I will willingly do so," I reiterated.

"Right then, Miss. You can tell your father that we're starving on account of him and his rotten cruelty. You tell him that he's a cold-hearted so-and-so. Five kids, I've got. I'd like to see your mother put up with what I got on me hands."

I reeled with shock at her words and the sharpness with which she had spoken them, and I certainly did not tell her that I have no mother.

"Baxter's the name." This was yelled like a hurled stone into my retreating back. I barely heard it at the time. I am not even sure now if I have correctly remembered it.

Suddenly, Jones, with his kindly manner was at my side and he led me away.

"Did you hear what she said about Papa?" I muttered. I don't know if any other words were exchanged after that. The next I knew I was walking into the dining room as Jones guided me to my usual seat.

"What was that about?" I asked weakly to anyone who was paying me attention.

"You shouldn't have gone to hear her but now that you did, you don't want to take notice of a woman like her, Miss."

"Why not, Jonesy?"

"She's abusive. A striker's wife, no doubt, with a foul mouth and foul manners," snapped Cook who was delivering a dish of buttered spuds to the table. Her manner shocked me almost as much as Mrs Baxter's.

I barely touched a bite of my lunch and my lessons were a struggle all afternoon, but I fought hard not to expose the extent to which the exchange at the door had unsettled me. Above all, not because the lady who called herself Mrs Baxter was ugly in the manner in which she spoke – which she was – but because, and God forgive me for thinking let alone writing this, I dreaded, and still do, that there might be a grain of truth in her outburst.

I cannot discuss these feelings about Papa with anyone, not even dearest beloved and wonderful Grandmama. For some inexplicable reason, I feel a real and deep longing to be in the company of Mary Kingsley. She has been in my thoughts ever since I returned upstairs to my room this evening. I have now put her book with its ink-inscribed dedication to me on my pillow at my side. I have been weeping for the loss of her and yet she is a woman I met but the once and I cannot help feeling that my tears are not for her at all. If I could have any wish in the world right now, it would be to have my mother sitting here calmly, in my room, on the edge of my bed, and me kneeling at her feet, with my head in her lap. I long for her in a way I have never known before; I long for her to stroke my hair and listen to my confusions. And to reassure me that my father is not a cold and cruel man.

17th July 1900

The strike is over. Father says that the men are returning to work in "dribs and drabs. They have learnt their place." The whole affair was never more than a "whimper" overshadowed by the great events taking place in South Africa. Father says the failure of the strike is a triumph for the employers. The men will accept the terms and salaries they are offered now with a little more gratitude. "It has taught them their place and they will think twice next time before they challenge the gentlemen who give them work."

I feel less at ease about it, not having forgotten the incident of "the thief" at the port. And that woman, Mrs Baxter, who came to our door.

I have also been reflecting on Grandmama's reaction to Papa when he told his story about ordering all the flags to be hoisted the length and breadth of every ship in dock. Is it possible that his intention was not to celebrate the achievements of the soldiers at war, but to take the attention away from the dockers, to weaken their cause? No, it could not be. How can I think such thoughts about my own father?

20th July 1900

We have passed a very jolly few hours. An outing to a West End theatre this evening where we saw a performance of *The Man of Destiny*, written by the Irish playwright, George Bernard Shaw.

During the interval, Grandmama took me by the arm and led me off, away from Father and Henrietta saying, "I want to introduce you to someone. Come with me."

Standing at the foot of the stairs which reached up to the dress circle was a young woman, not much older than Henrietta, engaged in conversation with two others.

"Christabel, this is my granddaughter, Flora Bonnington."

We shook hands and the lady, Christabel, said to me that she hoped to meet me again. "Your grandmother speaks very proudly of you. Perhaps you will come to one of our meetings, will you?"

I nodded, feeling rather shy in their presence.

"Deeds not words, Violet," she said to Grandmama as we stepped away.

"Who was that?" I asked as we left the three women to their conversation and made our way back through the throng.

"Her mother is a friend of mine from years back. I met her when she was still a young girl attending her first suffrage meetings. In those days, she was called Emmeline Goulden. Later, she married and became known as Emily Pankhurst. And the lady you have just been introduced to, Christabel, is her daughter."

"What did she mean by her remark to you, 'deeds, not words'?"

"I will explain, but not now. Look, your father and Henrietta are calling us. The play is about to recommence."

I glanced in Father's direction once or twice during the performance. He was smiling and looked as though he was thoroughly enjoying himself but when I asked him later what he thought of the play he said that it was not his cup of tea. "I prefer something a little more patriotic. He's a bit of a troublemaker that Irishman, Shaw," he said.

I suppose Papa was smiling because he is relaxed now that the strike is over. I wonder what happened to that Baxter family. I would like to talk to that woman again.

24th July 1900

I have been reading Miss Kingsley's book. It is quite wonderful. Her words have transported me to another world entirely. West Africa is a place that in my wildest imaginings I could never have pictured. Think how it would be if I could bring those images alive and show them here in England. Would the likes of Lady Duncan reconsider their cruel comments about the tribes peoples? Could moving pictures bring people closer together, towards a better understanding of the differences between us?

What is inspiring about Miss Kingsley's book is that she went out alone and created her own work. She followed her dreams and turned them into *her destiny*.

Oh, that I might one day have the courage to do such a thing!

3rd August 1900

Grandmother invited me to a meeting attended by herself and many other suffragettes. "You are fifteen. You are old enough to know your own mind and I believe you are ready, but obviously, it is up to you, Flora. Would you like to come along?" I told her that I would like to very much, and so it was agreed.

"As long as your father has no objections, that is."

"Oh, please, don't tell him!" I cried out. The words were spoken before I could think to stop them.

Grandmama frowned. "Why ever not, dear?"

"I would … prefer to tell him later," I stammered. "I would like to surprise him." But my excuse was a lie and I knew it. The truth is, I fear Father will disapprove.

We set off after tea. The meeting was held in a small, rather draughty hall towards the south of London in a place known as the Elephant and Castle. I cannot recall ever having been to that district of our city before. I did not like it much for it was very down at heel. But I have no right to judge it for that reason.

Christabel Pankhurst, the lady Grandmama introduced me to at the theatre a short while ago, seemed to be in charge of things. At least, she was the one who spoke the most and her oratory was given in a very impassioned and rather dramatic way.

"The vote for women is the symbol of freedom and equality," she cried, arms raised above her head. And others called back to her, loudly voicing their agreement. I looked around the place and was surprised to see women with their hair cut short, others who were smoking, still others who had a rather bohemian style of dress, but there were many who looked and behaved in a normal way. Many of the women quite obviously came from the same background as Grandmama and me. One of these was a very kind lady, about Gran's age, who was introduced to me as Millicent Fawcett. I liked her very much. She did not speak a great deal but when she did, her words were carefully considered and intelligent and the others present listened to her with a great deal of respect.

All in all, it was an interesting and colourful mixture of women of all ages, middle-aged like Grandmama, and younger. There were a few men amongst the crowd, too, which quite surprised me because from all that Gran has said to me I had thought that *all* men would violently disapprove of this women's suffrage stuff.

"Any class which is denied the vote is branded an inferior class. Hence women are judged inferior and the inferiority of women is a hideous lie! It teaches men arrogance and injustice!"

"Yes!!" The voices were shouting. Others were cheering and stamping and waving their arms. Their cries rang loudly like bells chiming. The energy was thrilling and I could not help myself being carried along with it. Within no time I was cheering too, although I did not always understand precisely what was being said.

After, hot tea was served from huge pots and we stood around in groups chatting. I say *we* though I did not speak much. In fact, I barely said a word. I was far too fascinated watching what was happening and listening to everyone's ideas and opinions.

The expression, *deeds, not words,* was spoken by several of the women. Both in conversation or when they were on the podium addressing the group at large. I thought it must be their motto.

Later, during the ride home in Grandmama's carriage, soothed by the soft clip-clop of the horses' hooves against the damply cobbled streets and the gentle sway of the carriage, I asked Grandmama again to tell me what the expression meant. *Deeds, not words.*

"There are many women who feel that the fight has been going on too long. The government is not taking us seriously and now is the time to begin to publicize our cause. Some feel we need to be more unionized to fight for our rights."

"Unionized? What do you mean, Grandmama?"

"That if women banded together in groups and fought

together their requests would be listened to. Others, like Christabel, believe we should go out on the streets and begin to march and make ourselves and our grievances known everywhere."

"You mean marching like the dockers have been doing in the East End of London?"

The carriage was approaching Hyde Park. Grandmama glanced out at the wet night and then back at me. "Yes, exactly like that."

"But they lost," I said earnestly.

"Not because they took to the streets. Their defeat was brought about by other circumstances."

"Such as?"

"Support for the Boer War."

"I don't understand," I said, but a part of me feared that I did.

"Most people would rather donate any spare money they have to help our soldiers abroad than help their fellow workers and their families and the less fortunate at home."

"Why?"

"Because the ordinary citizen believes that our British soldiers are fighting to maintain Britain's position as the greatest empire the world has ever known."

"Aren't they?"

"Yes, they are, but…"

"Well, what's wrong with that?"

"Most people do not seem to realize that, in many instances, this country that they feel so public-spirited towards is governed and controlled by those same men who refuse to give them fair wages and better working conditions. It is ruled by the men who keep them poor."

I fell silent thinking on all this. Is that what Mrs Baxter was trying in her own way to tell me about Papa? Is that why Papa requested the flags be flown? If people gave their money to the war widows they would have nothing left to support the dockers and then the men would be forced back to work to support their starving families. The more I thought about it, the more fitting it seemed that women should have the right to vote. It would be one step nearer to a more fair-minded and equal society.

"Well, I'll march, if you will," I replied.

"Done!" laughed Grandmama and hugged me tight.

5th August 1900

Father has cancelled our trip to Suffolk. He says that he has far too much business to attend to here in London and cannot possibly get away.

Grandmother said that he would be disappointing both

Henry and me, but we both shouted our disagreements. Henry has been moping for days at the thought of spending a month away from Archie. From my point of view it was one of the few attractions the holiday held for me: no Lydia, no Archie! If Henry ever found this diary and read it, she would hate me for ever more.

6th August 1900

This morning, after Jenny had woken me, while she was pottering around in my room and then preparing my bath, I began to watch her in a way I never have before.

"What are you looking at?" she giggled. I shrugged because I was embarrassed that she had caught me staring.

It was simply that it had never occurred to me before to consider Jenny's position. I don't mean within our household. What I was thinking as I studied her was what would happen to her if things ever got bad for us and Father was obliged to ask his staff to leave. I know that she is only a year or two older than Henrietta – twenty, I think – and that her family are poor and she was born somewhere in the East End of London. She has little, if any, formal education, but I have no idea what sort of wage Father pays her. She can read,

I know that too, because I have seen her from time to time with letters which, once read, she slips into her apron pockets like sweets to be consumed later when no one is looking. Are they from a boyfriend? Is she to be married? If Father were to throw her out on the street, which I know he wouldn't, what rights would she have? What prospects? I fear, none.

If I understand correctly, from what one or two of the women were saying at the meeting the other evening domestic servants are not members of any unions. Hence, Jenny has no rights whatsoever.

"Do you have a boyfriend, Jenny?" I asked eventually. She was bending over at the time sorting through petticoats in a drawer.

"Your question is a bit personal, don't you think?" But her response was said with warmth and a glint in her eye. "Yeah, I have."

Then I wanted to ask her how she pictures her future and what, if any, ambitions she has. But I was unsure whether or not she would think those questions too impertinent. Would she judge me horribly inquisitive?

How shocking it is that I have always taken it for granted that there should be maidservants in our house to care for me and my needs, but that their concerns should be of no matter to me.

"Will you leave here and marry your boyfriend?"

She howled with laughter. "He hasn't asked me yet!"

"Do you love him?"

"What do you want to know all this for?"

"I was thinking about your rights, Jenny. You know, if you should ever leave here…"

"My rights!" she scoffed. "Don't be so daft. What rights do I have?"

"That's exactly what I mean," said I, leaping off the bed to my feet. "If you joined the suffragettes…"

"You've gone loopy, you have. Suffra-what?"

"Votes for women, Jenny. Unions for domestic servants. The right not to be kicked out of your job. Fair wages."

"I think you should get in your bath. Your towels are warmed." And, with that, she disappeared from the room, shaking her head and muttering: "Rights for domestics, I don't know."

But I had meant it. I shall talk to Gran and see if we cannot persuade Cook and Anna and even Jonesy to accompany us to a meeting.

9th August 1900

Henry has received an invitation, along with Archie and the rest of the Marsh family to go to Ireland to stay at Wyngard, the famous country estate which belongs to Earl and Lady Londonderry. Father thinks that it is a splendid idea and has said that she can go at once. Jenny will accompany her. Our house is a-bustle with activity. Cases and clothes are everywhere as they both prepare for Henry's departure.

15th August 1900

I have been thinking about what Grandmama said in the carriage the other evening, about how we could best publicize the suffragette movement, aside from marching on the streets, that is. And I have had a most wonderful idea! How would it be to cinematograph one of the meetings? Then we could find church halls, institutions, local meeting houses, any place where the windows could be darkened, to exhibit our moving pictures. Women all over the country would be able to find out what is happening. They could hear what the suffragettes are saying and what they – no, WE – are fighting for. Surely, that is more efficient than giving out leaflets or marching? The problem is that I don't have a cinematograph camera. And the cinematograph does not have any sound, so we could not reproduce the discussions at the meetings.

Still, there must be a way to put such an apparatus to this good use, and what a well-found opportunity it would be for me to learn the craft I am so hankering to be involved with!

17th August 1900

Before dinner this evening, alone in the drawing room with Grandmama, I confided to her my plan about the cinematograph. When I had finished, she sat very silently, frowning. Her silence was so long and so considered that I feared I must have said something terribly wrong, until she nodded. Slowly, at first, brow furrowed deep in thought, she eventually replied. "It's a brilliant suggestion, Flora. The question is how can we effectively put it into practice?"

"The first thing is the cinematograph," I replied excitedly.

"No, no, the first consideration is … how on earth do we go about finding someone who could operate the camera?"

My heart sank like a stone in a lake. "Me, Grandmama. I will work it out. That's the whole point!"

She turned to me in astonishment and looked me full in the face. "You, Flora?"

"But, of course!" I cried. How could she doubt me or my idea? My heart was pounding. "You can't take the idea away from me Grandmama, you can't! It's what I have been dreaming of all year!" I was all but yelling at her because I was so intensely afraid that my opportunity was about to slip right out of my fingers, stolen by my closest ally.

"Sssh, sssh, dear. I had no idea you felt quite *this* passionately about it."

"But, yes! Yes! I don't want to come out into society and spend hours being fitted for dresses. I don't want to marry a chinless man like Archie Marsh who has more moustache than brains. I want to be a suffragette. I want to be like Miss Kingsley and travel. I want to be like you and care about people and causes! I want to do something with my life!"

"Hush, child, hush."

I sighed and sank back in my chair. "Sorry," I muttered tearfully, "I didn't mean to shout at you."

"No, your passion is splendid. The question is how to put all that energy to practical and positive use. Even if we could find a cinematograph camera for sale..."

"I could return to Paris and ask that lady director working for Mr Gaumont..."

"Alice Guy?"

"Yes, I could ask her to teach me."

"Flora, you are fifteen years old. This is not an apparatus that you learn to use overnight. The suggestion is excellent but your ideas for the execution of it are impractical."

I wanted to weep and sorely wished that I had never mentioned it, even to Gran. I should run away. Go to Paris and sit outside Mr Gaumont's studio until they agree to take me in and teach me the art of cinematographs.

I *will* go to Paris!

20th August 1900

"Well, Flora, I have been making enquiries and, it seems, we might be able to find one of your cameras right here in London." This was Grandmama talking. She had asked Jonesy to fetch me to her study. When I entered I found her at her desk, her pince-nez dangling from a long golden chain. She was waving a sheet of paper at me which was covered with lines of illegible handwriting. She spoke in a matter-of-fact manner. It was as though she were describing the most direct route from point A to point B on one of the underground train lines, while I, amazed, was barely able to take on the reality of what she was saying.

"I think we should contact this gentleman. Wait, I have his name here somewhere. Where is it? Ah, yes, here we are! This is the fellow, Mr Birt Acres. He has been exhibiting his pictures at the Royal Photographic Society. They have given me his details so I think we should telephone him and ask to meet with him, don't you?"

"Oh, yes, please!" I cried.

21st August 1900

Grandmama spoke to Mr Acres on the telephone early this morning. He has advised her that there is a colleague of his, a Mr R W Paul, who is making and selling cinematograph cameras here in England. It is he who has been producing them for the French illusionist George Méliès.

Now, all I have to do is to try and persuade Father to buy me one!

Mr Acres has invited us to the Royal Photographic Society to see his film. I am thrilled. So is Grandmama.

"Well, Flora, I am looking forward to this outing. I hope that I shall be as taken with these moving pictures as you are."

Oh, I so want Gran to be inspired, and then she will want to support me and plead with Father on my behalf.

23rd August 1900

Thank heavens we did not go to Suffolk. If we had, Gran and I would have been denied the pleasures of today's outing. This afternoon, we visited Mr Acres at the Royal Photographic Society. And what an event it turned out to be.

Mr Acres has cinematographed a series of photographic images which he has entitled: *Rough Sea at Dover*. As with the earlier pictures I saw with Miss Baker, each frame follows on from the last in fast succession to create the idea of movement. The subject today was waves crashing against a sea wall and, my word, the illusion was magnificent. The waves crashed and the spray exploded in the air into white clouds of foam. It was so realistic that we actually feared we might get wet! Grandmama was as taken with the whole business as I am.

"I almost believed I was standing alongside that sea wall," she whispered to me as our host switched off his projecting machine.

Our afternoon was made even more special because we had the viewing to ourselves; with Mr Acres, of course.

Afterwards, we took tea together. Gran was bursting to know all about it.

"Well, I congratulate you, Mr Acres. Those pictures in motion are most lifelike. Please, will you be so kind as to explain to us exactly how the whole business operates because I would like to purchase one of your cinematographs."

"You will need a projecting system to accompany it, Lady Campbell."

"Yes, yes, of course. Whatever is needed. And an operator, of course."

"No," I hissed, but no one paid me any attention. When Gran is enthused by one of her good works or projects she pays no heed to anyone and, this afternoon, that included me.

"There are one or two methods in operation at the moment. We are working with the one that is known as '35 millimetres.'"

"Why such a name, Mr Acres?"

"Because, Lady Campbell, that is the width of the film we are using. Please, let me show you."

Mr Acres led us from where we had viewed his work through to a small area which he called the projection cupboard. There, with the apparatus in front of us, he expounded on several technical matters. I have to confess that, try as I did to follow, I was soon lost. He demonstrated how the movement of the film is made possible. The film, which rather resembles a long length of ribbon, has holes punched into each of its two borders. These clip in to sprockets which are attached to a kind of wheel. The wheel turns and with it go the sprockets which carry the film along. In this way the film is moved forward. It is quite ingenious!

Gran seemed to grasp the specifics of it all without too much difficulty. She was certainly asking a great many questions, such as who had created the idea of film in lengths of ribbons. An American company named Kodak, was Acres's response. She enquired after the price of the film, then the cost of this and that and wrote down various figures and names, even an address or two.

On our way home in the carriage, Gran was still scribbling notes. "There is a great deal to learn, eh, Flora?" I only nodded because I knew that my idea of owning a camera and simply taking pictures had been proved to be rather naïve, but I was thrilled that she was so taken with it all.

26th August 1900

Six days ago, one of Father's steamers, *India*, bound home from Java laden with 85 tonnes of sugar went down in heavy seas off the east coast of Africa. All passengers and crew seem to have escaped by the lifeboats so, thank the Lord, no casualties have been reported, but Father's entire shipment has been lost to the oceans. He must have known about it for a day or two because it was reported in *The Times* but he has said nothing to us which makes me fear that the loss is a big blow to him and his company.

I cannot possibly mention the cinematograph now! How selfish of me to think only of myself.

30th August 1900

Henry and Jenny are returned from Ireland. Clearly, they have had a splendid time. Henry is filled with the beauties of the Irish countryside and she never stops dropping the names of this or that Duke or Lord who she lunched with or took tea with. All that aside from several princes she was invited to dance with.

"So, did you find yourself a handsome beau? Will you marry a prince and become a princess?" I asked her, jokingly.

But to that she replied in exaggerated surprise, "Why, Archie Marsh is my beau. Who else do you suppose, you silly girl? You understand nothing of true love, Flora Bonnington!"

How I hate it when she patronizes me!

Jenny tells me that she has "never seen the like in sumptuousness as the Londonderrys' country estate. I could have slept in the stables; the place was that posh and comfy."

14th September 1900

Archie and Henry are to be married! Yes! Father has approved the match. What a positively dreadful business! I feel sure that if Henry waited, she would find someone far more entertaining to spend the rest of her life with. Oh, well, it's her life. I overheard Grandmama in the library expressing similar doubts to Father. I think his response to her upset me more than the thought of the marriage.

"Violet, Archie is a titled gentleman of means and an excellent catch. I feel that, under the circumstances and for Henrietta's sake, we should not allow this opportunity to slip by."

Lord, it makes marriage sound as tedious as cricket! I shall have none of it!

20th September 1900

Grandmama was talking to me of converting a part of her Gloucestershire estate into a studio for the use of the art of cinematography! I am so excited that she is enthused.

"It will be an expensive proposition, Flora, but I do believe there is something in your idea of using it to teach people and to show them marvels taking place elsewhere in the world. The pictures we saw the other day were very exciting, but you are quite right, Flora. One could go further. I am going to have a word with your father about it."

29th September 1900

Father is absolutely furious with me. Before Grandmama went out this evening, she recounted our plans to him. I had been intending to accompany her to a suffrage meeting but he forbade it and summoned me to his study. I seem only to be invited there when I am in trouble.

"What on earth do you think you are playing at?" he asked me brusquely.

"I don't know what you mean," I replied.

"This talk about moving pictures."

"But it is what I want to do," I answered nervously.

My response must have infuriated him because he slapped his hand hard against his desk and began to shout at me. "This is idle nonsense, Flora. I will have no daughter of mine involved with any of it, do you hear me?"

"But, Papa, there is no harm in it." Arguing was a fatal mistake. I had intended to simply state my case but it only enraged him further.

"How dare you speak back to me!" he shouted. He seemed unreasonably upset. "You are a young lady of breeding. I had thought that it was some fanciful notion that would pass. Do you think that I would ever allow my daughter to move in such a world? The idea that you harbour thoughts of wanting to work at all is bad enough, but in among vulgar folk who have been born to vaudeville and theatre and the like. It is a working class amusement, Flora. Fairground entertainment, nothing more. Do you think I want you to end up with circus people and freak shows? It is disgusting! I should never have allowed all this talk of women's rights in this house. I should have put my foot down and insisted that you behave yourself and concentrate your energies, like your sister, on the things that matter. I am ashamed of you. You will be thought of as little better than an actress and you will bring disgrace upon our family name!"

"But Grandmama is…"

"Go to your room!" he shouted.

I was stunned by the force of his temper. As I turned to go, he told me that I am forbidden to leave the house without his approval and consent. I have spent the evening alone by my fireside, crying.

1st October 1900

I could not sleep at all last night and, eventually, got up and went downstairs to the kitchen for a glass of milk. As I was passing by the library, I heard voices from within, speaking sharply. I had not intended to eavesdrop, but the door was ajar and my attention was caught by the conversation taking place. It was between Father and Grandmama.

What I heard has shocked me so deeply. I wish I had not been witness to it because now I am at sixes and sevens and I have no one to confide in. I need to try and remember the exchange word for word, as best as I can, to make some sense out of it and to calm the torrent of feelings that have arisen within me and distressed me since the hearing of it.

Father was the one talking as I was passing, before I stopped to listen. He sounded irritable and his words were spoken in an impatient way. He said something like, "Violet, if you have no further use for your estate, then why not offer it to Henrietta and Archie as a wedding gift?"

Grandmama was calmer. "No, Thomas, I will not. Your treatment towards Flora is quite unreasonable and if you so stubbornly and cruelly refuse to encourage her attempts to expand her young mind and to seek out her creative direction, then I intend to assist her myself. Besides, I am in agreement with her. I believe these pictures in motion have a future and, if intelligently developed, could do much good in the world. Like Flora, I also want to share in this new discovery. You should be proud of your daughter, Thomas, not punishing her. She has a fine imagination and it should be encouraged."

"In the same disastrous way you encouraged Millicent. Is that what you are trying to tell me?"

Even from beyond the library door, I could almost hear the shock in Grandmama's silence.

"If it hadn't been for you, Violet, egging your daughter on to works that were quite inappropriate for a young mother and a pregnant woman, I believe that Millicent would still be alive today."

I could hardly believe what I was hearing. My heart was pounding and my head was swimming in a sickly way. I was shivering with cold.

"How can you even contemplate such a thought, let alone voice it?" Gran spoke slowly, in a considered manner, but I could tell from her deep gravelly tone that she was hurt or angry and was fighting to remain calm. I longed to open the door and rush in and speak out for her, but I could not bring myself to move; I was shocked rigid.

"You know yourself that what I am saying is true. Millicent wore herself out supporting you and your preposterous, no, dangerous, suffrage schemes. Her place should have been here at home at my side, caring for me and her small daughter, Henrietta. Instead of which, you filled her head with nonsense, rushed her from one meeting to another where useless females filled their empty heads with ideas about votes for women and blathered foolishly about opportunities to study the law or medicine. The very notion of a woman as a doctor goes against the natural order of things. I find it obscene. Such ambitions should have no place in a woman's world…"

"Thomas, you are…"

"And now, you are doing the same with Flora. Flora's tragedy is that she resembles her mother too closely. I had hoped that she would change as she grew older. I kept silent, thinking it would pass, but that was wrong of me. She has inherited her mother's passion. And you encourage her. But, this time, I refuse to stand by and watch while her head is turned by you and your compatriots; women who do not know their place or are simply sad unmarried creatures who have nothing better to do with their lives!"

"I cannot believe what I am hearing, Thomas. I have always judged you a reasonable man…"

"The moment my shipment of gold bars arrives from Africa and I have received payment for the delivery and sale, I shall refund to you every penny you have invested in my company, and you will be free to leave this house. Now, if you will excuse me, I have work to do."

There was a long silence – I supposed Gran was taking on the reality of all that Father had just told her – followed by her response, softly spoken. I detected no anger in her tone but, I fancied, a certain sadness.

"Unlike others less fortunate, I am not in need of the money, Thomas. If you want to return it, you may do so, whenever you see fit, and I shall accept it as your wish to settle all outstanding financial matters between us, but, please, do not jeopardize the stability of your business for my sake, particularly in the light of your recent losses at sea. In the meantime, I shall make plans to leave this address, but I shall do so discreetly and in my own time. I shall try to choose a moment which will not encourage gossip nor cause unnecessary distress to the household. Goodnight."

I heard Gran's footsteps crossing the study and I fled – not to the kitchen where I had been headed, but back upstairs to my room – before the door opened and I was discovered.

Now what? A life without Gran is too ghastly to contemplate. Am I really so like my mother? How I wish I could talk to her, just for fifteen minutes! And what of my father? I have never heard him utter such cruel and unkind thoughts before. Never. I want to write that I hate him, but I cannot. I do not.

18th October 1900

Our house, our home is cheerless. Nothing has been mentioned by anyone about the exchange I overheard all those days, weeks, ago and I cannot bring myself to let Gran know that I am party to it all. Actually, the days are a curious mix of moods; joylessness on the one hand and happiness on the other. Henry scoots about chirping merrily, making plans for her spring wedding, blind to the family undercurrents. Meanwhile, dear, wonderful Gran goes about her affairs in a quiet gracious way, but her eyes have lost their sparkle. I can see it. And what of Father? He has grown even more distant and unapproachable.

I want to burst with the weight of it all. Might this state of affairs pass? I pray that it will. I hope that Father and Gran can find a way to heal the rift between them and that we remain none the wiser (officially, that is). Still, the idea that Father could blame my grandmother for the death of my mother is horrible.

28th October 1900

Yet again, London is proving itself the capital city of the "world's greatest empire". Everyone is talking about the Boer War because a ship named the *Aurania*, carrying soldiers returning from a tour of duty in South Africa docked in Southampton yesterday. These soldiers, who sailed from Cape Town on October 7th, have been involved in combat and are to be given a hero's homecoming. The soldiers left London for Africa last January – I wonder if any of them was nursed by Miss Kingsley?

A parade through the streets of London is being arranged by the Lord Mayor of London. The soldiers known as the City Imperial Volunteers have been brought by train to Paddington Station instead of more directly to Waterloo because Paddington is the Queen's station. It is more prestigious and the surrounding neighbourhoods are less seedy and down-at-heel.

It is to be called the City Imperial Volunteers March and

Father says we must go because it is history in the making. Archie and his sister Lydia will be accompanying us. Of course, we will not line the streets and wait with the crowds for the passing of the procession. Apparently, there is to be a reception which will be held at the Guild Hall. I believe the Queen will be in attendance, and Father has been invited. He is planning to take us in his automobile. We will follow the procession and, after, we will attend the reception. I have no idea if Grandmama has been invited but, in any case, she is not coming with us.

"Why not?" I asked her when I found her alone in the study answering her mail.

"Because I have something else to do, dear."

"Couldn't I come with you?" I asked her. "I'm sure I'd rather."

"No. Your father is perfectly right. It is history in the making and, one day, you will be grateful that he took you along," she replied without enthusiasm.

"Pictures in motion and suffragettes are also history in the making and you know it. I don't care about the war any more than you do."

"You are wrong, Flora, I do care about the war. I care that people are dying needlessly. And I rejoice for each of those soldiers who has returned home safely, as well as for their families. And I believe that if women were given the vote there would be less fighting, less need for bloodshed."

"Are you really going to leave us, Grandmama?" I asked, almost without realizing what I was saying. She looked up from her writing, pen in hand, and stared at me with an expression which was both surprised and suspicious.

"What makes you ask such a question?"

"I overheard you and Papa arguing in the library."

Grandmama placed her pen slowly, thoughtfully, on to her desk. "Were you eavesdropping?"

"No! Of course not. I couldn't sleep. I was on my way to fetch a glass of milk."

"Sit down, Flora," she said, pointing to a chair which I drew up alongside her, next to the writing bureau. "Your father is right to care for your future welfare, and I … I was wrong to fill your head with ideas that you are too young to be a party to…"

"That's rubbish, and you know it!" I was on my feet, flustered and tearful. I felt as if I was losing my only ally and that, in a way, Gran was betraying both me and her principles.

"Don't lose your temper, Flora. If you want to discuss this, then you must behave like a young lady and not a petulant child."

Her manner was sharp and chiding and made me want to cry, but I took a deep breath and sat down again. "I am fifteen and a half. Henry is barely more than three years older than I am and she is getting married. So, if she is old enough to know her own mind…"

"In my opinion, she isn't!"

"I want to know what happened to my mother. And why Father holds you responsible."

"That is for him to tell you, Flora."

"But you know he won't! I have a right to know."

"Very well," she sighed. "Your mother caught pneumonia in the last days of her pregnancy. Her body was not strong enough to fight the infection. She grew weak and died shortly after you were born. There, you have it."

I sat staring at her, waiting for her to expand on what she had said but she did not. "Now, please, Flora, I must continue with my letters."

"Why did she catch pneumonia?" My grandmother made no response. "Please, Gran. Was it something to do with you and the suffrage movement?"

"Yes."

"What happened?"

Again, Gran sighed. She did not want to be pushed into a corner but she was too gracious to reject me and I had to know.

"She was canvassing with me. She shouldn't have been. She was eight months pregnant with you, but that was why she felt so strongly about the cause, don't you see? Women did not have sole custody rights over their own children. She believed passionately that, in the case of the death of a husband, every woman has the right to bring up her own children in the manner that she sees fit. Thomas forbade her to continue with our work. He said it would tire her. She did not heed him. We were walking from house to house, knocking at people's doors, trying to explain to them what it was we were fighting to achieve, and to ask them to sign our petition. The weather grew dark, the sky louring and an unexpected downpour drenched us both. Even with my carriage waiting at the end of street, we got soaked to the skin.

"By the time we returned here, Millie was shivering and chilled through. Cook and I put her straight to bed. Thomas was not at home. I sent immediately for Doctor Hubbard, but there was nothing he could do for her. Within a matter of days, she had developed pneumonia. She must have picked up the virus somewhere while we were out canvassing. You were born, a little prematurely but not seriously so, and five days later Millie, weak and feverish, died. So, in a way, your father is right. I was to blame and I have no right to encourage you along the same path."

"No, Gran, you're not to blame. You didn't force my mother, did you?"

Gran shook her head and smiled.

"And you are not forcing me. You said yourself that it was something my mother believed in passionately. How would Papa have felt if, after the loss of my mother, someone had come to him and said: *You do not have the legal right to bring up these children without a guardian who we consider* is

137

better able to look after them than you are? Don't you think he would have lost his temper and fought for his rights, too? I think what my mother did was courageous and I am only sorry that I cannot tell her so. And as for forcing your ideas upon me, it was me who introduced you to moving pictures, so there!"

Grandmother leant forward and stroked my face. "You are so like her," she whispered, and I swear there were tears in her eyes.

"It would be terribly wrong of me, and a betrayal of the memory of my mother, not to follow the path I passionately long to follow. But what you have told me has also helped me understand Papa a little better. He has always been so distant with me. It has hurt me so much. I feared he did not love me the way he loves Henrietta. I have always feared that he thought less of me and that I disappoint him in a way I could not understand, that I have let him down."

"No, Flora. I think that when he looks at you, he sees the beautiful woman he loved so deeply and, though he has never for one second blamed you, he lost her when you came along."

I nodded, kissed Gran on the cheek, whispered a barely audible *thank you* and left her to her letter writing.

29th October 1900

Today is the City Imperial Volunteers March. I have promised myself that I will be agreeable and do whatever Papa asks of me. I shall even be as nice as pie to Lydia and Archie.

30th October 1900

Yesterday was LONG! We set off from home a little after ten with Papa in his automobile. Archie sat next to him in the front and I was seated in the middle between Henry and Lydia. Every square inch of London seemed to be taken up with people. I had not imagined how crowded it would be. At every turn there were soldiers in their various uniforms lining the routes. Military bands were performing *Soldiers of the Queen* as well as other patriotic airs. The public were everywhere, herded together along the pavements, packing the taverns and coffeehouses. It was almost impossible to creep forward at any pace at all. Working people, delighted by the prospect of an unforeseen day's holiday, were perched in the branches of trees while dozens of children straddled the shoulders of their fathers, pointing in our direction. The routes were a living, moving sea of faces and bodies, cheering and eating and waving. It was very impressive, in a way.

Passing along Fleet Street, we caught sight of many journalists eager to find themselves a story. The down-at-heel pubs in that vicinity and the cafés were packed and noisy and doing a roaring trade. I longed to stop and take a tour and hear what they were all so busy talking and laughing about. Few seemed to have their eyes on the passing procession of City Imperial Soldiers who, whenever I caught a glimpse of one up ahead, looked quite bemused by the furore. I was transfixed by the number of people who had turned out for this event. Everyone was shouting "God Save our Queen" or "Rule Britannia" or "Long Live the Great British Empire", waving flags and bits of cloth or throwing their hats in the air, any old thing.

Suddenly, in the midst of all this, Henry said: "I suppose those soldiers are being rewarded for massacring hundreds of darkies." And then she went on to tell us, as though the two thoughts were directly connected, that she had read an advertisement in *Queen, the Lady's newspaper*, offering the services of a group of nigger minstrels called The Happy Darkies. "They can be hired for private parties," she said.

"Oh, how nasty to have darkies wandering about loose at a party! I would be so fearful," cried stupid Lydia.

"Of course, they are not real savages, Lydia," explained Henrietta, in an exaggeratedly patient way. "They are ordinary decent white men with their faces blacked up. I believe it is all the rage now. I think it would be a simply splendid and novel idea to have them perform at our wedding. Archie agrees and we intend to try and persuade Father to employ them for us. What fun!" I turned my attention elsewhere, remembering the promise I had made to myself – to be agreeable and nice to everyone. I concentrated hard on the world passing before my eyes beyond the automobile. There are times when I wonder if Henry and I were really born into the same family. The idea of such an entertainment struck me as horrid but my mind was distracted from such thoughts by an accident somewhere in front of us as we approached Ludgate Circus. I could not see what had happened but there were ambulance men everywhere and the whole procession seemed to have ground to a halt. I think it was because we were barely moving that I spotted the banners and was able to read the lettering so clearly though, try as I might, I could not see who was carrying them. But there they were, waving in the wind high above the sea of heads, clear as daylight. I was on the point of shouting out, but contained myself for I knew my joy would not be well received. There, in amongst the throng of people, were the placards with slogans saying VOTES FOR WOMEN and others with IF WOMEN HAD THE VOTE, WE WOULD VOTE AGAINST WAR. I thought of Christabel Pankhurst and her words to Grandmama, *Deeds, not words, Violet,* and wondered if she were there somewhere in among the crowds bearing her message for all, including our Queen, to see. I felt warm and proud inside. I tried to kneel up and peered hard into the people but they must have been more than a hundred deep. It was impossible to identify anyone in particular. Might Gran be out there somewhere? I asked myself.

A little further along, amidst much pandemonium, I spotted one or two other placards. Their messages seemed to be protesting against the city council: THE LONDON COUNTY COUNCIL WANTS CHANGES AT THE EXPENSE OF THE RATEPAYERS, one stated. And another: LCC SHOULD CARE FOR THE HEALTH AND LIVING STANDARDS OF *ALL* ITS INHABITANTS. Archie interrupted his discussions with Papa and turned back towards us, saying, "Look, see there, Henrietta. The Socialists are making trouble again. Even on a day filled with national pride such as today, they cannot keep from complaining."

I bit back my desire to say something and thought instead of how wonderful it would have been to capture this day, the throngs of the people, the protests, this famous city of London in full sail, on my dreamed-of cinematograph. It would truly be history in the making. So many different points of view. I tried not to dwell too long on these thoughts for the fact that I will never have my camera only makes me heartsick and frustrated.

Still, what a fine tale to tell and, although the moving pictures would be in black and white, I should entitle it: *Our Colourful Empire*.

Finally, after St Paul's Cathedral where the Lord Mayor and some city sheriffs in brilliant red coats awaited the procession, we made our way to the Guild Hall. Upon arrival at the Guild Hall yet another band struck up the first notes of *God Save the Queen* and dozens of soldiers dressed in khaki began to troop inside, ready to be honoured. And so we followed on.

By the time the reception was over, I felt as if we had been to war ourselves! When we returned home, completely exhausted, Gran was not there. I thought nothing of it at the time. Only later, at dinner, when I asked after her and Father remarked that she had been called to her estate in Gloucestershire, did I begin to feel afraid.

After supper, I sneaked along to her room to take a look at what was there. Many of her possessions had been removed and her wardrobe was half-empty. My heart was beating so fast as I ran downstairs in search of Jonesy. Father and Archie and Henrietta were in the drawing room so I knew I could have a quiet word with him. Jones was in the kitchen polishing Father's shoes. If there was news, he would be bound to have heard it.

"Where's Gran?" I asked him.

I could tell by the strained look on his face that he knew.

"Tell me, Jonesy, please. Is she visiting her estate, or has she left us?" Without a word, he stuffed his hand into his trouser pocket and pulled out an envelope which bore my Christian name. Recognizing the writing, I ripped it open at once. Jonesy stayed at my side.

My dearest child,

You caught me at this letter yesterday when you found me in the drawing room and I suppose I should have been less cowardly and just downed pen and told you the truth, which is that I am leaving Cadogan Square for a little while. Do not be alarmed or upset for I feel sure that matters will resolve themselves quickly, and we shall all be reunited again before too long. Please do not blame your father. This is my choice and not of his commanding. I have work to do for the movement which, I fear, would only embarrass him. I also feel in need of a short holiday, though, heaven knows if I shall find the time to take one.

Work very hard with your studies, for a good education will stand you in good stead, whatever path you choose, remember that. Be brave and patient – your time will come – and I promise to buy you a cinematograph for your seventeenth birthday.

Gran xx

I looked up at Jones who must have known the contents for his expression was as bleak as I felt broken-hearted. My seventeenth birthday! Lord, that is eighteen months away.

"Do you know where she has gone?"

He shook his head.

5th November 1900

Today, tonight, is Guy Fawkes Night. On this night, everywhere in England, folk light bonfires and burn a guy. A guy is a stuffed thing, like a big floppy rag doll. It is an effigy of the man, Guy Fawkes, who in the year 1605 tried to blow up the Houses of Parliament, home to the British Government, in a plot which failed and led to his execution, The Gunpowder Plot. It is not an event that we, as a family, have ever celebrated. So, why do I mention it in my diary now? Because I feel that Father and everything he stands for should be blown up. Britain, the Empire, the lack of rights for women, keeping me away from what I care for and love, driving Gran out of our home. No, I don't want to blow up my father. I love my father. It is what he believes in that I want to destroy. Surely I am not alone? Whether I be born into an aristocratic family or I come from a very poor one, surely other young girls of my age experience the frustrations I am experiencing? If I had been sent away to school rather than educated by a governess at home, even though I really, really like Miss Baker, I would have other girls of my age to talk to. But would I dare voice the thoughts I am thinking?

Before dinner this evening, I was so downhearted by everything that I pleaded with Jenny to help me cut off my hair. She stared at me, as she sometimes does when she thinks I am talking like a wicked fairy who eats frogs. "What are you asking?"

"It is the latest fashion," I protested. "I want my hair cut short. Just below my ears, I think." And so, Jenny, reluctantly, with a little assistance from me, chopped off my locks.

My appearance is most unladylike and, I think, rather splendid, but what a to-do this evening when I went down to dinner. You might think by the expression on everyone's faces that I had sliced off my head.

"What have you done to yourself?" asked Papa with a face as white as a sheet.

"I have cut my hair," I replied, in my most matter-of-fact manner.

"Oh, Flora!" shrieked – literally shrieked – Henrietta. "No, I don't believe it! How could you have done such a thing! You will be a disgrace at my wedding. Worse, you will bring disgrace upon our family. How could you have been so thoughtless and selfish!"

"Henry," I answered in a tone which I hoped might calm her. "Your wedding is not until March. If I wish it, my hair will have grown again by then. Please don't be so upset. It is my appearance, not yours."

"You are a witch," she screamed, and ran from the dining room.

"I will see you in my study after dinner," pronounced Father, as he does when he has something monumental to say but prefers to save it for later so as not to disturb whatever is currently in progress, which, in this instance, was his dinner. We ate in silence, until Henry returned and made such a theatrical display, addressing all her conversation to Papa just as though I did not exist at all.

Jones, when he came in to serve at table and caught sight of me, nearly dropped the platter of lamb. His face, trying not to express his shock, made me want to burst out laughing, even though I knew I was in for big trouble later. In fact, my encounter with Father was nothing out of the ordinary. He asked me what I had been thinking of and why would I want to deliberately spoil what he described as my "pretty feminine looks".

My only response was to shrug. I was unable to say the things I was bursting to say. Father is a very imposing figure and when he is angry, he can be quite daunting. I suppose I had hoped that I would be able to pour my heart out to him. Part of me was longing to confide in him but, as it was, I just stood there with my head bent, silent and unhappy. My punishment is the same as before. I am housebound and can only go out with his permission.

"And that, young lady, will only be given when I am satisfied about where you are going and with whom. Now, go to your room and stay there."

10th November 1900

Father has dismissed Jenny. I cannot believe it. On account of my hair. I found her sobbing her heart out in the upstairs laundry room.

"But, how can he possibly blame you? I never mentioned to him that you had anything to do with it," I assured her.

"When he asked me outright, I was obliged to tell the truth and admit that I did the chopping of it. Then he said to me that, as your maid, I should have been keeping an eye on you, not encouraging such carryings on. He told me to be out of here by Friday. He'll give me a month's pay."

"That's ridiculous!" I cried. "Please, don't be upset, Jenny. I'll make him change his mind. Do you have a place to stay while we sort it out?"

She shook her head and wept more bitterly.

I ran along the corridor in search of Henrietta, but she was not in her room. Suddenly, it struck me how apart we had grown. When had we last confided in one another or giggled like sisters? It was my fault. I was to blame. She must have sensed how much I dislike Archie. She must have been hurt by my aloofness, by my unwillingness to share in her happiness. While I was thinking all of this, I was running to and fro, opening doors, peering in rooms, trying to decide what I could possibly do. There is no way in the world we can allow Papa to dismiss Jenny. She is part of the family and, more importantly, she HAS NO RIGHTS. How could I have been so selfish as to involve her in my prank, my rebellious act against my father? If Gran were here none of this would have happened. I thundered down the stairs in search of Cook or Jones, threw open the kitchen door and there they both were, looking grim. The news had obviously reached them. Jenny had probably told them first, and their sympathies would lie with her. Whatever loyalty they felt towards me or my family, or any other individual within it, they were the employees and we were their employers.

I could see by the expression on both their faces as they glared at me that already something had changed. They had taken a step away, a step towards the safety of their own ground, and I was not welcome to intrude upon it.

"Where's Gran?" I asked. But I could tell at a glance that they were neither of them willing to get involved. Leaking such information to me – the troublemaker, the rebel – could cost them their jobs.

"She's the only one who can plead for Jenny," I pressed. "I telephoned Gloucestershire but she's not there."

Still they did not respond. I stared in shock for an instant and then fled the room. Miss Baker. Where was Miss Baker? I glanced at our grandfather clock in the hall. It was almost ten. Any second now she would be arriving. Normally, she would have been here by this time. She was late. Or had Father sacked her as well? I hovered in the hallway and, as she opened the front door, I all but pounced on her.

"Flora!" she shrieked. "You gave me a scare."

"Where's Gran?"

She looked completely bemused. Her blue eyes were dancing and staring in a very puzzled way. "What's wrong?"

"Papa has dismissed Jenny. I need to find Gran."

"Jenny? But why?"

"Because of me and my constant talk of the cinematograph and because I cut my stupid hair and I hate Archie Marsh and I DON'T KNOW WHERE GRAN IS!!" I was yelling and sobbing, out of control.

Miss Baker took me by the hand and led me through to the drawing room. She took off her coat, folded it neatly and placed it on the arm of the sofa. "If it were about the cinematograph and the moving pictures, I think that he would have asked me to leave, don't you? I don't know where your grandmother is. But have you spoken with anyone at the Suffrage Society?"

The words were like magic to me. "It never even occurred to me to ask there. But, of course. I'm going there at once." I rose to leave but before I had taken a step Miss Baker took me by the arms.

"Flora, wait! You know that you are forbidden to leave the house without permission. Do you wish to have the entire household thrown out on the street? Stop, take a deep breath and let us think this through in an intelligent manner."

"I have to get a message to her. She must come back and beg Father to change his mind. If he wants someone to pack their bags and leave, then I will."

"Be quiet, Flora. Stop this nonsense and let me think!"

Reluctantly, I sank back in to a chair.

"I have it," she said. "At midday, I have a mathematics lesson with Henrietta. Until then, I am supposed to tutor you. History, followed by geography. I will set you the work I had prepared for us to study today and then I will slip off. If, for some completely unexpected reason, your father should return, then you must tell him – it's a lie, I know it – that I was forced to go to the dentist. But, you must promise me to stay here and study. If you disobey me, you will make things impossible for all of us. And, Flora, I do not approve of lies on any account, but I cannot bear to think of Jenny without employment, do you understand me?"

I nodded, and then shook my head. "I am coming with you," I said.

"No!"

"Yes. I have caused this situation and I want to do my best to sort it out, and I want to see Gran."

"Flora—"

"Telephone Papa, *please*, and request permission for us to leave the house."

"Flora, you are putting my job in jeopardy, as well."

"No more than if you had gone to the dentist. Telephone him and I will call for a carriage."

Father agreed that Miss Baker could take me on a trip to the Natural History Museum, and so we escaped.

The Society headquarters were situated in a small mews house in Chelsea. Grandmother was not there but Christabel Pankhurst was. I requested to see her and, at first, was refused but when I explained my dilemma, the young lady at reception agreed to call her. Christabel recognized me at once and then, to my utter amazement, embraced Miss Baker as though they were old friends.

"Deeds, not words," they muttered to one another as though exchanging their secret code.

Christabel sat with us in the reception while I explained our plight. Once our story had been told, she agreed to get in touch with Grandmama immediately who, she informed me, "is holidaying in Venice, Italy. Meanwhile, the society will organize a bed for your housemaid, Jenny, until matters are resolved", which, she assured us, would be very soon.

December 1900

Matters have been resolved and in a most admirable fashion. Gran returned from Venice and has moved back in with us at Cadogan Square, denying that she had ever intended to leave for any length of time. She received a warm and hearty homecoming from us all. Her intention had been to speak with Father on Jenny's behalf, but, I am pleased to say, I had already resolved the situation. After Miss Baker and I returned from the London Headquarters of the Suffrage Society, I went looking for Jenny and found her slumped like a bundle in a corner of the laundry room. Her face was puffy and blotched red from crying and I felt guilty and ashamed, having come to understand the real delicacy of her situation and the trouble I had caused.

"You have nothing to fear, Jenny," I told her, intending to comfort her. "You will be taken care of."

But my words did nothing to alleviate her distress. She wept on, telling me that she could not return to her parents, her boyfriend had not proposed to her and in any case matters were not going too swimmingly between them and she did not believe that he wanted to marry her and she wished now that she had never met him in the first place. "I'm jobless and homeless," she wailed.

I was responsible and I knew that it was for me, not Gran, to put the affair in order, and I resolved there and then to do so. When Father came home, distracted and filled with work concerns as usual, I requested the time to talk with him. At first he was grumpy, as though I was interrupting his train of thought, but when he saw my face and the gravity of my intent, he nodded and led me through to his study. I sat down, facing him. My heart was beating like a kettle drum. Papa must have sensed my fear and discomfort but he did not make it easy for me.

"I'm waiting," was all he said.

I knew this was my moment and that if I did not open up to him now and stop fighting him, the opportunity might get lost and we might never be friends or understand one another. There was so much to say I hardly knew where to begin, but I took a deep breath and started, falteringly, to pour my heart out to him. He never once interrupted, so I had no notion of how my words were being received, but on I went. I recounted how I had overheard the dispute between him and Gran and how I had blamed him for her departure. I tried to explain to him how deeply I wanted to pursue a career of my own and not be married off like

Henry. I apologized for cutting my hair which had been an act to spite him and I made it clear that Jenny had been in no way responsible. Still he said nothing but his face, I was sure of it, had softened a little and he was listening earnestly and patiently.

Finally, I came to my mother. Father's hands which had been resting clenched on his desk were withdrawn and I knew that I was treading on delicate ground. I begged him not to hold me responsible for her death, nor Gran either. And I begged him not to judge me harshly because, apparently, I resemble her.

"Please, don't judge me in an unkind way because I don't aspire to the things you believe in. I am headstrong, Papa, I know it," I said, "and perhaps that is not always such a good thing. On the other hand, I believe passionately in what I want to achieve and without such passion and drive nothing in the world can be changed. Please, Father, don't deny me my chance."

"And what is it exactly that you want, Flora?"

"I desperately want to make moving pictures and, like Gran and mother, I want to fight for a redefinition of the roles available to women in our society. And I want almost most of all, for us – you and me, Papa – to be friends." A lump caught in my throat, and I fought back my tears. "I want us to love one another."

He said nothing. We sat either side of his desk in silence,

like strangers, but he never took his eyes off me. Two islands floating in different directions, until he whispered so softly that I barely heard him, "Come here."

I got up, shakily, and moved round the desk to his outstretched hand. He took hold of me, pulled me towards him and hugged me so tight that I thought I would stop breathing. "Thank you," he murmured in my ear.

The upshot of the whole affair is that Jenny will not be leaving us. In fact, after Christmas, she will be accompanying Miss Baker and me to Paris where I am to be educated for the coming year. Obviously, we will all be returning for the spring holidays and Henry's wedding to Viscount Archie Marsh.

In the meantime, Father has written a letter to Mr Léon Gaumont and to his lady director, Alice Guy, requesting part-time lessons for me in the art of cinematography. We are awaiting their response.

SUFFRAGETTE

28th March 1909

Lady Violet Campbell, the owner of this Georgian manor house in the depths of the Gloucestershire countryside, was buried today in the cemetery of the church at Dymock. Lady Violet, whom I loved with all my heart, died peacefully in her sleep six days ago after a short illness.

Many of her family and friends travelled up from London yesterday to be here for the service this morning, and tonight the house is packed to the rafters with sleeping people. Most of them know nothing of my existence and I am keeping myself well hidden.

I made my way here by train from Cheltenham to pay my respects. Charlton Kings is where I live during the week. I lodge with a kind-hearted family who were chosen by the late Lady Violet to look after me during school term. I could have boarded at my school, the Cheltenham Ladies' College, but Lady Violet decided that it would be better for me to share the company of a family.

"Because you have lost your own, dear," she reasoned.

You would assume from reading this that I am from a wealthy family, that I was born into the upper class, known here in England as the privileged class, but that is not at all the case.

My name is Dollie Baxter. I am fourteen-and-a-half years old, and I am the only daughter of a working-class man, John Baxter, who spent all his life labouring for a pittance at Bonningtons, one of the two biggest dockyard companies in London. But my father, who was a stevedore by profession, has been dead these past four years. I was ten years old when he passed away and his leaving us changed my life more than I could ever have dreamed was possible. I was uprooted and, quite literally, furnished with a new existence. All that was left of my past were my memories and my name.

So you see, I am a working-class girl of no means, and the knowledge of this fact might better explain my plight now that dear Lady Violet has passed away.

My mother is illiterate. Not a single syllable can she read or write, and nor does she have employment. The opportunities were never made available to her. Still, in a roundabout way, it is due to her illiteracy that I have been given this new life, this splendid opportunity. When my father died she was grieving and almost destitute. The only path open to her was to give me away. Lady Violet offered to take me, in a manner of speaking, and, eventually, my mother accepted.

I have four brothers, all of whom are older than I am. I never see them because they live in the same area as my mother in the East End of London. They have followed in my father's footsteps and are all employed at the Bonnington dockyards. I suspect that they disapprove of this gift of education that has been settled on me. Perhaps they blame my mother for what she did? Who can say? I cannot answer because I don't know. The important thing for me is that I don't blame her. I firmly believe that she judged it to be the best course open to me and, in any case, she had no real choice.

Lord, I am exhausted. All these memories are distressing. But if I don't write about my situation how else will I ever come to terms with it? I have no one now. I am alone and must find a way to fend for myself. That is the reason for this diary. I shall use it, these blank pages, as I would a friend, a kindly ear, as Lady Violet has always been for me.

There's someone knocking at the door! I'd better stop writing and turn down the gaslight. I will continue later or tomorrow.

Later, almost midnight

That knock gave me quite a fright, but I had no reason to worry. It was Rachel and Sarah. They work in the kitchens here and were bringing me a tray of food. They knew that I had not eaten since before I set off this morning. I could not be more grateful for their kindnesses. They made up this room for me and welcomed me as the regular visitor I have always been to this house. Of course on previous occasions I had my own suite of rooms and tonight I am up in the staff quarters, but that doesn't really bother me.

Rachel and Sarah sprawled on the bed and chatted while I devoured my vegetable soup and roast chicken. I was ravenous.

"Who's stayed over?" I asked.

"The whole bloomin' family," replied Sarah.

"Lady Flora, too?"

"She's in the room beneath. What a beauty she is. Slender as a stalk of hay." This was Rachel, who always worries that she is fat and plain and will never find a husband. "Are you going to introduce yourself to her, Dollie?"

I shrugged. "Not yet. It's too soon."

"What are you going to do then?"

"I don't know," I answered.

"Don't none of them know about you?"

I shook my head.

"Same boat as us you're in then. Out on a limb. We don't know if we'll have jobs this time next week."

"Whoever inherits this house will keep you on. Cook will speak up for you both," I assured them. "I'd help you, if only I could."

They wished me goodnight and we all expressed the desire to meet again before too long when, I hope, all our circumstances will have improved.

They will find positions, no doubt about it. My own situation is more awkward and I have no idea how it will be resolved. You see, I was Lady Violet's secret.

29th March 1909, before dawn

In spite of tiredness, I cannot sleep, so I shall write on.

Yesterday morning I was in a real sweat. I was running late because my journey took longer than I had anticipated. Starting out from Cheltenham, I was obliged to change trains in Gloucester. Unfortunately my first train was delayed, so I missed my connection and had to hang about for the next one. Once aboard I settled to the journey. It was a beautiful morning. Everywhere the fields were carpeted with daffodils. Staring out at the rolling green hillsides, the fresh spring growth, the orchards in bud, ponds with ducks and clear streams with men on the banks fishing for trout, I was marvelling at the sharpness of life beyond the carriage window, while I was en route to say my farewells to the woman who has lavished more generosity on me than any other. As my train drew closer to its destination, I spied the steeples of the neighbouring parishes, all of which I have explored many times so I know their streets and leafy lanes by heart. It's a glorious sight, I said to myself as the train steamed along. I shall miss it all horribly.

Upon arrival at Dymock, I hared up the hill, muttering crossly to myself about not having taken the dawn train. By the time I reached the village church, which is set back from the road and hidden behind spreading chestnuts and a splendid yew tree, the service was already under way. Try as I might I could not squeeze my way in. It was jam-packed. The crowds were spilling out of the great Norman doorway, pressed up tight against one another on the gravelled path, straining to hear the sermon. Finally I gave up, stepped away from the path and settled on the grass beneath a chestnut tree adorned with sticky buds.

Once the service was over, groups of people began to make their way across the cemetery to the graveside, where the sight of freshly dug earth heaped high made my stomach tight. There must have been more than 400 present. I held back, not only because I had arrived late and felt ashamed for it, but because there were so many faces I wanted to see in the flesh for the first time and because my emotions were at sixes and sevens. What would be my role in this county of Gloucestershire after today? Would I ever set eyes on this place again? I speculated. Who, if I had stepped forward and announced myself, would have opened their arms to accept me as a Bonnington? Many of the Bonnington clan, as well as the staff from their family house in Cadogan Square in London – all great admirers of Lady Violet – were present. I recognized Flora the instant I set eyes on her.

Well, it was not so difficult. Her picture has frequently appeared in newspapers due to her activities as a prominent suffragist and because she is carving a career for herself in the modern industry of the art of the motion picture. Also her grandmother, Lady Violet, kept dozens of photographs of her all over the house. There's a stunning one on the grand piano in the music room. She spoke of her favourite granddaughter endlessly and with enormous affection and pride. Sometimes it made me quite jealous.

So even though I was seeing Flora for the first time, I felt as though I already knew her. I watched her intently, scrutinizing her. She is every bit as lovely as the world says. How I longed to move up close but, sensitive to her loss and grieving, I kept my distance.

Flora was accompanied by two young men, both of whom are writers and applauded for their poetry: Rupert Brooke and John Drinkwater. Each of them has a small house only a few miles distant from the village of Dymock and they were frequent guests at Lady Violet's dinner parties. I stepped back into the shade as the trio, deep in subdued conversation, passed by. It was not that I wished to avoid them. On the contrary, they are both fascinating company, but I was not prepared in that moment to be introduced to Flora. It was not the right occasion.

Following behind were Mrs Millicent Fawcett and her equally celebrated sister, Dr Elizabeth Garrett Anderson. Both visited the house during my years there and I was presented to them, but only for split seconds. They worked and campaigned alongside Lady Violet. They are suffragists. In fact, Mrs Fawcett is a very famous name in the fight for women's votes. I have many newspaper cuttings about her and her sister in my suffrage scrapbook.

The Bonnington family and friends encircled the graveside. I easily recognized Henrietta, Flora's older sister, and her husband, Viscount Marsh. He was born in this county – his family own vast acres of arable farmland here – and he and Henrietta met at Lady Violet's many years ago. Their two small sons flanked them. They were also in the company of an elderly, stooped gentleman with grey hair and moustache. I felt my heart race and my blood boil as I stared hard at his face, at his impassive features. Sir Thomas Bonnington, Lady Violet's son-in-law, founder of the Bonnington dockyard empire and my mother's enemy. How she hated him! The accursed man who, she claimed, drove my poor father "to an early grave".

If I stepped forward and announced myself, would the name Baxter mean anything at all to him? That was what I was asking myself when, all of a sudden, as the vicar was on the point of a prayer, a hush descended even more awesome than the reverence of mourning. A late-arriving carriage had drawn up and out stepped a very stylish woman in her early fifties, dressed in black satin – Mrs Emmeline Pankhurst, the leading figure in the fight for women's votes. She strode purposefully along the stone pathway. I turned quickly to observe the crowd gathered round the graveside. Many eyes were upon her. Wherever she goes Mrs Pankhurst is greeted with a mixed response. There are those who are full of admiration for her work, for her charismatic manner and her courage and, above all, for the way in which she energizes women of all ages and class to join her cause. Then there are those – and I caught sight of a few of them yesterday morning – who despise her for what she does, for the fact that she, a respectable and well-bred woman, was imprisoned twice last year.

"We are here not because we are law-breakers; we are here in our efforts to become law-makers." These were her last words to the magistrate at her trial before he found her guilty and ordered her to keep the peace for twelve months or spend three months in Holloway. She chose prison, saying that she would never keep the peace until women were given the same voting rights as men.

Yesterday, Mrs Pankhurst ignored the reactions of the mourners. Instead, she made her way proudly towards Flora and positioned herself like an older, caring sister, behind her.

To see her standing there, not 50 yards away from me, made my heart quicken. She is a heroine to me. Lady Violet has talked to me on many occasions about the history of the women's movement and the directions the struggle is taking, but I still have much to learn. One day soon, I intend to join them in their fight. Their cause will be my cause! It is already in my heart.

As the coffin was lowered into the ground and the mourners, led by the vicar, recited the final prayer, I kept my distance and my face in shadow. Several local people spied me and nodded to me, but the family paid me no attention. If any had raised their bowed heads and glanced in my direction, they would probably have taken me for a local girl who worked as a kitchen maid up at the manor house. Not in their wildest imaginings could they have guessed what my place in the life of this lady had been.

Once the funeral was over, the crowds began making their way in dribs and drabs through the noon-day sunshine to the carriages and motor cars awaiting them beyond the lych-gate at the end of the stone pathway. I hung back until the cemetery had emptied. I wanted the opportunity to say a private and heartfelt thank you to the woman closed within that coffin.

I stayed a while, kneeling on the grass, talking to Lady Violet as though she were present and listening to all that

I was confiding to her. I could picture her grey-haired head, tilted sideways, her deep-blue eyes. It was the way she always looked when she was concentrating. No matter how occupied she was, she always found time for me.

Afterwards, I made my way on foot to the manor house, trudging slowly to the servants' entrance where I knew I would find a welcome. Agnes, the cook, promised to send up a square meal after the guests had all been fed, and Sarah and Rachel hurried away to find clean sheets.

So, here I am, bereft in this attic room. I shall stop writing now and try to get some sleep because I must take a train back to Cheltenham later this morning.

1st April 1909

I am back at school, but I don't want to be here any more. I keep thinking about my family. But I can never go back. I promised my mother she'd never see me again. I feel lost, rootless. I want to run away. Perhaps I should change my name, make my way to London and join the Women's Social and Political Union (the WSPU).

I copied a newspaper article pinned to the bulletin board this evening. It reported that twelve female suffrage demonstrators were arrested outside the House of Commons yesterday. What must it feel like to be arrested?

My English teacher, Mrs Bertram, was not at all cross that I had not written my essay for this afternoon's class. She is usually so strict, but all she said was, "The end of the week will be fine." Mrs Partridge, our headmistress, must have told her about Lady Violet.

19th April 1909

I was searching through *The Times* in the library during break this morning when I spotted an article reporting that Mrs Emmeline Pethwick-Lawrence, the treasurer of the WSPU and a personal friend of Emmeline Pankhurst, was released from Holloway prison three days ago after serving a two-month sentence. One thousand supporters were waiting at the gates to cheer her as she walked to freedom. What a splendid moment that must have been. How I would have loved to have been there.

I was about to copy the details into my scrapbook when Miss Manners, the librarian, leaned over. "You have a visitor," she whispered. "Come with me."

I was surprised because I had not been expecting anyone.

She led me to the waiting rooms that adjoin our headmistress's offices and instructed me to wait. About five minutes later, the door reopened and in walked Mrs Partridge followed by Lady Flora! I was amazed.

"Stand up please, Dollie," said Mrs Partridge. "I want to introduce you to Lady Flora Bonnington. She has travelled up from London to speak to you. I shall leave you with her. Remember to deport yourself in the manner of a young lady who is both educated and respectfully modest."

I nodded, and with that we were left alone. I felt awkward and shy, yet thrilled to be standing there with Flora. She stepped forward and brushed her elegant fingers lightly against my cheek.

"Do feel at ease, Dollie. There is no need for us to be formal with one another." She sat as she spoke and gestured to me to follow suit, which I did. "Do you have any idea why I am here?"

I panicked, tongue-tied. I had no notion what she might have learned of me, or what I was expected to answer. So I made no response besides a shrug.

"I think the name of my grandmother, Lady Violet Campbell, means something to you, does it not?"

"But of course," I stammered.

"You were her ward, isn't that so?"

"Yes, I … I was." I felt the tears welling up in my eyes. Was she here to inform me that I must leave the school? I would not have minded now that Lady Violet was no longer in Gloucestershire, but where was I to go?

"Mrs Partridge tells me that my grandmother was the one who placed you at this school. She says that you are a hardworking and very gifted student and that you have ambitions to become a journalist. Is that true?"

I nodded.

"Splendid. I also gather that you requested two days' absence from school to attend Lady Violet's funeral. Were you there?"

Again I nodded.

"I am sorry that you did not make yourself known to me or to another member of my family."

"I wanted to, but I didn't feel that it was correct to intrude."

At this, Flora smiled. "Forgive my asking, Dollie, but are you an orphan?"

"No. Well, not exactly. My father died a few years ago but my mother, as far as I know, is still living."

My answer seemed to confuse her. She frowned, fathoming the puzzle – if I had a mother why did I need a guardian?

"This was among my grandmother's papers," she said. She fished into her velvet handbag and pulled out an official-looking document. "It is a letter, hand written by her to her solicitor, Mr Makepeace, giving clear and precise instructions for your future."

I felt my stomach tighten and the palms of my hands go sticky.

"My grandmother has set aside sufficient funds from her estate for your board and keep and for your education through to and including university, if that is where your ambitions lie. She mentions that her personal preference would be for you to attend St Hilda's College at Oxford but she states that you must be free to choose and to follow whatever path you believe is yours. She has also requested that the sum of two thousand pounds be invested for you. You are to inherit this sum plus the monies that it will have accrued on your 21st birthday."

I was dumbfounded. I have never had one penny of my own and the very idea that Lady Violet would think of me in her last moments left me speechless. More embarrassingly, it reduced me to tears.

Sitting there, just a few feet away from Flora, I bowed my head, desperate to hide the rush of tears rolling down my cheeks. I was crying for the unexpected generosity shown to me by someone who had already been so kind to me and because I'd lost her. In all these weeks since I had been told of her passing away, it was the first time I had allowed my emotions to express themselves. I sniffled an apology for my foolishness and dug about in my pockets for a handkerchief. Flora offered me hers, a lacy one, then waited while I regained my composure.

"May I ask how you first came to know my grandmother?" she eventually inquired and with warmth. She didn't seem to be the least bit put out that a healthy sum of what should have been her and her sister's inheritance had been willed to me.

"She came to our cottage," I muttered. "My father was not there. He was out with my four brothers. They were marching with the strikers. Being a girl and the youngest, I was home with Mother. I cannot remember the exchange that took place between Lady Campbell and my mother during that first visit, though I stayed close to my mother's knee throughout their interview. I was only five at the time. What I do recall, though, is how she smelt."

"Whatever do you mean by that?" exclaimed Flora.

"She smelt so sweet. Of eau de Cologne. Perfumes and scented waters were all quite unknown to me then. In our neighbourhood, other less pleasant odours mingled and filled the air. But your grandmother did not seem to be disgusted or shocked."

"Disgusted by what?" asked Flora. It was evident from her questions that she had never visited areas of London where the very poor live.

"Well, her graceful manners and the finery of her clothes were quite at odds with the surroundings in which she found herself. She wore leather gloves and a hat decorated with glorious purple plumes and she had arrived in a motor car.

It was driven by a man in goggles who stepped out to open the door for her and draw off the blanket that was covering her; a protection against the wind, I suppose. Her arrival remains vivid to me even to this day because I had never seen a motor car before. It was autumn and the air was chilly. She bent to ask a group of children playing in the cobbled lane which cottage was ours. They stared, stupefied, and then I saw one of them point with filthy fingers towards our open door. Your grandmother thanked them with a bag of boiled sweets."

"Have you any idea what prompted her to pay you a visit?"

I hesitated. I feared my answer might offend Flora.

"It seems that my mother had turned up unannounced and uninvited at your family home in Cadogan Square and had made a rumpus at the door. She can get very riled sometimes and I remember that she was spoiling for a fight on that day."

"Really? Why?"

"She had been determined to see Thomas Bonnington, who, she was informed, was not at home."

"Whatever would she have wanted with my father?"

"It was during the dockers' strike of 1900. We had no money. My mother was angry but, more importantly, she was frightened and desperate, worrying how to feed us children and pay our rent. I don't know how your grandmother came to hear about my mother's visit to your house, but she

175

did. She came, she said, because she was concerned for our welfare. She offered help, but my mother sent her packing. Mother said we weren't in need of charity and certainly not from a member of the Bonnington family."

As I recounted this incident of almost a decade earlier, I caught my breath. Flora's father had brought so much misery and hardship upon my family. Still, I have never held Flora responsible and was about to say so, but she interrupted me.

"Baxter, of course! *Dollie Baxter*! How foolish of me not to have made the connection earlier. Your mother is Mrs Baxter. Good Lord, yes! I remember her visit to our home very well indeed. I remember her, too. And, yes, your father is a docker, employed by my father and –"

"He's been dead these past four years."

"I'm sorry. Yes, you told me that. Please go on with your story and forgive my interruption."

"In spite of my mother's rejection, your grandmother came back to visit us from time to time, over many years. She talked to my mother, asked her questions, listened to what she had to say. It was suggested that she would like to see me educated. I was the youngest and the only daughter. I couldn't go to work on the docks. Lady Campbell painted a picture of a life for me that my mother could never have dreamed of. 'Think of it, Mrs Baxter,' she said, 'if Dollie could read and write and in due course earn her own living, it would give her the opportunity to become an independent woman.'

176

"What your grandmother was saying rang true, but my mother was defensive. She refused outright and with harsh words. 'We don't need your kind here,' she declared. As far as I know she never discussed it with my father and I am not sure she ever really comprehended why your grandmother would want to waste her resources on a family like ours. 'Working class, that's what we are, Dollie. The bottom of the heap,' she used to say to me. 'Derided by the rest of society.' But at some point she began to trust Lady Campbell and little by little came round to the idea. 'And there's precious little future on offer for you elsewhere,' she'd mutter. It was as though she was trying to convince herself that she was making the right decision. But it wasn't until I turned ten, a short while after the death of my father, that my mother finally made up her mind.

"She woke one morning full of resolution. 'Come along, miss,' she announced. We walked for miles, looking out for a place where she could telephone to ask Lady Campbell to drop by. When your grandmother arrived a few days later, my mother explained her predicament – that she had recently lost her husband and was penniless save for the sums two of her sons brought home (my other brothers had married and left by then). She feared ending her days in the poorhouse and had come to realize that here was an opportunity for me to have a better life.

"'I'm doing this for you, Dollie,' she said the evening

before I was due to leave. 'I want you to have a future. God knows, I don't want you to end up like me.'

"The following morning we said our goodbyes. I watched her struggling with her emotions and hugged her so tight. 'I'll come back soon,' I whispered, choked with my own.

"'No, you won't,' she barked. 'Forget me. Forget all this. I don't want to see your face here again. Promise me you'll never return.'

"'But...'

"'Promise, Dollie.'

"I nodded, failing hopelessly to fight off tears."

"What happened then?" asked Flora.

"I was driven in a chauffeured motor car to Paddington Station, given a ticket and put on a train to Gloucestershire. It was the first time I had ridden in a train. I was headed for your grandmother's estate. When we arrived at the country station where I had been instructed to get off, a porter met me. I remember how puzzled he was that I had no luggage, no belongings of any sort. He hailed a horse-drawn cab and within the hour I was with your grandmother."

"But how absolutely extraordinary that she never mentioned a word about you or any of this story to me," mused Flora.

"I have often wondered why she bothered with me, but on the few occasions when I begged her to tell me she fobbed me off without giving me a satisfactory explanation."

"I think I might know the answer," said Flora.

"Really? What is it?"

"Let's leave it for another day, but I will tell you when the time is right. Meanwhile, please, tell me all about your life at this famous school. Are you happy here?"

"I am very fortunate, though I am a bit of a square peg in a round hole."

"I don't follow."

"I'm the only girl of working-class origins here."

"Ah, I see. Yes, that could be difficult. How long have you been here?"

"Two years. Before that, while I was at living at your grandmother's, I was tutored by a governess. I couldn't read or write when I left home. There was a lot to learn. I had to work very hard. Then I attended a school in one of the neighbouring country towns for a short while and only later, when it was agreed that I would be able to keep up, was I enrolled here. But, in answer to your question, yes, I was happy here until Lady Campbell died, but now I feel…"

"What?"

"Cut off. Alone. For the first time since I arrived in Gloucestershire, I am really homesick. I long to return to the city."

Flora rose, took me in her arms and embraced me like a sister. "You are never again to consider yourself alone. I am certain, Dollie, that you and I will become the best of friends. My grandmother's wish is that I replace her as your guardian.

On a temporary basis, at least, until you and circumstances choose us another direction. What do you say to that? I realize that we are as yet barely acquainted, but I would like you to think of me as a sister, or if you feel that I am too old for such a role then how about a kindly aunt?"

"Sisters!" I exclaimed. "Oh, yes, please."

"And how would you like to come and stay with me for a few days at my house in London? We could organize it for May."

I was overwhelmed. Such a generous offer was unexpected.

"What do you say, Dollie?"

"I would love it," I answered shyly.

"Then it's settled. I shall speak to Mrs Partridge and arrange everything."

"Thank you. Thank you so much."

We said our goodbyes and I hurried back to the library, where I had left my books. I was horribly late for maths, but I didn't care. I could hardly believe my good fortune. It was as though all that I had been longing for was suddenly being offered to me.

17th May 1909

Flora's home is in Bloomsbury, a district of London slightly north-west of the city centre. A horse-drawn cab awaited me as I came out of the station at Paddington the day before yesterday. It delivered me right to her door. She was waiting there with open arms to greet me, and since then I have not found a single minute to write my diary until now.

I have never visited such a place before. It is a tall, narrow house in a terraced row. There are five storeys, and my room is on the fourth. The place is spilling over with visitors and guests. I feel SO SHY. But what a splendidly lively environment! Each room is chock-a-block with fine furniture and furnishings, including Art Nouveau lamps and chairs and goodness knows what else. (I had never heard of Art Nouveau until Flora showed me some examples.) The dining table is carved mahogany and has twelve matching chairs. The curtains are of a printed fabric from a famous department store in Regent Street, Liberty's.

Writers, designers and film-makers are endlessly around. Almost all of them are from Europe or America. One or two of them are staying here, while the rest drop by to discuss their ideas or to be introduced to like-minded artists. Flora says that she sees her home as a focal point for creative thinkers. It is all dazzlingly bohemian.

Every room I enter, I discover gaggles of artistic folk bawling good-naturedly in an assortment of languages. French seems to be their common ground, not English, while Flora skips easily from one to the other. Yesterday, she introduced me to two French film-makers: Alice Guy, a highly regarded director who taught Flora in Paris, and Max Linder, a dapper, internationally famous actor and director. Cecil Hepworth, a British producer, was also present.

"Has anyone seen his new picture, *The Lonely Villa*? You must! You simply must!" Hepworth was shouting, while waving his arms to emphasize his point. "It's a magnificent example of intercutting, Alice! And what drama his techniques create!"

His comrades were deep in debate. It transpired that their passionate exchange was about an American director called DW Griffith who, Alice explained to me, is revolutionizing the technical language of motion pictures. "Intercutting", "close-up figures". I did not understand these terms because I have never seen a motion picture, but I didn't own up to it.

France, someone claimed, continues to be the most important film-producing country in the world, and its film business is rapidly expanding. Another woman, an American with a necklace of large amber beads and smoking a cigarette, disagreed loudly. She claimed American Biograph was the most innovative film company in the world.

Flora spoke of her high hopes for England. "And what of London? It is the financial centre of the world, but I dream of giving it equal status as an artistic centre. I want to live in an England where women's rights and talents are recognized and thoroughly exercised. Today, there is not one woman working as a director of films here, but I intend to change that."

Lord, I was exhausted just listening to them. Such intensity and passion! Oh, I adore it here. There is much I shall learn and, for the first time in ages, I feel light-hearted.

18th May 1909

I slept for ever and woke late! I hadn't realized that I was so tired. There has been so much coming and going that I didn't notice until this morning, when the house was calm, that Flora has two truly gorgeous silver-blue cats. I found them curled up asleep on one of the Liberty chairs when I went in for breakfast.

19th May 1909

We had luncheon today with a journalist friend of Flora's who writes for the *Times Literary Supplement* and lives round the corner from here in Gordon Square. Her name is Virginia Stephen. She is a rather delicate-looking lady with wistful eyes and a pale face shaped like a long leaf. She and her sister, a painter called Vanessa Bell, along with several other friends of theirs, are the founders of a locally-based society known as the Bloomsbury Group. Flora is also a member. Among the other guests at lunch was a Labour politician from Scotland, Keir Hardie. He is a well-known supporter of the women's movement and a great friend of the Pankhursts.

"What does your group do?" I asked Miss Stephen. "What is its purpose?"

"We are all of us passionate about the arts and believe that the highest form of social progress is the accessibility of art to everyone. All society should be entitled to enjoy the pleasures of human intercourse and the enjoyment of beautiful objects."

I could not always follow the subject matters but the

discussions were very lively. The talk was of social progress, sexual equality and the "strictures of the Victorian Age".

From time to time I nodded and tried to look intelligent. I agreed with much that was said, particularly about sexual equality, but I remained silent. I felt too shy to speak.

By then it was about time for tea. The others left and Flora invited me to her study. It smells of leather from the big chairs and the hundreds of books lining the shelves. I was glad everyone had gone because we had barely seen one another since I arrived.

"When I was your age, Dollie," she said, "one of my favourite pastimes was afternoon tea with Grandma. Cook would serve us my favourite home-made biscuits and then, once we were settled and I was tucking contentedly into the goodies, Grandma would encourage me to talk. She wanted to know all about my worries and my hopes and joys."

"Yes," I said. "She used to ask me the same."

"Do you intend to try for Oxford, as my grandmother obviously hoped for you?"

I do desire to go to university, but I did not have the confidence to say so. How could a working-class girl like me, even with the special opportunities that have been bestowed upon her, dare to count on the possibility of Oxford?

"I am very touched that Lady Campbell has made such a path available to me," was my response. "I will work hard and do my best."

185

"Have you decided what you will read if you are accepted there? Or do your imaginings take you travelling? Perhaps you fancy studying medicine or law?"

I hesitated. So many questions.

"What do you hope for, Dollie? What do you dream of achieving? Do tell, darling."

"I intend to be a journalist."

"Ah, yes, I had forgotten. And what will you use your pen to fight for?"

I was a bit sheepish about divulging any of my secret plans but eventually, because Flora continued to press me – "Tell me every detail and I will do my utmost to assist you." – I confided that I wanted to follow in the footsteps of Lady Violet, and of Flora herself. "Your grandmother always taught me that votes for women are essential, but that the vote is only the beginning. And that is what I feel, too."

"Indeed, Dollie, it is only the beginning. Once we have won the right to vote, we will have been given the opportunity to voice our opinions and to be heard throughout the Empire. We can make a difference."

"Do you believe that one day it will be possible to offer every woman the chance of a decent education? To give them self-respect and equal rights with men?"

"Yes! We will put women into Parliament, Dollie. Think of it. Women contributing to the way our country is governed. Women like my great friend Christabel Pankhurst.

She has a degree in law and showed her skills with such brilliance when she defended both herself and her mother at their trial last year. But do you know that she is barred from practising her profession as a barrister for the simple reason that she is a woman? Her qualifications and talent, which are outstanding, count for nothing. When we have the vote such sexual injustices will be swept aside."

"England was the first country to grant women the right to practise medicine, wasn't it?"

"Yes," smiled Flora. "Yes, Dollie, it was."

"So why not law? Or politics? It doesn't make sense," I added.

Flora poured me another cup of tea and glanced across to the grand piano where a splendid silver-framed photograph of Lady Violet took pride of place. "My grandmother dedicated her life to the Votes for Women campaign and working for those less fortunate than herself," she continued. "As did my mother, I believe. Sexual equality was their goal, as it is mine. So you dream of being a suffragist, Dollie?"

"No, I intend to be a suffragette."

Flora stared at me quizzically. "A suffragette? Do you understand the difference between suffragists and suffragettes?"

"The *Daily Mail* christened the women fighting for votes 'suffragettes' and, like you and your grandmother, I want to wear that name honourably. You ask me what I dream of? Well, I want to fight, too. I want to see women such as my mother given the opportunity to learn to read and write, to be more than the domestic help in the home, to be treated decently, equally. Never to be..." I paused because I was about to touch upon a private matter that I am not ready to discuss, not even with Flora.

Flora sensed my reticence. "Never to be what, Dollie?" she interrogated.

"Never to be subjected to male dominance, never again to be at their beck and call. It is a question of human rights and, if necessary, I will give my life to the cause," I confided.

Flora laughed in a kindly way and suggested that perhaps I should not consider such dramatic resolutions. "I doubt that any of us will be called upon to give our lives, Dollie. At least, I sincerely hope that we won't."

I did not feel it polite to remind her that Mrs Pankhurst has described her organization as a "suffrage army fighting in the field" and so I kept quiet.

Flora promised to give me all the support she could. She explained, though, that she is with the constitutionalists not the militants. "We of the National Union of Women's Suffrage Societies, the NUWSS, are suffragists, Dollie, not suffragettes. We advocate legal means of campaigning such as parliamentary lobbying, whereas the more militant activists, those in the WSPU, the organization founded in 1903 by Emmeline and Christabel Pankhurst, are the women the *Daily Mail* dubbed 'suffragettes'. It was intended as an insult because they are judged unladylike and because they are willing to break the law to achieve their goals."

"Yes, I know that the WSPU is the more militant of the two leading suffrage organizations," I countered, for I didn't want Flora to believe me ignorant. "And I know exactly what first caused them to become more extreme," I added.

"Really?" she replied with surprise.

"On 19th May in 1905, a group of ten women went to speak to the Prime Minister. Amongst these women was 76-year-old Emily Davies who handed the women's suffrage petition to the Prime Minister. His answer to them was, 'Be patient.' This was not the response they had expected. Women (and some men) had been actively campaigning for votes for women since the 1860s and they were tired of being patient. And so the movement grew in momentum and it became militant."

"Well, yes, Dollie, that is one of the incidents that fired the desire to fight harder and more vehemently. But my way, the way of the NUWSS, headed by Millicent Garrett Fawcett, is equally active. We have the same burning ambition to see women enfranchised. Why not consider allying yourself with us?"

"But if both organizations are fighting the same battle...?"

"They are, but their approaches are different, and although Christabel and I have known one another since I was your age and she is a dear friend whom I admire, I do not always agree with the means she uses. And I think it is important you know that my grandmother was a suffragist. She was never a suffragette."

I was taken aback. I had always assumed that Lady Violet was a suffragette.

20th May 1909

This morning Flora took me shopping to buy clothes that she feels will better suit my needs here in London.

"But I am only staying ten days!" I exclaimed.

"Well, you can leave them in the wardrobe for your next visit," she laughed. "That blue bedroom is now exclusively yours."

We travelled to Knightsbridge in a hansom. This is a long, low vehicle that holds two passengers with a driver seated on a high deck behind. It was the first I had ever been in. Before being set down outside Harrods, a terrifyingly posh and shockingly expensive store, we made a short detour to Cadogan Square.

"My father lives there." Flora pointed to one of the tall, elegant houses.

I felt myself stiffen. "Are we going in?" I asked nervously.

"Another day, perhaps. I wanted you to see where your mother came during the dockers' strike. I was descending the stairs, I remember it clearly, and I saw her waiting at the door. I went to ask if I could help her, but she refused point blank to deal with me. Eventually one of the staff turned her away.

"I think the reason my grandmother made the journey to the East End in search of you all was because I had told her about your mother's visit. The incident had troubled me greatly. I had not known what to do for the best. I brooded over it until, eventually, I turned to Grandma."

"And you think that your meeting my mother was what prompted Lady Campbell to visit our home and offer us assistance?"

Flora considered my question. "It was a part of the reason. And now see, Dollie, after all these years, here we are together like sisters. An odd turn of events, don't you agree?"

And I do agree. Still, I sensed that there was more to the story than Flora would tell. I love her already, though I am deeply conscious of our differences. We are poles apart! Even when we were looking at clothes today, I preferred the simpler, practical dresses, while Flora was excited by flamboyant and ornate gowns. But she did not insist and bought me those I chose.

After we returned from our shopping expedition and I had thanked her for my two new outfits – they are lovely – she promised that before I left she would take me to the

Prince's Skating Rink, which is also in Knightsbridge, quite close to Harrods.

"But I can't skate."

"No, you will see. A grand bazaar is being held there, or an Exhibition as everyone is calling it. It has been mounted by the WSPU to raise money for the cause."

I cannot wait! I shall be surrounded by real suffragettes. All those women I have been reading about for so long. Flora tells me that they have been advertising it in the streets with their very own band.

21st May 1909

I have a desperate urge to contact my mother. I promised never to return, but only because she practically forced me to give my word. Would she hold it against me if I broke that promise now, after four years? Does she miss me? Does she ever think of me? Is she still alive? I would so like to share with her all that is happening to me, to introduce her to my new life.

23rd May 1909

It is settled. Tomorrow, we will visit the Exhibition. That's the exciting news. But after that, in two days' time, I must return to school. The prospect makes me very downhearted. I am having such a wonderful time. The country means nothing to me without Lady Violet there to encourage and befriend me. Here, with Flora, I feel as though I have found a real sister.

Later

A lady called Katherine Mansfield came by this afternoon to lend Flora a volume of John Ruskin's work, *The Stories of Venice*, because Flora is planning a trip to Italy later this summer. Miss Mansfield was invited to stay to tea. I rather liked her. She is originally from New Zealand.

"Do you know the writings of Ruskin?" she asked me.

I confessed that I did not.

"Ah, he is one of the greatest writers of English prose. You must read him, particularly if you have ambitions to be a journalist, Dollie. His earlier works on travel and art are quite exceptional."

Then the discussion turned to a Debussy concert she had attended yesterday evening at the Queen's Hall. This was followed by passionate complaints about the stench and pollution caused by motor cars. "There are so many of the blasted things now. Everywhere in this city, the streets reek of petroleum," she cried. "It is not at all like my home town of Wellington. I positively refuse to use one. If I take a cab, it must be a hansom."

Flora hooted with laughter. "Oh, Katherine, my dear, I fear that you will never visit me again!" And she confessed that she has ordered a Fiat motor car, which will be arriving any day now.

Miss Mansfield then told us that in Australia and New Zealand women are far better regarded than in England. In those two far-off antipodean countries, women have already won the vote!

"Melbourne, the last state on the Australian continent to concede it, gave women the vote last year.

Here in England we females are disgracefully discriminated against and oppressed by men," she lamented, and continued by saying that until we have the vote and a voice of our own, nothing will change.

How I agree with her sentiments!

24th May 1909

The Exhibition! Oh, the Exhibition! What sights I have seen and what a secret adventure I have made of it.

First, we visited two replica prison cells. I went inside one of them and walked around. It was eerie! And so cramped. They had been constructed to demonstrate what women are suffering on our behalf, the conditions they are being forced to endure for the sake of what they believe is our right. And it *is* our right. Women should have a voice in this country. In every country.

Afterwards, to brighten our mood, we ate the most delicious ice cream from a stall set up by Americans, and then we paraded up and down the alleys, in amongst the busy throng of chattering people, peering at all the goods on offer. Of course I had no money to buy anything, but I didn't care. I was there to look, gaze and breathe it all in. We visited stalls with displays of exotic pieces of jewellery, and all sorts of handicrafts. I have never seen so many lace pillowslips and tablecloths! There were kindly stallholders selling books, flowers, herbs, needlework, chinaware, fancy hats and Lord knows what else. There were bands playing rousing music, tables laid out for tea. We made a stop at a booth for the Actresses' Franchise League. Flora, of course, knew everyone and was greeted with much embracing. She introduced me to a group of her actress friends. I do not remember all their names, but Elizabeth Robins, the American woman with the amber beads who was at Flora's the other day, was one of them. Several others were fluttering around a tall, skinny gentleman with a beard. He was wearing a tweed suit and seemed to be holding court, talking rapidly in a thick Irish accent.

"Who's he?" I whispered to Flora.

"His name is George Bernard Shaw, a rather well-known music critic and playwright, and an active supporter of women's rights. He wrote a play two or three years ago, *The Doctor's Dilemma*, whose leading character is named Sir Bloomfield Bonnington. He swears he didn't steal the name from Father," she grinned.

Then, while Flora chatted animatedly to her colleagues, I stood gazing in every direction. There was such a buzz of energy fed by the excitement and the determination to win this battle against the current Liberal government. Well, against all anti-suffrage governments. In fact, against anyone who claims that women are lesser citizens than men and are not capable of understanding politics. Suddenly, my eyes lighted on a stand where a large white, purple and green banner had been hung.

"Do you know what those colours represent?" Elizabeth asked me.

"They are the colours of the Women's Social and Political Union."

"Yes, but why those three in particular?"

I shook my head.

"Purple stands for dignity, white for purity and green for hope. But why don't you go and find out for yourself? Don't worry, I'll tell Flora where you've gone."

"Thank you," I said, hurrying off through the crowds. There were quite a few people queuing to ask questions but eventually I was able to push my way forward to a desk where a red-haired woman with pince-nez was presiding over piles of pamphlets. Her job was to explain to all those interested what the aims of the WSPU are. I told her that I knew all about the fight and that my dream was to become a member.

"Well, why not join now?" she replied in a broad Scottish accent.

"Might I?" I was thrilled at the prospect but also a bit scared. I can't quite explain why. Well, yes, I can. I think it was because I felt as though I was being treacherous to Flora, who had made it clear that she is a suffragist not a suffragette, and that Lady Violet had also leaned towards the less militant approach. Then I reasoned that Lady Violet would want me to be true to myself. Above all else, I believe that is what she would demand of me.

But will it make that much difference if I join? I was asking myself. And my silent response was that these are the women I admire and want to be affiliated with. These are the women, if any, who could change the hardships that housewives such as my mother are forced to endure.

The Scottish lady handed me a form, which I filled in and signed after barely a glance before thrusting it nervously back at her.

She read my name and said, "Welcome, Dollie Baxter. We are delighted that you are with us. Feel free to visit our offices at 4, Clements Inn, whenever you fancy. Think of it as your home. My name is Harriet Kerr and I am the office manager."

"I'll be there, Miss Kerr," I said, and I hurried away in search of Flora.

On our way home in her new Fiat motor car Flora told me more about her Irish playwright friend, Mr Shaw. He's a Socialist and a fighter for the rights of the poor. I am not madly interested in plays – actually, I have never been to a theatre show – but I would dearly love to meet him and ask him many questions.

25th May 1909

Flora is my very best friend and I love her like a sister, but I have not yet plucked up the courage to confess to her that yesterday I joined the suffragettes. Though I did feel desperate enough over breakfast to blurt out my desire not to return to Cheltenham.

"But it is a very fine institute and your education is of the utmost importance, Dollie. Surely you realize that? And Grandma went to such lengths –"

"Yes, I know, but without her close at hand, it will never be the same again. If it's possible, I would prefer to continue my education here. I feel at home in London. Oh, Flora, I would so like my future to be here."

"Well, there is Croydon Girls' High School or Blackheath, but they are long distances out of town. I will make some enquiries. There are sure to be several excellent girls' schools in the city centre, though it may mean that you will need a tutor until we find the right one for you. Leave it with me."

"Thank you. I will be closer to my roots and relatives. Well, to my mother…"

"Is it your wish to return to your birthplace and live with her?"

I remained silent. How many times recently have I asked myself this question? Of course, I know that I cannot stay on indefinitely with Flora... But how can I go back? I know so little of my mother's way of life now; I have become estranged from my past. The fact is, I belong nowhere.

"I don't think so," I answered eventually, "though I long to see her again, to have news of her."

"Have you visited her while you've been in town?"

"Not yet."

"Then why don't we go together? Tomorrow morning, directly after breakfast, we'll take the Fiat and..."

I hesitated, remembering my vow. Flora mistook my hesitation for an unwillingness to include her.

"How thoughtless of me! No, you must go alone. I won't intrude on your life. I only want to assist you as my grandmother has done. When you are ready, let me know what you have decided and I will do everything I can to help you. In the meantime, you are welcome to stay here for as long as you please."

I nodded and smiled at the touch of her hand on mine.

Flora is splendid, but we are so different. Her world is exciting and international, but it is not my way forward. I must make my home where my heart is, where I feel my commitments lie. But first I must learn whatever news there might be of my mother.

26th May 1909

I don't know where to begin to express what I am feeling tonight and all that I have witnessed during the course of this day.

After breakfast, I walked to the southern end of Holborn and from there found a bus that was heading east out of the city centre. I chose a seat by the window so that I could peer out at all the London streetcars and the thoroughfares and the people bustling by. Many of the main roads have been furnished with electric lights now, but there are gas lamps down the narrower side-streets. I needed distraction. I was making my way to the district of my old home in search of my mother and my heart was beating fast with the anticipation of what lay ahead.

The change as we approached the poorer regions of London was obvious to anyone with half an eye. The buildings grew uglier. Even the sky seemed darker as blocks of flats, cheaply constructed and over-populated, closed out the light. The pavements were a sea of concerned faces. We drove by an open market, where children and grown-ups alike were rooting hungrily through garbage piles, salvaging vegetables and fruits and stuffing them directly into their mouths.

Once I stepped off the bus, I meandered for a while up and down the cobbled lanes, lost in the stream of shabby people. I was scared of going to my address, scared of what I would or would not find there. I could not say if, during that walk, I more greatly desired to find my mother or not.

I remember my earlier life as a time of endless hardships. I have grown used to another standard of living and it has softened me. But the trick these past four years has played on my memory was a greater deception than I had bargained for. Today I came face to face with much that I had wiped out. I had forgotten the day-to-day struggles of the thousands living and starving in such nook-and-cranny quarters. Crowds everywhere. Sad, pinched faces with desperate or drunken eyes. All of them facing destitution. You cannot get away from folk in this part of London town. A heaving mass of humanity struggling to make it through one day to the next.

I could not help but see the streets, the lodgings, the second-hand clothes shops, the people sleeping rough without so much as a blanket to keep them warm and dry – the world of East End London in all its sordid detail – through Flora's eyes, not my own, and I felt shame. Not for my kin, but for the fact that the entire locality is shockingly down-at-heel and smells so foul you want to hold your breath. Squalid is the adjective that sprang to mind.

I passed a man swaying on his haunches, trying to mend his shoes. Shoes that weren't fit for the dustbin.

A small grocery store, one of the few I spotted, had signs in the window stating the various prices of the goods on sale. I paused to look. Tea – 1d, Sugar – 1d, Bread – 3d and Butter – 2d.

Usually it had been me who was sent out to buy a small something or other, because I was less likely to be refused the paltry morsels needed to keep our hunger at bay until Father received his next inadequate pay packet.

"Give us tuppence worth of this or thruppence worth of the other," I'd beg the storekeeper. "Mum says she'll square it with you Friday when Dad brings home his wages."

I remembered how two ounces of boiled ham for "tea", our evening meal, was a sumptuous banquet, shared out between the seven of us. A penny tin of condensed milk was also a huge treat.

I walked on, passing by a narrow lane known as Milk Lane. Washing was hanging out to dry in the alleyways. There was not a flower or a plant in sight. The brick houses are built alongside one another, packed tightly together. Unkempt children were playing in the passageways. These infants are not scruffy urchins because of neglect but because no one has enough resources or time to take better care of them. They stared hard and mistrustfully at my passing silhouette or chased after me gazing in awe, holding out their filthy palms, eyes peering out of underfed faces, in the hope of a coin.

It was my clothes that gave me away as a "foreigner". An outsider from the West End. There might as well be a wall between the two London towns.

I passed a young woman with flushed cheeks whose hair was going grey even though she could not have been more than 30; she was stitching the seat of her son's breeches right there in the street. I bent to tighten my bootlaces, an excuse to observe her and to ask myself: Was that how my mother had looked to the Bonnington family that midsummer day in 1900 when she went knocking on their door? She would also have been about 30 at that time.

Finally I turned a corner and came face to face with our cottage. How small it seemed to me today! The door was ajar. I hung back and took a deep breath. My hands were clammy as I lifted my fist to rap on the wood.

"Who'zere?" was the response called from within. It was followed by an awful bout of coughing. Without a word I pushed the door and stepped inside, for I had recognized the voice of my mother.

Her face was pastry-pale, lined and aged almost beyond recognition. Before me stood a stooped old lady. She gazed at me in blank amazement.

"Christ Almighty! Dollie? No, it can't be you."

I noticed bottles of stout, both full and empty, littering the floor. How can she afford such indulgences? I was smiling nervously to encourage the situation. Is she spending whatever food money comes her way on stout? She was painfully thin.

"Yes, it is." I heard the quaver in my speech.

She scrutinized me hard. "Well, take a bloomin' look at yerself. All dressed up."

"I hope you don't mind… I know I promised not to return, but…"

"Quite the lady you've become, eh?"

I looked about me, lost for words. Her scullery-cum-parlour room – there is only the one living space – was hideously cramped and it smelt of old mushrooms. I felt a rush of shame. Not for what I was witnessing, but for the privileged existence I have been living. The private rooms with private toilet facilities that I have begun to take for granted. How could I have forgotten so many details, and so quickly? The primitive and inadequate lavatory accommodation out back alongside the coalhole. Cockroaches running haywire up and down the walls.

Mother's room contains a sink, dingy-brown from years of use, which serves for both cooking purposes and washing facilities. Along one wall is a broken-down dresser. On the table stands the same big, enamelled teapot we used when I was a small child.

"I know I promised not to return—"

"So what are you doing here and what the bleedin' 'ell are yer staring at?" she snapped, without the slightest glimmer of warmth.

I wanted to burst into tears. My desire was to run away, to be shot of this scene as soon as possible, but then I reminded myself: *This is your mother.*

I took a deep breath and the reeking odour all but burned my nostrils. "Lady Campbell has passed away," I said.

"Well, there's nothing for you 'ere. I can't keep you. I can't keep meself. It's your brother John what's lookin' after me. I gave you yer chance. If you've made a hash of it…" And as her fury rose, so her breathing grew more irregular and she doubled up with another fit of coughing. I forced her to sit, to be still and silent for a moment. She raised a hand to her mouth. I took a step towards her but her gesture was brusque, warning me to keep my distance.

"I have not come here to be a burden to you," I began firmly. "I only wanted you to know that I shan't be returning to Gloucestershire. I intend to continue my education in London. I intend to find lodgings close by and I thought that…" My sentence dried like wood chips in my mouth. Her hand was still clamped against her lips as she struggled for breath. "Lady Campbell has left me some money. I am not entitled to touch it until I reach 21, but … I want help you. To find you somewhere else to live, to take you away from…"

Her eyes rose to meet my gaze as her hands fell into her

lap. I saw then how sick she was. Small and vulnerable like a bird caught in a trap, dying.

"The best thing you can do for me, Dollie, is to make your own way. Don't, for the Lord's sake, get yerself sucked back into any of this."

"What about my brothers? Do they visit and care for you? What are you living on?" I persisted, but she waved her hand in a dismissive way.

"I don't want to see yer here ever again," she rasped, and rose unsteadily to shove me off back into the street. Of course, she had no strength but I went anyway. Perversely, I did it to please her.

But what must I do? How can I help her?

27th May 1909

I woke feeling a heavy responsibility hanging over me. Forcing myself to be decisive, I bathed and dressed quickly. I was intending to discuss my mother's situation with Flora and ask her advice but she had left early for rehearsals of a new film she is involved in, so I skipped breakfast and set off for Clements Inn, to the offices of the WSPU, my thoughts still troubled by my visit of yesterday.

"The abyss" is the phrase coined by certain writers and journalists to describe the conditions of the life of the poor in this country. "The people of the abyss" wrote the best-selling author, HG Wells, when speaking of Britain's working class. And how right he is!

I know for sure that *when* women are given the vote the living conditions of the poor will be one of the first problems to be addressed. And that is why I decided to call at the WSPU today. If there is one thing that I can do for my mother it is to fight for women and our place in this society. And, once that fight has been won, then we will be well placed to look to our society. A society that is sinking at its foundations.

I reached Clements Inn, opened the door and found myself in a large, immaculately tidy room, where girls at typewriters were clacking busily. There were posters on all the walls, stacks of newspapers on the floor, neat piles of banners, legal books and social texts everywhere.

I enquired for Harriet Kerr, who welcomed me as though I were a friend and then introduced me to a middle-aged woman, Miss Baker. Astoundingly, I learned that she had been Flora's governess for many years. Now she is employed as a member of the staff for the movement, or "the Cause" as they all call it there.

"How old are you, Dollie?" asked Miss Baker.

"I have just turned fifteen," I fibbed. In fact, I shall be fifteen in November.

"Why aren't you at school?"

I considered her question. The quarter of London where I originally came from has no library. Why would it have? Most women in such districts are illiterate. A few of the men can read a newspaper and write their names, even a letter if they are obliged to, but what time do they have for reading? Children leave school at eight or nine and go out to work because the families desperately need the pittance of income their offspring earn. My brothers were all working by the age of ten. I would have been engaged in domestic work if Fate had not taken a hand. I wanted to tell all this to Miss Baker, but I liked her and decided not to be cheeky. "I have recently moved back to London and hope to start at a new school in the autumn."

Miss Baker screwed up her brow. "You should be attending school."

"I believe Flora is looking for a temporary tutor for me," I answered.

"I see. Well, while you have time to spare, just say the word and we'll take you on as a volunteer."

"What would it involve?"

"Can you type?"

I shook my head.

"Never mind, there are plenty of other duties to be carried out. But only in your free time. One of our goals is to encourage women's education, not to hinder it, do you understand me?"

I nodded.

"How about selling copies of our suffrage newspaper, *Votes for Women*? It means going out on the streets. Or if you are too timid for that we could put you to enrolling new members. Or interviewing local MPs."

"I can't afford to get into any trouble…"

Miss Baker laughed loudly. "Not all of the ladies here are of a militant mind, Dollie. Harriet, who enrolled you at the Exhibition, left her secretarial agency in Aberdeen to come and work here, but she has made it a condition of her employment that her work is exclusively administrative."

"I would be honoured to help out in whatever way I can," I replied.

"Excellent! Why don't we start with something straightforward such as the door-to-door distribution of handbills, or…"

"My dream is to become a journalist, so why don't I try my hand at selling the newspapers?"

"Splendid! Now what are you doing for the rest of the day?"

I shrugged.

"Then why don't we begin immediately? This was going to be a free day for me and I was on my way to a new Monet exhibition at the National Gallery, but that can wait. I'll go later. Are you familiar with the work of the French Impressionists?"

I shook my head.

"Even better. I will accompany you on your newspaper expedition. Just this once, mind, so that you get the hang of it, and while we are out and about I can answer any questions you might have about the Cause. Then later this afternoon, we'll make an outing together to the National Gallery." And, with that, Miss Baker flung a huge batch of papers at me, shoved a hat carelessly on her head, wrapped a light shawl round her shoulders and we stepped out into the street.

We made our way by underground to the corner of Tottenham Court Road and Oxford Street. "This will be your pitch. Be warned, it's a busy one. You'll sell a good stack of papers here and you will almost certainly get asked questions about our work. So you'd better have your facts straight. No, don't stand there. It is important to position yourself in the gutter. Never stand on the pavements."

"Why ever not?" I asked, fearing the passage of hansoms and, worse, of motor cars.

"Because you run the risk of being charged by the police with obstruction."

"Oh." This news made me a little panicky. In my heart I want to be a true and brave suffragette, but in reality, I cannot afford to get myself into trouble.

"Don't be anxious. There's nothing to worry about. Here comes someone. Offer the paper."

And before I knew what was happening I was selling my first copy to a smiling, elderly lady who donated not the requested one penny price but a full shilling and then complimented me on the splendid work we are doing!

Later, over a mug of tea near Oxford Circus, I was introduced to another newish recruit, Mary Richardson, a Canadian, who has been in England since 1900. Mary is selling papers a little way up the street from my pitch.

"The main thing is not to be shy and not to take any abuse hurled at you personally," she advised me.

"What sort of abuse?"

"Now, don't go scaring our Dollie away," laughed Miss Baker. "Mary was bombarded with rotten fruit by some women working in the Crosse & Blackwell factory."

"Whatever for?" I was beginning to doubt my commitment to the Cause!

"There are many women and men too, who continue to believe that our sole purpose on this earth is to breed and be perfect wives. They see our work as a threat. Or they have the notion that we are demeaning ourselves, giving females a bad name. 'Respectable women stay home,' they say. 'It is only the other kind of woman who makes a spectacle of herself in the street.'

"Others declare that our force is made up of spinsters and widows, that we are women lacking men. All nonsense, of course, and makes me quite furious, but we must be patient. Sooner or later they will come to see that our place is right alongside men, making decisions, weighing up the choices, taking responsibility for the way the world works. I personally believe that when that day comes, folk will see that there are certain areas in the public arena that will be better handled by women."

"Such as?" I asked.

"Well, we are not warmongers, for a start. We don't run round with weapons. I think the chances of international peace would be increased if the government had women in the cabinet negotiating on their behalf. Who knows, we might have avoided the Boer War."

Gosh, I had never considered such a notion before, but it made sense.

Miss Baker then recounted to us the episode of last year when she and several other WSPU colleagues went to Downing Street where one of their suffrage sisters was intending to speak. Miss Nell chained herself to the railings outside the Prime Minister's front door so that the police could not move her along before she had finished her speech. She was keen that the Cabinet, who were in session, as well as the crowd gathering in the street, would hear her words without interruption. "And what an impassioned address it was!" grinned Miss Baker.

"What did she say?" I asked.

"'Each and every female in this country of eighteen years and older should have the right to vote in this nation's political elections. We have the right to be equal with men.

We are the equal of men. It is they who are denying us our rights and our true position in the society that we are also building. This battle is about more than the vote. It is about equal opportunities!' She was quite remarkable. A blazing force wrapped in chains, a human letter from us all. Flora was with us in the crowd on that occasion. I wish she'd come along more often. Soon another woman, a nurse, Olivia Smith, rushed forward and followed Miss Nell's example. Imagine it, Dollie, two women chained to the railings in Downing Street. The police could do nothing. The crowd grew excited. Some were angry and jeered as the women spoke out. Others were cheering them on. It was a thrilling and a dangerous moment. I rushed forward, intent on joining my sisters, but Harriet held me back." Miss Baker paused and took a sip of her tea.

"Why did she do that?"

"I explained to you earlier, Harriet is not militant and she believes that there is important work to be done behind the scenes, in the offices. I am needed for that work because as a trained teacher I can write the pamphlet literature, and correct the spelling and details."

"What happened to the two women?" I asked.

"They were arrested. And two others with them. The police hauled all four off to Bow Street Magistrates' Court, where they were charged with disorderly conduct, found guilty and sentenced to three weeks' imprisonment or to pay hefty fines. All chose prison because it creates publicity for our cause. Good Lord, look at the time! We must dash, Dollie, if we are to make the gallery. Now then, Mary, you take Dollie's remaining newspapers and sell them for us, will you, dear? Thank you. We'll see you tomorrow."

And with that we were gone and off to the Monet exhibition. It was quite wonderful. Such colours, soft as butterfly wings. But I will have to write about that adventure tomorrow because now I am exhausted. My feet are killing me and Flora has guests for dinner. I intend to wear one of my new frocks.

28th May 1909

I spent about half an hour yesterday standing in front of a painting entitled *Waterlilies*, painted by Claude Monet in 1903. I don't think that I have ever seen anything so lovely. It is curious because when you move up close you can see clearly that the canvas is a mass of painted dots. The idea is that, joined together, they give the impression of a shape or a colour or a scene. That is why he and other artists painting in the same style are known as "Impressionists". According to Miss Baker there is an entire school of painters in France who have been christened "French Impressionists". Not "school" as in my one at Cheltenham, but as in "school of thought": a way of thinking. The Impressionists have a way of looking at light and its effect on objects and nature. Wandering through the exhibition, gazing at all those canvases, it was as though someone had drawn back the curtains on to a new world, a new mode of *seeing*. I have never perceived life, looked at nature, from such a perspective before. It was so beautiful. It really lifted my mood.

I so like Miss Baker. It would be too wonderful if she could be my summer tutor. I shall suggest it to Flora.

29th May 1909

Trying to find time to spend with Flora is so difficult. She has been busy working on a film and there have been so many visitors. Luckily, this evening I found her alone in her room. She was curled up in a flowery kimono, on her chaise longue, hair flowing long and loose, barefoot, reading a script, with the two Russian Blue cats, Strindberg and Ibsen, dozing at her side.

I wasted no time in asking if I could possibly withdraw a portion of the money that Lady Violet put in trust for me.

Flora looked astonished. "It is not within my power to authorize that," she said. "Is there something you need?"

I explained that I had been to see my mother. "I fear she may be seriously ill and needs urgent medical care. I must have money to help her."

Flora tossed her script to the carpeted floor. "But, Dollie, it is locked away. The terms of the will have to be respected; that is the law. But I can come with you to meet your mother. I could bring a doctor who can examine her. Then we'll know what needs to be done. And you are not to concern yourself with the costs."

I stroked one of the cats, thinking about what Flora had offered. "I don't know that my mother would be willing to see a doctor."

"A close friend of mine, Caroline Sturge, is a doctor. She's very kind. Why don't we give her a try?"

I agreed that we should, and once I had made the decision I felt as though a great load had been lifted from me.

"That's settled then. Now, please be a sweetheart and take me through my lines."

30th May 1909

I entered the cottage first, intending to prepare Mother for the arrival of the others, and was utterly shocked by what I saw. I could not believe that she had deteriorated so quickly, nor that she had been left alone in such a condition.

"Who's been looking after you?" I cried. "Where's John?"

"What're yer doing bringing those bleedin' toffs here?" she hissed as Flora and Doctor Sturge entered. "Who are they?"

I did not dare to give Flora's family name. I asked after my brother again, but Mother could barely talk. I think her initial outburst had weakened her. I glanced about but saw no signs of a male presence. At least he must be feeding and keeping her or she would have found herself on the streets, in pauper lodgings or the workhouse long ago.

Judging by the grave expression on Doctor Sturge's face, she seemed to recognize the nature of Mother's sickness even before she had examined her.

"She needs immediate medical care," she said.

"Is she going to die?" I croaked.

"Not if we get her to a hospital right now."

It was a real battle to move her. She may have been weak

and very ill but she put up an almighty resistance. "The only way you'll get me out of 'ere is in a bandbox," she rasped.

"What's a bandbox?" whispered Flora.

"A coffin."

Eventually she agreed to go. As they carried her out on the stretcher, I saw the dark vermilion stains on her fingers and realized she must have been coughing up blood. Thank Heaven we got here in time.

31st May 1909

My mother has been taken to St Thomas's Hospital. Whitechapel would have been closer but both Flora and the doctor agreed that it is desperately overcrowded and both staff and facilities are inadequate.

I visited her there today. Dr Sturge and another doctor were examining her and I was only allowed to stay for a minute. She seemed pleased to see me though, and I promised to return again soon.

2nd June 1909

Dr Sturge telephoned Flora late this afternoon. She confirmed that my mother's lymph glands are very enlarged and that she is suffering from a form of tuberculosis.

"Promise me she won't die," I cried when I heard the diagnosis.

"We are doing everything we can," she answered.

I felt totally depressed when I put down the phone and spent the evening alone in my room.

6th June 1909

Flora and I have been to visit two schools. The headmistresses interviewed us, asked me questions about my time in Cheltenham and requested a report from my former school. One is in Hammersmith in the west of London and the other is in Camden, a little north of Flora's house. St Paul's, the one in Hammersmith, also made me sit a short written exam. The paper was not difficult, but my heart was not in it. I cannot stop worrying about my mother. Both schools said they would be writing to us shortly.

11th June 1909

NO new school has been settled yet, so Flora was delighted at the suggestion that Miss Baker should tutor me in the meantime.

"But how did you come to meet her, Dollie?"

I could not lie. I owned up to the fact that it was a contact made on the day we visited the Exhibition.

"I see. Well, she is a brilliant woman and a first-class teacher. I only hope that she does not allow her allegiance to the WSPU to colour your studies. I will need her assurance on that point."

12th June 1909

Miss Baker came to have tea with us. Flora and she were obviously delighted to see one another again and they have settled on an arrangement. Five sessions a week is what they have scheduled, so that I don't fall behind with my lessons. We will study in the living room between eight and ten each morning. The hours are a bit early for my liking but Miss Baker needs to be at the WSPU offices by half-past ten.

13th June 1909

Lessons began today with a series of oral tests: maths followed by French. Then Miss Baker quizzed me on geography, a bit of English literature and history and, to round it all off, German verbs.

"Mmm," she pronounced. "Your maths and German are extremely weak. Your geography is reasonable, your history is rusty and English literature quite good. We have a lot to do."

Once all that was over, she set me pages of questions to prepare for tomorrow's session.

When Flora asked me later how the session had gone, I told her, "Miss Baker is horribly keen on German."

She laughed and said that she remembered that.

14th June 1909

I went to the WSPU today and helped to prepare pamphlets for distribution. Miss Baker and I sat cross-legged on the floor, slipping them into envelopes while she took me through some Latin grammar. I have forgotten everything! After we had completed several boxloads we stopped for a cup of tea and she and Harriet astounded me with episodes of their suffrage experiences.

I learned that on 11th October last year, Emmeline and Christabel Pankhurst, together with another suffragette, Flora Drummond, addressed huge crowds from the plinth of Nelson's Column in Trafalgar Square. Thousands of handbills were distributed. They were printed with the message: *Men and Women, help the Suffragettes to Rush the House of Commons on Tuesday Evening, 13th October 1908 at 7.30 pm.*

Miss Baker remembered that it had been a warm day, the end of a long hot summer, and all the while she was distributing her leaflets she had been aware of the eyes of the police upon her. They were stationed everywhere.

"The bobbies were keeping track of us, Dollie. By then we

were beginning to realize that they had been ordered to spy on our every meeting, to keep abreast of what we were up to. Two days later, on 13th October, the WSPU held their demonstration as planned, but the bobbies were waiting and there were violent clashes. The police had instructions to keep the women out of the House. Twenty-four women were arrested, including Emmeline Pankhurst, who was sentenced to three months in prison. Over the remaining months of 1908 suffragettes continued to attempt to gatecrash Parliament. The police, both on foot and on horseback, began to respond with violence. Women were hurt. Many were arrested and imprisoned.

"Until last year, 'Deeds not Words' had become a passionate call but had remained a non-violent interpretation of what was needed to bring about change. Now we feel we must go further," said Miss Baker, "in order that the Cause be brought to everyone's attention. We are frustrated by the deaf ears of our Parliament but we remain resolved. Our government will hear what we have to say even if we must break the law to make them listen."

Harriet went on to explain that some Union members have been disguising themselves as waitresses and messenger boys, jumping out of delivery vans, hanging from the windows of the House of Commons, entering from the River Thames, haranguing MPs wherever and whenever they can. Nothing will stop them, not even the prospect of months behind bars.

"But if the law forces us to serve sentences, what we are insisting upon is to be classed as First Division prisoners. That is to say, political prisoners rather than common criminals."

"I don't understand the difference," I replied.

"Well," said Miss Baker, "First Division status gives us certain rights or privileges that are denied to Second or Third Division offenders. For example, First Division prisoners are not searched when admitted to jail. They can order in food if they wish to, and most do because prison food is terrible. They are allowed visitors, books, newspapers and writing materials, and they are allowed to pen articles for publication. Also they are free to spend time with fellow inmates. Last year, when Christabel and Emmeline were in Holloway, they were separated. Emmeline was tagged a 'dangerous criminal' and kept in solitary confinement. This meant no exercise, no chapel, no companionship, for days at a time during her sentence."

"That's horrible." I was beginning to understand the sacrifices involved in being a true suffragette. If I was faced with such horrors I am not sure that I would have the courage to stand them.

15th June 1909

At the hospital this afternoon one of the nurses warned me that Mother's condition is rather advanced, but she assured me that she is comfortable and they are doing everything they can.

I sat with her for a little while but she was weak and her eyes were closed most of the time – she was dozing, I think – so I just held her hand and kept quiet.

23rd June 1909

I sat in on a thrillingly heated debate at the WSPU offices yesterday. The subject was: How to guarantee that any sentenced suffragette will serve her term as a First Division prisoner.

"I intend to write a letter to Parliament demanding that our status as political prisoners be recognized," announced Miss Baker. This was received by applause.

"Throughout the civilized world, male political offenders are given special status and we have the right to receive the same treatment as men," a woman whom I had not seen before called out.

"Yes!" a chorus of voices rejoined, including mine.

Someone suggested, and it was backed up by Mary Richardson standing near me, that the younger, stronger women should volunteer to serve the prison sentences, which are debilitating for the older women.

"That's a good point," Harriet Kerr said. "We all know that Emmeline's health is not what it was."

I knew I should volunteer, but after all that Miss Baker had told me I felt too scared. Solitary confinement would terrify me. A few put their hands up and called out their names. I did not, and then the moment was lost because a Scottish woman whose name is Marion – she's a painter or sculptress, I think – hurried to the front of the room, signalled for quiet and began to speak.

"Ladies, I think there are two issues that need to be considered here. The first is that the government's treatment of suffrage campaigners is barbaric. Of course, we are not thieves or murderesses. There is no question that any status given to us other than that of political prisoners is a deliberate misinterpretation of the law. We are fighting for our rights, and that is not a crime." There was cheering and waving from the entire room, but Marion raised her hand for hush. "Wait, wait. Because this is about much more than what status we are given as prisoners. The fact is we shouldn't be thrown into gaol at all. *We are legally entitled to petition.*" Marion's speech was wildly applauded and the evening ended on a very upbeat note.

Walking to the bus I was still asking myself whether or not I should volunteer. So far I have done little for the Cause besides sell newspapers. But if I did have to go to prison, what about my school work? Or even worse, what if something were to happen to my mother and I wasn't there?

24th June 1909

Marion Wallace Dunlop, the Scottish painter who spoke at the debate yesterday evening, rubber-stamped a message across one of the walls at St Stephen's Hall in the House of Commons this morning. The extract is from the 1689 Bill of Rights:

It is the right of the subjects to petition the King, and all commitments and prosecutions for such petitioning are illegal.

Of course, she has been arrested. But what is excellent is that she is stating a very important point. What is more, she is not alone in claiming that we have every right to protest and that we cannot be arrested or imprisoned for the simple act of petitioning.

25th June 1909

Flora told me this morning that she is leaving for Italy at the beginning of July. She is intending to visit Florence and Venice, and expects to be away for a couple of months. She invited me to accompany her but I declined, which surprised her.

I want to be close to my mother, I told her. Also, I feel there is too much happening here to go off travelling. This is a very important time for the Cause and I want to involve myself more deeply. Marion Wallace Dunlop's claim that it is our right as citizens to be allowed to protest is being taken up as a legal battle among the suffragettes. If the Cause wins this point, none of us can ever again be imprisoned for demonstrating for our rights.

I would certainly feel less guilty then about the fact that I have not volunteered for anything more dangerous than office work or newspaper-selling. And I thought I was brave!

30th June 1909

Marion has been sentenced to serve a month in Holloway Prison on a charge of wilful damage. She has been classed as a Second Division prisoner but is fighting against such treatment and insisting that she be moved to the First Division. The request has been refused by Mr Herbert Gladstone, the Home Secretary.

A letter from the school in north London arrived today. Flora said that they have not accepted me. No reason was given.

"Don't be disappointed. There's still St Paul's," she said. "If not, we'll try others. And Miss Baker will continue to tutor you until you are settled."

Lord, I feel a real failure.

5th July 1909

Something quite extraordinary and unforeseen has happened. Marion Wallace Dunlop has thrown away the food that has been brought to her and decided on a hunger strike. This is her own idea. No one at the WSPU knew a thing about it. Several members spoke of the dangers to her health when the news reached us, but most of us saw it as an act of real courage and daring.

The prison authorities are threatening to force-feed her through her nostrils with a liquid mixture of egg and milk. Ugh, how disgusting!

6th July 1909

Miss Baker told me that the wardresses have been leaving trays of food in Marion's cell in the hope that she will weaken and break her fast. So far she has stood firm. We are all keeping our fingers crossed that Mr Asquith will relent and improve her prison status.

Flora set off on her travels this morning. I was really sad to see her go. I hugged her tightly and thanked her for allowing me to remain on here, and for all her many kindnesses to me and to my mother, who has grown a little stronger these last few days. When I visited her this afternoon she was quite chirpy and talked about going home soon. I pray it won't be too long before she is allowed to leave the hospital, but I hate the idea of her returning to the East End.

When I arrived back at the house, it felt so empty. I wandered about from room to room, not knowing what to do with myself. Then I sat on the sofa with the two cats at my side and read *A Midsummer Night's Dream* – Miss Baker is going to set me an exam on Shakespeare.

I have promised myself to use these weeks fruitfully, to work hard at my studies and prepare myself well for whichever new school takes me.

9th July 1909

Marion has been released! After 91 hours of fasting, almost four days, the Home Secretary has set her free.

Emmeline Pankhurst, who is away, travelling from one corner of Britain to the next, talking to groups, at societies, and raising the profile of the Cause, has stated that this act of Marion's has lifted "our militant movement on to a higher and more heroic plane".

I am so proud to be a member of the Union.

When I popped into the hospital to see Mother I was dying to tell her some of the WSPU news and all that is happening to me, but two of my brothers were there with their wives and children and Mother looked tired and weak again. So I only stayed a while and came home.

I feel very distanced from my family and I suspect my brothers resent me. I know my oldest brother's wife, Clara, does. I can tell by the way she looks at me. And one of my nephews, Henry junior, said to me, "You talk funny."

20th July 1909

Talk at the WSPU offices today was that Marion's example has been followed by other imprisoned suffragettes. Fourteen women who were convicted of stone-throwing on 12th July have taken up her baton. When their request to Mr Gladstone to be transferred to the First Division was turned down, they refused to wear their prison clothes or to clean up their cells. They have broken windows to get fresh air and the prison authorities have responded by throwing them into punishment cells for their disobedience.

"We are political prisoners and you are treating us like common criminals," was the women's response. They have all decided to go on hunger strike.

26th July 1909

The women have been released.

This is being hailed as a triumph for our cause because although the authorities threatened forcible feeding they have not carried out the threat. The general consensus seems to be that they do not dare because it would be barbaric and illegal, and would cause public anger.

I received a letter from Flora this morning. It was sent from Paris. She has been staying for a few days with Alice Guy on her way south. Flora sounded very happy about a scheme she and Alice have for directing a film together. I wonder if this means that she will be away longer than she originally intended. I hope not. I miss her and I want to talk to her about my mother's future.

A letter also arrived from St Paul's in Hammersmith, addressed to Flora. I am *dying* to know what it says.

14th August 1909

After lunch, I took the bus to St Thomas's and went to visit my mother. She was very pale, but although still frail she looked a little plumper. She coughs incessantly, but tries her best to make light of her pains in front of me. I think I am rather bad at hiding my feelings; and she senses how upset I get.

We talked of when she leaves the hospital. I suggested finding her a little flat near to Flora. "We'd share it," I promised, but she flatly refuses to move from that horrid damp cottage. How stubborn she is and how frustrated it makes me. But I must be positive. It is wonderful to see her growing stronger and to know that she is going to get better and that somehow or other we will work the other problems out.

20th August 1909

It is now illegal for women to attend public gatherings, particularly those events organized by or involving the Liberal party. The government is embarrassed by the heckling they are receiving.

As a protest, a group of us, including Mary Richardson and Miss Baker, hid in the bushes last night outside a hall in Kentish Town where a Liberal meeting was assembling. While the hall was filling up we tried to make our way inside, but we were forced back out on to the street. So we remained outside, shouting, "Votes for Women!"

"Why don't you treat imprisoned suffragettes as political prisoners?" I called nervously. My heart was beating fast. I've never heckled before.

Mary followed with, "Put your Liberal principles into practice."

"Justice, and the vote for women!" That was me again. I was beginning to gain confidence.

"Give us the vote and we'll go home," yelled Miss Baker. What a booming voice she has!

People in the hall turned their heads in horror. "Get those

blasted women away from here!" A short, bald-headed chap instructed as the doors were closed in our faces. We tried one more time to get in by beating our fists against the doors, but we had no luck. We hung about outside in the street, shouting and kicking up a racket, until eventually, hoarse and hungry, we took a bus back into town and went for soup and ice cream and cake at Mary's. All of us were laughing, buoyed and exhilarated by what we had done. It felt so daring.

21st August 1909

Mr Asquith, the Prime Minister, was interrupted during his speech in Liverpool last night. To protest against the bar on women at public meetings, a few suffragettes broke windows and threw stones. They were arrested.

At the office this afternoon, Mary Richardson said to me, "Next time, we'll break a window or two. It's what we should have done last night, eh?"

I shrugged, but I'm not sure I'd dare go that far.

1st September 1909

Flora is back, looking radiant. It was wonderful to see her.

"How's your mother?" she asked me during dinner.

"They say she'll be coming out of hospital very soon," I replied.

"That's wonderful news, but you don't look very happy about it, Dollie."

"I don't want her to go back to our old home," I said. "She'll only get sick again." But I refused to discuss the subject further. I fear Flora will think that I am angling for more assistance, which I am not.

2nd September 1909

Miss Baker was taking me through her corrections on a Charles Dickens essay she had set when Flora came bursting into the living room waving a letter.

"Forgive me for butting in, but this was among my pile of post. It is from St Paul's. You've been granted a place.

Well done! Their new year begins on 10th September, which means that we have a mountain of things to organize."

Gosh, school. I have enjoyed all these free days and was beginning to hope that it would never happen.

10th September 1909

It feels so strange to be back in a classroom. I have grown used to a life in London that does not include uniforms, morning assemblies, chapel and structured timetables and I don't like being back in the system one bit. I would far rather Miss Baker continued to tutor me, but I daren't say so to Flora who has gone to such lengths to get me here. We seem to have done nothing but traipse round the shops buying clothes and sportswear and pens and books.

I am one of two new girls. The others in my class have all been here for several years. I am reminded of my first days at Cheltenham Ladies' College and how out of place I felt. Once again, I appear to be the only girl from a working-class background. Of course, no one knows my history because my address is Flora's and my school records are from Cheltenham, but it still makes me feel awkward.

I really MUST NOT be so negative. I dream of being

239

... and of helping my mother. Without a decent ... ion I will have no chance, so I'd better make the best of it. And once I have made some friends, it will be different.

18th September 1909

I was going through my things last night and came across my suffrage scrapbook. I haven't looked at it since moving to London. It seems sort of quaint to me now that I actually know some of the women involved in the struggle. I shall take it to school and work on it as a modern history project – it will help me feel less distanced from the movement.

Asquith was speaking in Birmingham last night. Some regional WSPU members climbed up on to the roof of a neighbouring building, lifted off some slates and hurled them at his car as it drew up. Windows and lamps were smashed, but they were careful to avoid hitting the Prime Minister himself. Their intention was to be heard, not to cause physical violence. They yelled out to him that we won't give up until we have the vote. The police were called and hosepipes were turned on the women, who were driven down by the force of the water and by stones thrown at them. They were led away to prison, soaked to the skin, having lost their shoes in the struggle. One of them was injured, but the article didn't report the seriousness of the injury.

I almost wish that I had been there. I can't imagine myself smashing windows, throwing slates at cars or being arrested, but anything is better than sitting in a classroom all day. School is so lady-like.

21st September 1909

The Birmingham demonstrators have been arrested and have received sentences of three and, in Mary-Leigh's case, four months. They are now in Winson Green prison in Birmingham, on hunger strike. The authorities are refusing to release them. Instead they have begun the unthinkable: they are force-feeding our women!

Flora and I talked about the matter over breakfast after she had read out a letter in this morning's *Times* written by Christabel Pankhurst. Christabel has stated that women are being driven to stone-throwing by the government. They are banned from attending public meetings and Mr Asquith continues to refuse to meet with the Union and will not discuss the matter. Every avenue to the vote is being blocked.

acts will do more harm than good,"

ßut what else can we do?" I retaliated.

"We? I sincerely hope, Dollie, that you are not involved with such carryings-on. I told you that I do not approve of unconstitutional acts to win the vote. I am as passionate about our place in society as you are, but these methods will not gain us respect. In fact, I believe they will turn public support against us."

I finished my tea and set off for school without another word. During morning break, I asked one of my classmates, Celia, who seems rather nice, what she thinks about the Birmingham women's fate. Her answer was worse than Flora's.

"They deserve to be force-fed," she said.

I'd better keep my opinions to myself then.

24th September 1909

I attended a meeting at the WSPU offices this evening. It is the first I have been to since school began. Usually I arrive early and make tea. We always serve cakes on these occasions, but as a mark of respect tonight we drank water. The place was packed. Women had come long distances to be with us.

Christabel Pankhurst was chairing the evening. There was real concern about the welfare of the imprisoned women.

The meeting began with the reading of a letter written by our treasurer, Mrs Emmeline Pethwick-Lawrence, and published in today's edition of *Votes for Women*. Naturally, it denounces the force-feeding of women. It received applause and cheers. Questions followed. These were answered by Christabel, who assured us that her mother has a plan. She stated that, as leaders of the WSPU, she and her mother and Mrs Pethwick-Lawrence are officially supporting the acts of the prisoners, including the stone-throwing, and that they intend to make a public statement tomorrow.

During the break, the point at which we usually serve tea, I heard one or two members suggesting that Emmeline and Christabel had no choice but to stand behind the stone-throwers, even though the Birmingham women acted on their own initiative. I have no idea whether this is true or not.

Afterwards, another letter was read aloud to us, a truly shocking one. It had been written to Marion Wallace Dunlop by a force-fed prisoner and described her ordeal. When Marion had finished, the room was silent. Another lady, who announced herself as a doctor, rose to inform us that the inserted tubes used for force-feeding are frequently unsterilized and infection is possible.

I walked to the bus with Harriet Kerr, but we didn't talk much. I think we both felt sickened.

25th September 1909

Today Mrs Pankhurst, Christabel and Mrs Pethwick-Lawrence have publicly supported the imprisoned women and denounced the government for inflicting such pain and humiliation on them.

At school, one of the teachers talked about what was happening. It turned into a class debate and I was relieved to discover that many of the girls were strongly against the government's actions.

Celia and I ate our lunch together. She seemed less disapproving of the Birmingham women today – I think the debate this morning has made her reconsider her opinions – and I offered to lend her my suffrage scrapbook. "It might give you an idea how long this battle has been going on," I said.

I sat next to a sweet old lady on the bus this evening who said she "had never heard the like in all her years". Personally, I feel so angry and frustrated that it makes me want to run round the streets of London, breaking windows and shouting.

28th September 1909

When I arrived home from school this evening, Mrs Millicent Fawcett was visiting with Flora. Flora called me into the drawing room to be introduced. I did not mention that Lady Violet had presented me to her ages ago in Gloucestershire.

"I want you to hear this, Dollie," Flora said, and because their expressions were both so serious, I thought I must have done something wrong.

Mrs Fawcett then informed me that she had recently written to the Prime Minister requesting an audience with him.

"Do you know what he has answered, Dollie?" Flora asked me.

I shook my head. The way they both quizzed me I felt personally responsible.

"He has refused to see me," Mrs Fawcett explained flatly. "Do you know why?"

Again, I shook my head.

"His argument is that, although I am not connected with the troublemakers, the organization discrediting the case for women's franchise, he is too busy with urgent political

245

business to see anyone from any group connected to the Women's Suffrage movement."

I glanced at Flora who was staring hard at me.

"Forgive me if this sounds impolite," I said. "I really don't intend it to, but this government has slammed the door on all peaceable negotiations and now it criticizes us because we have been driven to other means!"

"*Us*? Dollie, are you telling me that you are involved in these terrible acts?"

I couldn't speak.

"Dollie, Flora has told me all about you and I think it is splendid that you are so committed to our cause," Mrs Fawcett continued quickly, "but won't you put your energies with us? We will win the vote, but we will do it without acts of violence and without turning the British public against us."

I agreed to think about it and then excused myself, saying that I had homework to do. I hurried to my room, feeling – what? Betrayed by Flora, I think.

29th September 1909

Mr Keir Hardie was one of the guests at dinner this evening. What a nice man he is! Inevitably the conversation turned to the hunger strikes and the government's response.

"I don't know how this Liberal government hopes to regain respect. Force-feeding women is barbaric." The voice of Virginia Stephen. "As an eminent Labour MP, Keir, what is your opinion?"

Mr Hardie then recounted how he had challenged the government in the House yesterday. "I begged to know how a Liberal government could justify an act of such cruelty against the female sex. In answer, I was informed by the Home Secretary's speaker that it is common practice in hospitals to force-feed patients when they refuse to eat."

Elizabeth Robins, also a guest, was furious when she heard this. "What nonsense!" she cried. "The only patients who are force-fed in hospitals are the mentally insane."

"Asquith is refusing to meet with Millicent, saying that if he sees her he must also give an audience to the WSPU, but, whatever his excuses, he will be forced to put an end to this inhumanity. His government is being condemned from every quarter," were Flora's words on the subject.

"Might the Home Secretary, the government and prison authorities judge suffrage women mentally unstable?" I ventured. "Perhaps that's the message they want to put across to the British people?"

"That's a very good question!" bellowed Mr Hardie.

I blushed, but was thrilled to have been taken seriously.

4th October 1909

No school today. So I went to the WSPU.

Miss Baker, who I haven't seen in ages, asked me about my new school. I told her it was fine but that I preferred being tutored by her.

"Have you made any friends yet?"

"There's a nice girl, Celia Loverton, but she isn't madly interested in our cause and she's posh, so... What's been happening here?" I changed the subject because I am fed up with everyone asking me about school.

"Letters are arriving by the sackload at the offices of all the national newspapers in protest against the treatment of the Birmingham women," Miss Baker said, handing me a copy of the latest issue of *Votes for Women*. "Emmeline has written an article in which she demands: 'How can a Liberal government in free England torture women in an attempt to crush their struggle for citizenship rights?' She intends to begin proceedings against the Home Secretary and the prison authorities on the grounds that a physical assault has been committed against these women. She is choosing one prisoner from the group, Mary Leigh, and will fight it as a test case."

"That's a terrific idea!" I cried. "She's bound to win."

6th October 1909

Asquith has received a protest letter signed by 116 doctors opposing the force-feeding of women prisoners:

> We the undersigned, being medical practitioners, do most urgently protest against the treatment of artificial feeding of the Suffragist prisoners now in Birmingham Gaol.
>
> We submit to you, that this method of feeding when the patient resists is attended with the gravest of risks, that unforeseen accidents are liable to occur, and that the subsequent health of the person may be seriously injured. In our opinion this action is unwise and inhumane...

I believe my mother's doctor, Caroline Sturge, is on the list.

Editors are resigning from their newspapers if their journal expresses support for the government on this issue.

It is true to say that this has caused a national outcry, both from suffrage sympathizers and opponents alike. And so it should. But the depressing fact is that the Prime Minister is still adamantly refusing to back a women's suffrage bill. Nothing we do or say seems to make any difference.

10th November 1909

My birthday. Fifteen years old. Flora has given me the most wonderful gift in the world. My very own typewriter! I cannot begin to describe how touched I am by her generosity. It made me ashamed for the anger I have felt towards her lately.

Celia gave me a new scrapbook. I was amazed. She really enjoyed my suffrage one. "I hadn't really understood before what it was all about," she said.

I invited her to come to Clements Inn with me, to one of the monthly meetings. She said that she'd think about it.

I visited Mother this evening. She looked much stronger and was happy to see me. We talked about school, but when I spoke of the WSPU she waved her hand impatiently.

"You'll end up in trouble mixing with that lot. I don't want you going against Flora," she warned. "She may be a toff, but you are bloody lucky to have 'er."

Sometimes I feel quite on my own. But I am happy about Celia. I want to introduce her to Miss Baker.

11th December 1909

What a bitterly disappointing end to one of the most pressing issues of this year. Mrs Pankhurst's case against the Home Secretary and the prison authorities, which she has been fighting for the past two months, was lost the day before yesterday. The grounds for the decision were that forcible feeding was necessary to save Miss Leigh's life. It was also stated that only the most minimal force was used. This means that the Home Secretary is within his rights to order the feeding of every woman prisoner who chooses hunger strike as a last means of protest.

Mrs Pankhurst is required to pay the court costs or face prison herself. She learned of this judgement as she disembarked from the ship that had returned her from a successful lecture tour of America. What a terrible welcome home!

12th December 1909

An unknown supporter has paid Mrs Pankhurst's fine. That is cheering, but I hoped that we would have so much more to celebrate by this year's end.

I must be positive! Mother's health is greatly improved and that is cause for celebration. She looked blooming this evening.

Celia Loverton told me today that she lives with her grandmother because her parents are in India. Her father is employed by the British Consulate in Delhi, and they are not coming home for the holidays.

14th December 1909

Everyone is preparing for a General Election early next year. There is hope that the Tories might win. My choice is Mr Hardie and the Labour Party, but the important thing is to oust this anti-suffrage lot!

15th December 1909

It has been snowing! I built a snowman in the yard and then Flora and I had great fun hanging Christmas decorations. She has invited Mother here for the festivities but Mother says she wouldn't feel at ease. These are the occasions when I feel torn between my two worlds.

I asked Celia where she feels she belongs.

"With grandmama, I suppose," she told me. "I rarely see my parents."

18th December 1909

We had a jolly "Bloomsbury Christmas Party" yesterday evening. Several of Flora's friends came over for supper. Among them were Cicely Hamilton, actress and novelist, Elizabeth Robins, who is writing now, and the Irishman, George Bernard Shaw – gosh, he's brilliant! Their conversation was of plans to form a Women Writers' Suffrage League. It is to be fronted by some of the most eminent literary figures of today, men as well as women. The idea would be to support all suffrage leagues, whether militant or constitutional. It's so exciting. Flora is right behind it, too.

"You see, Dollie," she said, kissing me goodnight. "We can win this battle with intellect and not aggression."

I wish I could believe her!

26th December 1909

It has been a splendid Christmas. Yesterday morning I went to the hospital to visit Mother. All my brothers and their families were there. I wanted to run off but of course I didn't and everything was fine. We all got on quite well and Mother looked really relaxed.

"All my families together in one place," she laughed.

Today, Celia came over for lunch. We had turkey and steaming baked potatoes and then talked in my room for ages. She told me all about her parents in Delhi and how much she misses them. She is really nice. I think we might have more in common than I supposed.

3rd January 1910

According to the New Year issue of *Votes for Women*, working-class suffrage prisoners are being treated far worse than their more privileged sisters. Reading such articles reassures me that I am right to fight with the WSPU.

24th January 1910

Saw Mother. She looked well and wanted to know what I have been up to. I told her all about Lady Constance Lytton who was in prison last year and who was released after two days of hunger strike without being force-fed. "She believes that she was treated with compassion because she is an aristocrat."

Mother frowned. "She probably was, but who cares about toffs like her?"

"She cares about us," I replied.

"Oh, yeah?" she scoffed.

"This year she returned to prison under the name of

'Jane Wharton', went on hunger strike and was force-fed on numerous occasions before her true identity was discovered. Yesterday she was released from prison. She has been giving interviews to the press. Her story has scandalized the nation."

"People of our class have no rights, Dollie. I don't have to be thrown in prison to learn that. It's why I want you to do good at your school and stop this nonsense."

"I do work at school but I also know that I have to fight for women's rights and that MUST include the interests of working-class women. Think, if you could read and write—"

"Keep your voice down," she snapped. "You'll wake the old girl in the next bed. You've the chance to rise above the abyss, Dollie. Grab it. Stop fussing about the rest of it. Fight for yourself."

Sometimes I think she'll never understand how much this matters to me, and why.

31st January 1910

A committee has been formed to draft a parliamentary bill. It will be known as the Conciliation Committee Women's Franchise Bill and, *if passed*, will offer voting rights to property-owning women. Married women and working-class women, which would include me if I were old enough and my mother, will still not be eligible to vote. The reasoning is that if we fight for all women, no one will get it.

I am disappointed by the narrowness of the Bill's draft because it goes against everything I want to see achieved, but Mrs Pankhurst and Christabel feel that our only chance is to win our rights by degrees. I trust them, so I will back them.

In order to help the Bill gain parliamentary support, Mrs Pankhurst has called a truce on all militant acts. We, the members of the WSPU, have agreed to uphold this. We will continue to lobby vociferously but without militancy.

Flora has declared the truce an excellent move. I do not agree with her. I am incensed by the treatment of suffrage prisoners, particularly those of my own class, who are suffering far greater measures of cruelty. But our debate on these issues today was friendly.

14th February 1910

I can hardly believe it! The Liberals have won the election, with the support of the Labour party. Perhaps this will force them to take notice of the women's issue.

Celia told me that her grandmother doesn't want her

to get involved with any political organizations. I tried to persuade her just to come along and hear what it's all about, but she said she didn't dare go against her grandmother.

20th February 1910

I believe Mrs Pankhurst is also troubled by the fact that this bill is so narrow, but she is keeping quiet because she does not want to upset the apple cart. She is determined that, one way or another, a bill will go through. Her policy is to think practically. Once the vote has been won for a few women, it will pave the way for the rest of us. If it goes through I shan't cheer too loudly because ALL WOMEN OF EIGHTEEN AND OLDER should be allowed to vote.

17th April 1910

Mother has been released from hospital! At last! I went in a hansom to collect her and we travelled back to the East End together.

"Please stay a while at Flora's?" I begged as we approached the slums.

She shook her head.

"You have nothing to worry about," I assured her. I reminded her of the money I shall receive when I am 21, and I promised, as I always do, that I will look after her. I offered again to move her to comfortable lodgings.

Her response was a shrug. "This is where I belong," she answered.

At least my brothers were there to greet her and welcome her home. But I left feeling troubled.

7th May 1910

The most unexpected news yesterday was the death of our king, Edward VII. He was not a supporter of our work and some say that he positively encouraged the government's decision to begin force-feeding, so I do not feel a great desire to mourn.

Visited Mother. She seems settled back at home but it worries me that the lack of comfort will make her sick again.

20th May 1910

As a mark of respect for the King, the mammoth peaceful suffrage demonstration that had been scheduled for the 28th of this month has been postponed until Sunday 18th June.

Saw Mother today. She was in one of her difficult moods. I think I grew over-enthusiastic again about my work with the WSPU. She retorted with dismissives about what she describes as "the crowd" I am involved with.

"Education has got you nowhere, my girl," she said to me. "Out in the streets with banners, ranting and raving about women's rights. I don't know what fancy notions have got into that head of yours. A woman's place is in the home with her family."

I sighed and attempted to explain again. "You were the one who sent me away. You were the one who thought that an education would give me opportunities."

"Yes, but I didn't think it would fill your head with all this nonsense and make you dress la-di-da. I hope you're not getting yourself into trouble with all your talk about women in prison. If I thought…"

"I am fighting for you!"

"But what's the point, Dollie? I don't vote."

"Because you don't have the right to, Mother."

"But even if I did, I wouldn't. What damned difference would it make to the likes of me? Poor is poor, whoever is running the show."

"Not necessarily! Think how different your life might have been if you had been offered an opportunity to study. If you could have earned your own living and not been forced to rely on Father. I know what he put you through," I said. "If you had been independent you could have chosen to leave." It is the first time I have ever dared to broach the subject and she pounced on me like a reptile after a fly.

"You watch your mouth, my girl! I won't hear a word said against your father in this house."

It was plain how she still misses him, though he has been dead for over six years now. Whenever I visit, she talks of him. "The life of a docker, the stresses and the booze sent him to an early grave. Just past 40-years old, he was, when he died. He was a good man," she says, more to herself than to me.

And so to change the subject and because it was almost time for me to leave, I stroked her cheek and said, "Next time I visit I would like to invite Flora, if you will welcome her. She has expressed a desire to see you again. May I?"

"You'll do as you will, whatever I say. You have high-class attitudes and think you know better than your own family, but if she wants to come then I'll not stop her."

"And perhaps you might consider coming to the West End and visiting us."

"Not bleedin' likely! And have all them posh Bonnington folk saying, 'She's not one of us.' No, I know my place, thanks all the same, Dollie. But yer a good girl. You're bright and I'm proud of yer."

I nearly fell over. She has never complimented me like that before.

14th June 1910

Great good news! At last the Bill is to be debated in the Commons. It will make Sunday's march an upbeat affair. I have persuaded Mother to accompany us.

"It's only to see," she said. "And to stop yer nagging me about not knowin' what's what."

I am so looking forward to sharing such an important part of my life with her. Celia has agreed to come along too.

"What about your grandmama?" I asked her, but she assured me that her grandmother sees it as a harmless "bit of fun" and a celebration of the new king.

18th June 1910

We marched from the Embankment to the Albert Hall. It was a glorious day. The sun shone warmly. Everyone was in good spirits. More than 10,000 people had come from all over the world and there were dozens of bands playing. It was incredible. Even Mother looked happy, she who has been so opposed to my involvement with the WSPU. I think the fact she agreed to march with us pleased me more than anything else. Her face was full of wonder. I had to take good care of her, though, so that the press of people did not harm her. She is still so frail.

I introduced her to Miss Baker and to Mary Richardson, and all of them to Celia. They were all lovely to Mother. We read some of the slogans out loud to her because she cannot read them for herself.

We waved banners, carried flowers, sang along with the tunes. Hundreds who have been imprisoned for our cause marched together in a powerful band. It was all very rousing to the spirit. I felt proud to be a woman, proud to be alive, proud to be a part of a movement that is fighting to make a difference.

When we arrived at the Albert Hall, Mrs Pankhurst rose to speak first. Cheers rang out from all around us. She opened with the statement: "One word: Victory!" And then she read an address calling upon the government to grant facilities for the Women's Suffrage Bill before the end of the summer session.

The crowds cheered her once again and laughed and shouted.

"Gosh, I can see why you're so enthusiastic," Celia shouted to me through the din. "Your friend, Miss Baker, has offered to tell me all about what's going on, and I think I should be involved."

I was so glad she wasn't disappointed.

Then a collection was taken for the Cause.

"Is that her then?" my mother asked. "Is that yer famous leader?"

I nodded. "What do you think?"

"Well, she's distinguished and she's got a way with words, I grant you that."

And I knew then that Mother was on her way to being won over. I stood watching as she gazed all around her, taking it all in, with astonishment. Her eyes were bright as round blue buttons. "I thought it'd be a load of toffs," she murmured, "but it's a real mixed bag, all right. See over there."

I turned to where she was pointing and saw a gaggle of young women giggling and chattering together.

"Them's a bunch of seamstresses from the East End. I 'eard 'em talking back near that Marbled Arch." She smiled at me and we hugged one another tight.

A sea of women, and men too, rallying for a new future. It seemed to me as though we could taste victory this afternoon.

19th June 1910

The procession of yesterday was two miles long and the collection raised £5,000 for the WSPU campaign. We are all quite staggered and exhilarated.

Mother was exhausted by the time I got her home last night, but admitted to having enjoyed it much more than she had expected.

I'll make a suffragette of her yet!

12th July 1910

The Bill has passed its second reading in the House today with an excellent majority of 109. Not surprisingly, both our Prime Minster, Mr Asquith, and his Chancellor of the Exchequer, Mr Lloyd George, voted against it! And Mr Churchill has also voted against it. If that does not prove how anti-suffrage the leaders of this country are, I don't know what does. But with a healthy majority, we can still get this bill made law.

School broke up for the summer today. I invited Celia to the rally next week, but her parents have just arrived from India and they are taking her to Italy for six weeks. "But I will come again," she promised. "It was great fun last time."

23rd July 1910

Another splendid rally today, out under the blazing-hot sun. This time the march took us to Hyde Park. There must have been close to a quarter of a million people present. There were Men's Leagues and Women's Leagues from all over the world, banners in every direction brilliantly displaying our Union colours and large signs inscribed with the word *Justice*. Flora and Elizabeth Robins led the Actresses' Franchise League.

Everything remained peaceful and people are sticking to the truce, but there was an air of restlessness and concern.

Asquith is creating obstacles for the Bill; he is stalling for time. Many believe that these are tricks of his to block the Bill's hearing before the end of the summer session.

24th July 1910

I was at Clements Inn this morning when I heard the news. Asquith has announced that the Conciliation Bill will be given no more time this session. This means that, at the very earliest, we must wait until the House reconvenes in the autumn.

Everyone was bitterly disappointed. Emily Wilding Davison, a brilliant woman and one of our most militant and devoted members, and Mary Richardson were among those who called for the truce to be lifted and a return to militant acts of demonstration, but Mrs Pankhurst said no. "Let us wait and see what happens in the autumn."

So even the most extreme among us have agreed to wait, but it is deeply frustrating.

The offices will operate for most of August with only a skeleton staff because many of the women, including Mrs Pankhurst, are going away. I have agreed to lend a hand.

30th July 1910

Flora has been trying to persuade me to go travelling with her. Part of me would enjoy it, but I refused. I feel I should stay in London and be close to my mother, and I want to keep my promise to help staff the WSPU offices.

12th August 1910

London feels quite empty already and I am rather lonely, but I have managed to catch up on a heap of school reading. Once the vote is through I will need to concentrate on taking my exams and getting into university. So these long-drawn-out days have a useful purpose.

I took the bus over to see Mother this evening. I came up with the most wonderful plan and can't think why I haven't thought of it sooner. I could teach her to read and write. But when I suggested it, she shook her head. "It's too late for all that, Dollie."

"It's never too late," I retorted, but she refused to discuss the matter further. There are days when her stubbornness exasperates me.

23rd August 1910

Miss Baker returned from visiting her family yesterday. This afternoon we walked in sunny Green Park together and caught up on all our news.

A postcard arrived from Flora saying that she will be back by the middle of September.

18th October 1910

Flora gave a party at the house this evening in honour of her friend, Edward Morgan Forster, who published his new novel today. He is a writer I enjoy. Or, to be truthful, although he has published three previous works I have only so far read his last, *A Room With a View*, which was great fun. Much of it is set in Italy, a country loved by my dearly missed patron, Lady Violet. But I did not attend the *soirée* because I spent the evening at the Union offices. Everyone is agitated about what will happen when Parliament reconvenes. Mrs Pankhurst has written to Mr Asquith to forewarn him that if no time is made for our bill then militant demonstrations will recommence.

10th November 1910

Today is my sixteenth birthday. Flora burst into my room this morning with a mountain of lovely gifts for me. A silk kimono from Japan, embroidered Indian slippers, French cologne and Forster's latest novel, *Howard's End*. Apparently, it is causing quite a stir. "Edward has written a dedication to you and here, look, I cut out this splendid review from the most recent issue of *The Spectator*."

I was rather overwhelmed by it all.

"I hope you like his book. I devoured it at one sitting and believe it quite excellent. You look tired, Dollie. You never stop studying. How is it going?" But she did not wait for my response. "Have a splendid birthday, my dearest." And she was gone to have her bath.

It's true; I have been swotting late into the night. I need

to create as much free time as possible to devote to my Union duties. This is a critical time for us, as we await the news. After school, I attended a big meeting at the Albert Hall in support of the Conciliation Bill. £9,000 was raised. Wonderful! Emmeline in her address to the crowds said that if the Bill, in spite of our efforts, is thrown out by the government, then it will be the end of our truce.

Flora made me delicious hot chocolate when I arrived home. "You look frozen, dear. Have you had a lovely birthday?"

I thanked her again for my presents.

"Were you at the Albert Hall?"

I nodded, but did not elaborate.

"It is not my place to tell you what or what not to do, but your involvement troubles me. You know that, don't you, Dollie? If the Bill does not go through, I fear trouble from the militants."

12th November 1910

Mrs Pankhurst is reminding Mr Asquith regularly that Parliament must set aside time for the Conciliation Bill. There has been absolutely no assurance from him that this will happen, so she has called upon members to mass together on the 18th for a special deputation. The march is to coincide with the reassembling of Parliament.

I will have to skip school to be there.

14th November 1910

I confided in Celia today that I won't be at school on Friday. When I explained why she expressed a wish to march. "I haven't dared join the WSPU yet, but being there will be like creating modern history."

18th November 1910

Celia and I met outside the tube station at Tottenham Court Road.

"I brought sandwiches," she said. "Isn't this exciting? I've never played truant before."

Arriving at Caxton Hall we found a crowd of several hundred women. "There has been bad news," Ada Wright informed the members.

Then Emmeline, with Christabel at her side, rose to speak.

"Earlier this morning, Mr Asquith opened his first parliamentary session by informing the Commons that negotiations with the House of Lords have broken down and Parliament is to be dissolved by the King on 28th November. He went on to say that between now and that date, priority will be given to government business. No mention whatsoever has been made of our conciliation bill."

Cries of disappointment and anger rang through the crowds. Mrs Pankhurst held her hands high, requesting silence. She then made it plain that, in spite of this news, the demonstration was to be peaceful. "I will deliver the following Memorial to our Prime Minister, and we will make our point. But there are to be no acts of militancy." She read out to us the Memorial she had been intending to give to Asquith:

This meeting of women, gathered together in the Caxton Hall, protests against the policy of shuffling and delay with which the agitation for women's enfranchisement has been met by the government, and calls on the government at once to withdraw the veto which they have placed upon the Conciliation Bill for Women's Suffrage, a measure which has been endorsed by the representatives of the people in the House of Commons.

There was general cheering and support and then, led by Emmeline, Christabel and Elizabeth Garrett Anderson, about 300 of us, including Mary Richardson, Ada Wright, Miss Baker, Celia and myself, marched from Caxton Hall to Parliament. Although determined in our purpose, we were all good-humoured. We walked in bands of twelve or sixteen, many arm in arm. Celia ate one of her sandwiches, offering me the other, but I was nervous and not hungry. All was harmonious and pleasant until we reached the steps of the House of Commons. There we found lines of police waiting for us, and our mood immediately darkened. I heard later that many of the bobbies had been brought in specially by the new Home Secretary, Mr Winston Churchill, from the district of Whitechapel (where they are used to rough work).

Before any of us could reach the House of Commons we had to face organized gangs of both plain-clothes police and those in uniform. Suddenly, as we moved forward, they began to shove, push and accost us. Some women got frightened and began to scream. Celia was one. I saw her panic, turning in circles. It was horrible. Friends all around me were being hurt. Celia was manhandled by a bobby. She screamed hysterically. I tried to reach her but it was chaotic. I couldn't get through the press of people. Men shoving, women being pushed. Then I felt a hard blow against the base of my neck and fell to the ground. A man's boot kicked me in the ribs. A hand hauled me to my feet again.

By that time Mrs Pankhurst and Mrs Garrett Anderson had got through, but I had lost all sight of Celia and I was scared for her. Several policemen a few feet away from me began tearing women's clothes, touching them in improper places. Foul words were spoken. I was very afraid and deeply shocked. I yelled out, "Celia!" but it was hopeless. I began to feel sick.

Though trembling, I moved on forward alongside Ada and 50 or so others until we reached the steps. As we did so we were forced back by the police. It was like a human wall pressing against us.

A female voice I didn't recognize called out: "This way! Follow me."

A small band of us turned left. We were to enter the House by an underground passage that was known to some, though not to me. Unfortunately the police pursued us and the scene that followed was ghastly. We were attacked and, in certain cases, sexually molested by members of the police force. Their manners and their tongues were brutal and indecent. I cannot even write the words I heard spoken by those men. I myself was grabbed by the hair and dragged back out on to the street where I was pushed until my knees buckled and I dropped to the ground on all fours like an animal. Even then I was beaten hard. I was not arrested but kicked back into a jeering crowd, bleeding and bruised.

I made my way back to Bloomsbury alone. My clothes

hung from me like rags, my legs were sore and I was fighting back tears. Fortunately, Flora was out when I arrived home. I would not have wanted her to see the condition I was in, nor to know that I had not attended school. I dread to think what Celia's grandmother will say if she has arrived home in a similar condition.

19th November 1910

A photograph printed in this morning's *Daily Mirror* shows Ada Wright thrown to the ground, beaten and hurt. The paper headlined yesterday's incidents "Black Friday", and so we will christen the day. The number of women arrested is recorded as well over 100. And at least 50 women were seriously injured. How is it possible that our police could behave in such a disgusting way?

I am covered in scratches and bruises and had horrid nightmares. Thank Heaven it is Saturday and there is no school, except that there is no news from Celia.

I skipped breakfast and avoided Flora all day. If she had seen me and guessed where I had been, she would have been furious.

22nd November 1910

No one has even mentioned my absence from school, but there is an uproar about Celia who was arrested on Friday. Apparently her grandmother was summoned to the police station and, after various formalities, Celia was released without being charged, because of her age.

She looked pale today and she has several cuts on her face. "I didn't mention you," she whispered at break. "There was no point in getting us both into trouble. I have been forbidden any involvement in suffrage activities. My grandmother says I have acted like a hooligan and disgraced the family name."

"But you haven't! What happened on Friday wasn't your fault. It was a peaceful demonstration until the police became aggressive."

"I know, even so…"

"Thank you," I said, and I hugged her because I thought she was going to cry and because I feel horribly guilty about her.

14th December 1910

The weather is endlessly wet which seems to more than match the mood of these days. The police are claiming that it was not they who touched women indecently on Black Friday. A report from the Commissioner of the Metropolitan Police denies all accusations.

Mr Churchill has stated that the only ones to blame for the disagreeable scenes on 18th November were the "disorderly women themselves". What a truly horrid man he is!

17th December 1910

School broke up today. Celia told me that she won't be coming back next term. Her parents are returning to India and she must either go with them or be sent to a boarding school outside London.

Life feels grim. We are about to face our second General Election within a year.

20th December 1910

Asquith has been returned to power. Again! Oh, why could we not have been given lovely Mr Keir Hardie, along with his colleague George Lansbury? They and certain others in the Labour Party are so much more sympathetic to our cause. Asquith's majority remains very small so I must take heart from that.

Flora's father, Sir Thomas Bonnington, was here. I was on my way out of the door to see my mother when he arrived. Obviously, Flora introduced me. I nodded and then hurried away as soon as I could. He is an old man now but there was a look in his eyes that made me shiver. My father used to speak of him as cold and heartless. Seeing him today, I understand why.

21st December 1910

Flora handed me a very elegant invitation this morning. Sir Thomas is giving a New Year's Eve party. It is to be a very splendid affair. Flora insists that I attend. "Does he know whose daughter I am?" I asked her.

"No, of course not. You were my grandmother's ward and my family accepts that. It is holiday time, Dollie, and I think you working too hard with your studies and … everything else. It will do you no harm to meet a new circle of people and we can both have great fun dressing ourselves up in splendid evening gowns."

27th December 1910

Flora told me this morning that Mrs Pankhurst's sister, Mary Clarke, died quite suddenly on Christmas Day. She had been released from prison only two days earlier. I wonder what part the shocking conditions of prison life have played in her unexpected death? I am typing a condolence letter.

(I mustn't boast, but my typing is rather skilled now. I love Flora for buying me such a present.)

Christmas and New Year's Eve are behind us, and what a whirlwind of activities I have been caught up in. I even begun to ask myself whether Flora wasn't keeping me occupied on purpose, to take my mind away from my WSPU work. I think she knows more about my activities than she lets on, but even if she does she was very generous with me and gave me five pounds to spend on whatever I fancied. With such riches in my pocket, I was able to visit my mother twice and I spent the whole of Christmas Day with her. We took a bus, just the two of us, and went into the centre of the city where we wandered about the streets which were quite deserted, but it was great fun to be in her company and to see her smiling. My presents to her were woolly gloves, a rich plum colour, and a long matching scarf. It almost drowned her, she has become so slight, but she was well protected against the cold wind of the day and I was delighted to be able to give her some small gift. We ate a hearty Christmas lunch in the Strand at the new Lyons Corner House. The ground floor food hall with its bakery was not open because it was a holiday, but we were able to climb the stairs and eat on the second floor in a very capacious setting. It was packed to the rafters with diners; all very jolly, singing and carousing, and my mother's expression as she gazed about was a delight to behold.

The Corner House with its Art Nouveau decor was very swish, I thought, but it paled beside the gaieties and extravagances of New Year's Eve at the Bonnnington five-storey mansion in Cadogan Square. In spite of the time I have now been living in London I had never been back to Cadogan Square since the day Flora took me to Harrods – and then I didn't go inside. It is a very grand district of London and Cadogan Square is considered to house its finest addresses. The Bonnington home must be amongst the most luxurious, and I felt as though I was stepping into a fairy story as I crossed its illuminated threshold. Flora and I arrived together by carriage at half past eight in the evening. There were silver candelabras glowing everywhere. In the main sitting room with embroidered silk furnishings stood the tallest Christmas tree I have ever set eyes on. A trio of musicians in evening dress were tucked into a corner playing festive tunes.

The invitation stated that there would be champagne before dinner and then fireworks to celebrate the arrival of the new year at midnight. I have never tasted champagne before. It was served in tall flutes on silver trays. I accepted a glass but found it a rather sour drink and full of bubbles that went up my nose and made me want to sneeze. I was not too keen on the experience but I sipped at it anyway, slowly, to be a part of the occasion. Altogether, we were approximately thirty guests. I have certainly attended far larger gatherings, but never have I participated in anything quite so sumptuous. Flora, who looked astounding in a pale lilac evening frock, was very thoughtful and did not abandon me. She knew how nervous I was and must have understood that this was also an emotional trial for me. If my mother had never barged her way to the great wooden door, full of anger and frustration, fighting for her family courageously, I would not be here today. Nor would I have allied myself with the WSPU. So, I had a great deal to reflect on even while I was making small talk and watching everyone in their finery and jewels. Sir Thomas spent most of the evening seated on a Georgian chaise longue with a walking stick planted firmly between his knees. If someone wanted to converse with him, they went to him. I did not, of course, but my attention was constantly drawn to him and to the thoughts of what has happened to my family. After all, I have brothers still employed by this mighty firm. What would they think of me if they knew the company I was keeping? But what a frail figure the head of the firm has become.

A nice man called Jones, or "Jonesy" as Flora called him, kept an eye on me, making sure that I was never without someone to talk to. If I was left momentarily alone, there he was at my side offering me some sweetmeat or other. He is the family butler. Imagine it! Flora says that he and the cook, addressed merely as

"Cook" and as plump as a stuffed partridge, have been with the family since before she was born.

Flora's sister, Henrietta, is a marchioness and is married with two sons. I had spotted her with her family at Lady Violet's funeral but, of course, was never introduced. In fact, I found myself seated beside her at dinner and looked forward to getting to know her a little, but she was not terribly friendly, or rather I held little interest for her. "Oh, yes," she said. "I remember someone mentioning you. You were grandmother's ward, weren't you?" I nodded. "I hadn't realized you are still with us."

And that was more or less the sum total of our exchange. On her right side sat Baron Northcliffe who, along with one of his brothers who was not present at the party, owns Amalgamated Press. Press tycoons. They publish the hugely succesful *Daily Mail*, the *Times*, *Sunday Times* and *Observer* amongst other journals. He and Henrietta were deeply engrossed in a debate about Rolls Royce motor cars. I longed to butt in and engage him in conversation about his newspaper coverage of our cause – if the power of his pen were behind us we would win the vote in no time – but I had promised myself not to involve Flora's family or guests in my role as a suffragette. In any case, he never once gave me a glance.

By midnight I was fairly exhausted, but the firework display in the central gardens of Cadogan Square was truly splendid. Many neighbours and others came out to join us and all stood warming themselves around the roaring bonfire Jonesy the butler had lit for the occasion. Everyone ooh-ed and aah-ed and drank more champagne and cheered in the new year. Even the downstairs staff were with us, wrapped up in mittens and coats. All present except Sir Thomas who had retired earlier to bed.

When the bells chimed midnight, Flora hugged me and whispered, "I know what you wish for, my dearest Dollie, and I hope too that the vote is won this year, but in a peaceful fashion." I hugged her tight, thanked her for her generosity and said no more.

What an evening. One to remember for a long time to come, but if only I could have won the ear of Baron Northcliffe.

20th January 1911

At the WSPU offices there is talk that Christabel and Mrs Pankhurst will renew the truce. Although a great number of the members are pressing to return to militancy, the Pankhursts are holding them back. The organization is in dispute. There are many who feel that we have been betrayed too many times already – I am one of them! – and then there are those, loyal to the Pankhursts, who will follow their leaders' advice whatever. Others say Mrs Pankhurst is tired and sad. During this last year she has lost her only son, her mother and now her sister. Certain members feel that she wants peace at any price and an end to this interminable suffrage struggle.

Emily Wilding Davison asked me if I was sufficiently passionate about winning the vote that I would die for it. I couldn't immediately answer.

"The Cause needs a martyr," she said.

Suddenly I pictured Celia Loverton with her cut face. She, in a modest way, has become a sort of martyr to me. She is probably on the boat to India now. I miss her.

Others may feel as strongly as Emily obviously does. The overruling sentiment within the WSPU is that this government is deaf to our pleas and "it is time to go to battle". It is certainly what I feel.

21st January 1911

Flora took me to a concert this evening. It was a celebration for released prisoners. The music, *The March of the Women*, had been written especially for the event.

6th February 1911

Our new government has met for the first time. There is a move towards a new bill for us, a Second Conciliation Bill, though no mention was made of it in the King's speech.

15th March 1911

Serious criticism is being lobbied against our organization, of Mrs Pankhurst and Christabel, too. It hurts to read it, and I believe it confuses the general public. Even within the WSPU, disputes and alliances are dividing us. We should not fight among ourselves. It is important that our goal bonds us. Miss Baker assures me that Mrs Pankhurst is aware of the situation, but accepts that within any organization divisions and struggles are inevitable. It seems wrong to me.

16th March 1911

The Second Conciliation Bill is due to have its first reading on 5th May. Again it is disappointing because, as with the first, *if* it goes through, it will only allow the vote to women who are householders. The argument remains the same: its narrowness will secure its success.

Mrs Pankhurst has a new car. It is a Wolseley and jolly smart. She has her own driver, too – a woman, and the first to be admitted to the Automobile Association. Well, that is a move in a good direction, I suppose.

When my inheritance is paid, I might buy myself a car. I won't have a chauffeur, though. I rather fancy being at the wheel. I will be able to take Mother out, too. Anything to get her out of that horrid area.

19th March 1911

A national Census is due to be taken on 2nd April.

A boycott has been planned by all the various women's groups, constitutionalists and militants alike. Instead of completing the form, the recommended response, written boldly across it, is, "No vote. No Census."

It's an excellent idea. It appeals to Flora, too, and her passive approach. *The Times*, of course, has criticized us.

20th March 1911

Over breakfast this morning, Flora read aloud Mrs Pankhurst's reply to *The Times*, which is terrific!

"The Census is a numbering of people. Until women count as people for the purpose of representation in the councils of the nation as well as for the purposes of taxation and of obedience to the laws, we advise women to refuse to be numbered."

YES!

"What will you write on our household form, Flora?" I asked.

She laughed at my earnestness. "If Mr Asquith has not pledged, on or before the beginning of April, to allow women's suffrage I shall do as Millicent, Emmeline and Christabel and like-minded suffragists are advising. I shall write in large letters right across our form: No Vote. No Census. There, Dollie, does that please you?"

"Perfectly!" I cried.

3rd April 1911

I am EXHAUSTED. Last night was Census night.

No pledge had been forthcoming from horrible Asquith, so suffrage supporters held an all-night vigil. Flora and I attended a concert organized by the WSPU at the Queen's Hall (where the Exhibition was held two years ago). Afterwards, about 1,000 of us walked around Trafalgar Square in a circular procession for ages. It was magnificent. Everyone was so united. And then we went to the Scala Theatre, where there was entertainment until three in the morning. I have never been up so late before. Flora performed a pro-suffrage poem. What a splendid actress she is! After that, many of the supporters went on to the Aldwych Skating Rink for all-night skating, but we returned home. We walked all the way to Bloomsbury in the cold air, arms linked. Passers-by, who were nothing to do with us, waved and shouted their support. Even a few bobbies called out, "Good on yer!"

We stopped at an all-night café for mugs of scalding-hot tea and sticky buns.

"Your performance tonight was great, Flora. I would have loved my mother to have heard you," I said as we walked on.

"Thank you. Yes, I was surprised when you said she wasn't coming."

"She's been sick again. It's nothing serious but she does have to take care. I wish she'd leave that cottage. The damp gets in to her bones. But she seems happy and John is kind to her, even if he thinks I have become a 'stuck-up missie'. Lord, Flora, I hope I haven't."

Flora roared with laughter and hugged me tight. We were shivering with cold. "Is that why you are so passionate about all this?" she asked softly. "Is it all for your mother?"

"Maybe," I answered, but I wasn't able to explain more. It's funny; even after all this time I have never been able to open up to Flora about what drives me to this work. The only person to whom I ever confided the terrors of my childhood was Lady Violet.

The fact is that everything I am fighting for, the women's battle I am committed to, is fuelled by memories that will always haunt me. Those nights when Father came home drunk or deadbeat or out of work and took his moods and frustrations out on my mother. Sometimes he would hit her and those nights were the worst. I would lie in my bed, wanting to die. Sometimes I would get up and rush at him and beg him to stop, tears streaming down my face, but then he would turn on me, too.

I would lie awake listening to her sobbing and it devastated me that there was nothing I could do for her. Nothing that she could do for herself. Yet, even today, I do not believe that Father was a cruel man. My parents were caught up in a situation that they could not get free of.

My mother has sacrificed her life for him and the family. But I ask myself how it would have been if she had been educated and could have found independence, if she had not been financially dependent on him. Or how might it have been for him if she could have carried the financial load with him? What shame did he suffer knowing he could not feed his family?

4th April 1911

The news is that all across the country supporters held the all-night vigil to boycott the Census. A large midnight feast took place on Wimbledon Common where they tucked into roasted fowl, boiled ham, coffee and lashings of hot tea. What a fun way to protest!

Emily Wilding Davison hid herself in the Houses of Parliament. It had been her intention to rush into the House first thing on Monday when the Prime Minister appeared and shout, "Mr Asquith, withdraw your veto from the Women's Bill and women will withdraw their veto from the Census." Unfortunately, she was found by a cleaner in the crypt of St Stephen's Chapel. The police were called but she was not charged, though her name has been added to the Census numbers.

How daring, to stay there alone in the dark. I would have been absolutely petrified.

23rd April 1911

There was a meeting at the Queen's Hall this evening, which I missed because I had a mass of homework to catch up on. I heard later that Mrs Pankhurst gave a rip-roaring speech which finished with: "We believe that this cause of the emancipation of women is not only the greatest cause in the 20th century, but we believe it is also the most urgent and the most necessary."

Yes! It reminded me of Celia saying, "We are making modern history." I miss her.

5th May 1911

The revised Conciliation Bill passed its second reading in the House of Commons today with a truly excellent majority – 88 votes against and 255 in favour.

It looks as though, AT LAST, a handful of women are soon to win the vote.

The news was announced at a mammoth meeting at Kensington Town Hall, which Flora and I attended together. She accompanies me when she feels that the mood is determined but peaceable. I love it when she's there; it forms a bond between us.

Let's work as we have never worked before to get this bill passed during this session of parliament. That was the gist of Mrs Pankhurst's call to us all. Our cheers must have been audible all the way to Hyde Park.

Afterwards Miss Baker, Flora and I were invited to dinner with Emmeline Pethwick-Lawrence and her husband, Frederick. Their house is terribly posh but they are really nice and very generous and so committed to Christabel and Mrs Pankhurst and the Cause. Flora and Miss Baker started up a heated but friendly debate during the meal about the continuation or not of the present truce against militant action. Miss Baker and I were the two who most favour militancy. The Pethwick-Lawrences counselled caution and Flora remains firmly against it.

29th May 1911

Mr Lloyd George confirmed in the Commons today that Mr Asquith will make no time for a second reading of the Second Conciliation Bill this session. It will have to wait until 1912.

I hate those politicians. We have been cheated. This could end the militancy truce and might well affect the King's Coronation procession next month.

12th June 1911

Christabel informed a large gathering of us at the office last night that she has received sound reassurance that at next year's session our bill will be given all the time it requires to make certain of its successful passage. I think this news, coming from her, who would normally countenance militancy, has quietened the angry hearts of a few. Personally, I cannot help asking myself why the promises always remain somewhere far-off in the distant future.

17th June 1911

A stupendous procession took place today, which, although sponsored by us, was supported by 28 other suffrage groups. We named it the Women's Coronation Procession. It was the best ever. All the various suffrage groups united, and it went off without any violent incidents.

It began at the Embankment. Everyone walked seven abreast or rode on horseback – horses had been loaned to us by supporters everywhere. I spotted a chestnut mare eating the daisies off the straw hat of a girl in the crowd lining the pavements. When I pointed it out, my row got the giggles.

It was a cold, bright day but the exercise kept us warm. As we approached Piccadilly there were roaring salutes and cheers. I was puzzled. Then I spied an old lady sitting on a balcony, decked out in our colours. An inscription on the railing read: *The Oldest Militant Suffragette Greets You.* I couldn't believe my eyes. It was Elizabeth Wolstenholme Elmy. She has been a fighter for our cause for the past 50 years and was a great friend of Lady Violet's.

It brought home to me for how long and tirelessly women have been fighting for the right to be acknowledged as the equals of men.

22nd June 1911

Today was the official Coronation day. The crowning of King George V. In my opinion it was a shadow of our spectacular Women's Coronation Parade last Saturday; everybody is still talking about the immense support we received. Our procession was seven miles long!

24th August 1911

A very worrying article has appeared in the latest issue of our *Votes for Women* newspaper (which I am no longer selling because Harriet Kerr has promoted me to a summer typing job). It states that Lloyd George, speaking on behalf of the Prime Minister, has broken faith with the Conciliation Committee by suggesting that another bill of a similar nature could be given facilities next session. Our journal states that if he betrays women's suffrage societies, the WSPU will "revert to a state of war".

Mrs Pankhurst is away so we have not yet received her opinion. I haven't quite understood the implications. Harriet sincerely hopes that we won't be forced back to aggressive tactics. Christabel warns that we must be wary of Lloyd George, that he is an enemy of women's suffrage.

The problem seems to be that Lloyd George wants the Conciliation Bill to offer voting eligibility to a broader band of women. On the face of it, that sounds splendid. However, Miss Baker advises that this would almost certainly lead to the Bill's defeat. "The Liberals are terrified. Women all over the country have campaigned tirelessly against them because they have refused to give us suffrage rights. If this bill goes through, they know that every woman with a voice will vote against them and they will lose the next election. So, they have no intention of making it law."

7th November 1911

Asquith has announced that a Manhood Suffrage Bill, which would give the vote to a wider section of the male population, is to be introduced into the next session. The Bill will allow for an amendment, if the House of Commons supports it, for certain classes of women to be enfranchised.

Christabel has cabled the news to her mother, who left for the United States a month ago on a speaking tour.

We have been betrayed!

10th November 1911

It is my birthday. Seventeen. I'm getting old. I went and had tea with my mother. Two of my brothers and their families were present. One of them took me aside and ticked me off, saying that I caused my mother "nothing but worry with all your talk about women's rights".

I was speechless. I was sure Mother was beginning to support us.

12th November 1911

News from Mrs Pankhurst in the States affirms new and more militant activities. Christabel has announced that the WSPU is returning to an anti-government policy.

Flora was most upset when I told her this evening. "It will

do you no good getting involved with illegal acts. You must think of your education and your future."

"It is no future," I rejoined, "if I grow up into a world where women are not recognized as citizens and are not free to follow the professions they choose. A world where the majority of them cannot read, write or earn their keep."

17th November 1911

A deputation, led by Christabel and Mrs Pethwick-Lawrence, of nine suffrage societies, including the Actresses' Franchise League, was received by Asquith today, but he stressed that women's suffrage will not become a government measure while he is in power. The only path he will follow is the Manhood Suffrage Bill.

Flora was very depressed when she returned this evening, but she still maintains that militancy is not the direction. I DISAGREED WITH HER! We had a horrid argument and here I am in bed, writing my diary, feeling upset.

18th November 1911

The WSPU has issued an official statement. Hostilities are to be resumed.

21st November 1911

Mrs Pethwick-Lawrence led a march from Caxton Hall to the House of Commons today. I did not participate because I accompanied a smaller group of other militant friends, including Miss Baker. Armed with bags and pockets laden with stones – some of us had hammers – we smashed the windows of several city-centre stores. I broke the glass of two windows of Lyons' Tea Shop. Swan & Edgar, the department store, was damaged, as was Dunn's Hat Shop.

Others targeted newspaper offices, the *Daily Mail* and *Daily News*, while several men's clubs came under attack.

Over 200 were arrested, including Mrs Pethwick-Lawrence and Mary Leigh. I was caught, too, but when the bobby learned my age he let me go and I legged it home. I said nothing to Flora. She'd be livid if she knew. I have never indulged in illegal deeds before and I am shaken by the force of my anger today. Also, I have a deepish cut between my wrist and my left thumb. Still, I don't regret my actions. This has to be done.

23rd November 1911

At the Savoy Hotel this evening, Christabel publicly defended the violence of two days ago. She claims that men won their right to vote through riot and rebellion and we must do the same.

Flora interrogated me about my bandaged hand, and I lied to her. Oh, Lord. I think fibbing to her – she who is practically my sister – hurts more than anything. But what choice do I have?

28th November 1911

Many feel that the "vandalism" was inappropriate because it was carried out against *private* property, not public. The movement has never previously targeted personal possessions.

Christabel maintains that such acts may need to be repeated.

Flora is absolutely furious. She made me promise not to get involved. It was awful, making a promise I knew I would be obliged to break. I am in full support of more extreme acts, but I hate the deceit this is forcing me into.

4th December 1911

Mr Lloyd George has been publicly boasting that he has "torpedoed the Conciliation Bill". Horrid man. I want to torpedo him. It is no wonder that women's anger is reaching such a pitch of violence. The government betrays us and then gloats about it publicly. Mrs Pankhurst might cut short her trip and sail back to fight with us, though we are well led by Christabel.

15th December 1911

Emily Wilding Davison soaked strips of linen with paraffin, lit them and then thrust them into various pillar-boxes today. Some of us found this all a bit shocking. I don't think her actions were sanctioned by the WSPU leaders. She was arrested near the Parliament Street post office and has been committed to trial at the Old Bailey.

Emily is convinced that the publicity will bring us new supporters. She believes that only once we express the depth of our commitment will the government and the country really take heed and fully comprehend what we are fighting for, and how profoundly important to mankind our cause is.

I spoke to Flora about Emily's thoughts. "She goes too far," was her response, "and that is why she is no longer employed by the WSPU."

"She is still a Union member," I retorted.

"But she acts alone. She is a renegade and that is dangerous."

I did not dare reply that I think Emily and others of a like mind will go to even greater lengths if they deem it necessary. Am I one of those? I cannot be sure, but I think so and that scares me.

13th January 1912

Emily Wilding Davison has been sentenced to SIX months' imprisonment. We are all reeling with shock at the severity of such a sentence.

22nd January 1912

Mrs Pankhurst has returned from the States. She spoke at the London Pavilion, declaring that she will support nothing less than a government bill of full sexual equality. She applauded us window-breakers of last November. If we are not given the opportunity to be heard then we must find other means to express our discontent.

We will fight this government and every succeeding one if it does not take up our cause, was her message.

1st March 1912

"Why should women go to Parliament Square and be battered about and insulted and, most important of all, produce less effect than when they throw stones? The argument of the broken pane of glass is the most valuable argument in modern politics."

Emmeline recently made this statement.

Today, led by her in Downing Street, women broke windows all over London.

Charlotte Marsh, Emily Wilding Davison's friend, who prefers to be called Charlie, and I shattered an entire row of shop windows in the Strand. Shards of glass lay like hundreds of puddles on the street behind us. We kept our hammers hidden in our muffs and walked fast. It was scary.

Approximately 150 women smashed 400 shop windows today. Mrs Pankhurst has been arrested for inciting violence. The total number arrested was around 120.

2nd March 1912

At Bow Street Magistrates' Court today Mrs Pankhurst was sentenced to two months' imprisonment in the THIRD DIVISION.

Her speech was amazing:

"If you send me to prison, as soon as I come out I will go further, to show that women who have to pay the salaries of Cabinet Ministers and who pay your salary too, Sir, are going to have some voice in the making of the laws which they have to obey."

3rd March 1912

Skipped school again – I haven't been in since last Thursday.

Both yesterday and today, groups of us have been out smashing windows again as a protest against Mrs

Pankhurst's sentence. Many of the windows at Liberty's were broken.

Millicent Garret Fawcett spoke out against our militant acts and declared that the NUWSS stands where it has always stood.

Elizabeth Garrett Anderson has also condemned our violent behaviour and criticized Mrs Pankhurst.

4th March 1912

I was working at Clements Inn today when the police arrived, armed with a bunch of warrants. Both Mr and Mrs Pethwick-Lawrence were arrested. It was upsetting because Mrs P-L was only recently released from Holloway. Emmeline Pankhurst could not be arrested because she is already in prison, as is her comrade, Mabel Tuke. This left Christabel. A warrant was issued for her arrest, but she escaped.

Flora was telephoned. She agreed to give Christabel some contact addresses in Paris. The good news is that with Christabel still at liberty there is someone to direct the movement, even if it will be from a distance.

Annie Kenney, a great friend of Christabel's and the only working-class member of the WSPU leadership, says that we can continue to operate effectively. We must find a means of staying in contact with Christabel.

But the mood here is desperate. We feel cheated and betrayed.

7th March 1912

Flora is monumentally furious. The headmistress at St Paul's contacted her to find out where I have been. When she confronted me, I was forced to admit the truth. I can't keep deceiving her. Besides, I believe that what I am doing is right. VIOLENT PROTEST HAS TO BE MADE if we are to change the government's thinking.

"Why are you risking your future, which is so bright?" she shouted at me.

"Because without equal opportunities for women there is no future."

"But nothing justifies this violence, Dollie, nothing."

"It does, but you cannot understand because your life is comfortable and secure. You can work. You have money for food, even without the vote," I screamed back at her.

She was aghast. "Your fury reminds me of your mother when she turned up at our home during the dockers' strike.

She was angry and abrasive, and refused to discuss anything with me and it got her nowhere." How could I begin to explain to Flora about my mother's life or my early childhood memories? Never in a million years will she see my point of view. She has also forgotten that if my mother had not arrived unannounced at the Bonnington door Lady Violet would never have known about us, and I would not be here today, living this privileged life. So my mother's courage *did* make a difference.

"How far can you go for an ideal, Dollie? Think about it carefully, I beg you. What you have done is illegal. You could end up in prison, and then what will you have achieved?"

I left her and went to bed. I had no stamina left to fight with her, and besides it hurts me because I love her so much.

28th March 1912

A second reading was given to a barely revised Conciliation Bill and it has been rejected. I don't think our case has been served by an article in this morning's *Times*, which stated that our revolutionary acts prove that we are all mentally unstable and not worthy of the vote.

Mrs Pankhurst and Mr and Mrs Pethwick-Lawrence have

been committed for trial on charges of conspiracy, which means they are being charged with plotting to pervert the course of justice. That's really serious. Those who are left at Clements Inn are depressed. Our dreams of the vote for this year have been destroyed.

A massive turn-out tonight at the Albert Hall rally to support our leaders and to show our defiance at the decisions taken by this turncoat Liberal government.

30th March 1912

Mrs Pankhurst has contracted bronchitis in her cell at Holloway and an appeal for bail has been refused. We fear for her fading health.

4th April 1912

Mrs Pankhurst has finally been released on medical grounds. Thank Heaven.

14th April 1912

Christabel is continuing to write columns for our paper, *Votes for Women*, but they are published anonymously. Annie Kenney makes weekly journeys across the Channel to get instructions for us from Christabel.

I am channelling my energies into my neglected school work and am deep in history and English essays. I have so much to catch up on!

15th May 1912

The conspiracy trial began at the Old Bailey today. All the newspapers are reporting on it, which gives a very high profile to our cause, even though the thought of Mrs Pankhurst being committed to prison for a long term makes me miserable.

22nd May 1912

Mrs Pankhurst made a very moving speech from the dock yesterday in which she pointed out again that we have been fighting for the vote since before the Reform Bill of 1867. It is despair and frustration that have driven women to such acts of militancy, she argued. She also talked of the appalling conditions in which so many women and children live. It stabbed at my heart.

But, despite her fine words, the all-male jury found Mrs Pankhurst, her friend Emmeline Pethwick-Lawrence and her husband Frederick guilty. They were sentenced to nine months in the Second Division and ordered to pay the prosecution costs of the trial. The women were taken back to Holloway and Mr Pethwick-Lawrence to Brixton prison.

NINE months in the SECOND DIVISION. How unjust can a system be!

1st June 1912

The prisoners have threatened to go on hunger strike unless they are given political status. Several Labour politicians, including George Lansbury and Keir Hardie, and hundreds of famous people, Flora and many of her friends included, are supporting this request.

It is encouraging to feel the public response.

10th June 1912

All three prisoners have been placed in the First Division. This is the first time the government has ever recognized our cause as a political one. It is a TRIUMPH!

14th June 1912

Our "triumph" was shortlived. It turns out that only the three leading suffrage prisoners are being granted political status. The others, some 78 prisoners, must stay in the Second or even Third Division cells. So, after all, it is not that the government recognizes our status; it is simply that they wish to appease the public outcry.

19th June 1912

A hunger strike began today. Emmeline and the Pethwick-Lawrences are supporting the rest of the movement and striking with them.

22nd June 1912

Doctors and nine wardresses entered Mrs Pethwick-Lawrence's cell today and forcibly fed her. Afterwards they flung open the door of Mrs Pankhurst's cell armed with force-feeding apparatus. Forewarned by the harrowing cries of Mrs Pethwick-Lawrence, she received them with all her anger and indignation, grabbed a large earthenware jug, held it above her head and said, "If any of you dares take so much as one step inside this cell I shall defend myself."

They fell back and left her. When she entered her friend's cell, she found her in a state of collapse.

26th June 1912

Mrs Pankhurst and Emmeline Pethwick-Lawrence have been released from Holloway, for health reasons.

Mrs Pankhurst spoke of the prison scenes that took place around her as "sickening and violent". She claims that "every hour of the day" she woke from nightmares and the doctors had to be called to calm her. During her imprisonment, she was assured that she would not be force-fed, but there are many other women still behind bars who are being subjected to this foul indignity.

Yesterday the Labour MP George Lansbury warned the Prime Minister in the House of Commons, "You will go down in history as the man who tortured innocent women."

1st July 1912

Mrs Pankhurst has left for Paris to visit Christabel, travelling under the name of "Mrs Richards". Before she left, Flora met her and gave her advice on various French matters, including medical care.

Although Flora deeply disagrees with the violent tactics we have used this year, she remains a great friend of Christabel's and holds Mrs Pankhurst in the highest esteem. When she returned home, she said that Mrs Pankhurst looked very frail and must take time off to rest.

4th July 1912

Emily Wilding Davison threw herself down an iron staircase in Holloway Prison last night. She was protesting against the treatment the prisoners have been receiving. I was told, but I don't know how accurate this is, that her intention was to kill herself. She wants to become the martyr she passionately believes our cause needs. She did not succeed because she fell upon some wire netting 30 feet below, but she was badly concussed and has severe injuries to her spine. She had to be seen by the prison doctors. Even so, today, she was forcibly fed again. I travelled to North London, to Holloway, to see her but I was refused a visit. It looks so grim in there. I was glad to get back on the bus.

10th July 1912

The Pethwick-Lawrences left for France. They are travelling to the Hotel de Paris in Boulogne where they will meet up with Christabel and her mother who are arriving from Paris. They intend to spend a few days together, recuperating. The hunger strikes have taken their toll.

17th July 1912

Confusing news has reached us at Clements Inn. It seems that there has been a disagreement between Emmeline and Christabel Pankhurst and the Pethwick-Lawrences. Mr and Mrs Pethwick-Lawrence have criticized the excessive violence our Union has resorted to and they were distressed to learn that the Pankhursts feel we must intensify our campaign, or all our work will have been to no avail. When they expressed their objections Mrs Pankhurst requested their *resignations* from the Union. This is incredible.

I cannot bear to think what this might mean. Could it be the beginning of the end? If the Union splits, will our fight have been in vain? I pray that they will find a way to resolve their differences. I wish I could talk to Miss Baker on this matter, but she, like so many of my friends, is in prison, and there is no point in pouring my heart out to Flora. She agrees with the Pethwick-Lawrences. Of course.

21st August 1912

We are in the throes of moving offices to Lincoln's Inn House. The chaos of files, pamphlets, papers and notes seems to me to reflect the state of affairs. I am exhausted from filling boxes and stacking crates and I feel angry and worn out by the government's cruelty and stubborn attitude.

25th August 1912

I have just learned that Christabel returned to London recently in disguise to meet Frederick and Emmeline Pethwick-Lawrence. She has confirmed that both she and her mother wish them to leave our organization. We are all quite stunned because they have been such loyal workers and have offered us so much financial support over the years.

When I got in this evening, Flora greeted me with, "I insist that you renounce all connections with the WSPU."

"You can't ask that," I retaliated.

"You must concentrate on your school work if you are to gain a place at university," was her argument.

My marks have been consistently high and I have been working extra hard so that I would not fall behind, for the precise reason that I have not wanted her to use my studies as an excuse to make me resign from the WSPU.

"Even if you throw me out on the street," I told her, "I won't give up this fight."

"Oh, Dollie, I will never throw you out, but I dread the thought of you ending up in prison. It's because I love you that I am begging you to find another way to channel your commitment."

"If you love me, Flora, please try to accept me for who I am," I replied and went upstairs to take a bath.

16th October 1912

We are just about installed at our new office address. The split with Mr and Mrs Pethwick-Lawrence is certain. They came to a meeting the other night at the offices and the matter was discussed openly. I am very sad because I like and respect them both. The members are very divided on this matter.

17th October 1912

Flora took me to the theatre to see a French actress, Sarah Bernhardt. She performed in Shakespeare's *The Winter's Tale* and was magnificent. Afterwards, we went backstage to her dressing room. Flora knows her rather well. It was incredibly exciting and I felt that it bonded Flora and me again after all our arguing and bickering during these last six weeks. Elizabeth Robins was also in the audience. She was upset about the business with the Pethwick-Lawrences, but we did not discuss it in front of Flora.

18th October 1912

We have a new newspaper, *The Suffragette*. Its first issue appeared this morning. *Votes for Women* will be published by the Pethwick-Lawrences. They are continuing to support women's enfranchisement, but in their own, less militant, fashion.

Mrs Pankhurst's intentions for our future were stated clearly last night at a huge gathering at the Albert Hall, which I attended with Miss Baker who has just been released from prison. We are to show resistance not only to the government itself but also to the Irish and Labour parties who support the Liberal anti-suffrage policies.

Secret acts against public and private property, are what she counsels us to carry out. "Be militant in your own way," she said. "I incite this meeting to rebellion."

Flora, who has been spending time with the Pethwick-Lawrences, is horrified. She was mumbling something about sending me away to school. If she intends to, I shall run away.

24th November 1912

Mrs Pankhurst has been campaigning this month in the East End, in areas such as Bethnal Green and Limehouse. I have been accompanying her on several of these trips because I know the area a bit and because it is an aspect of the work that matters so deeply to me. Every time I hear her speak I feel the fire rise in my soul. She is very sensitive to the needs and disadvantages of the very poor.

Sylvia, one of her other daughters, has lived and worked

in the East End, among working-class women, for many years. She knows the dire necessity for women's rights there. I am very inspired by her.

George Lansbury, one of our greatest advocates, has been thrown out of the Labour Party because of his support for women's suffrage. He is going to stand as an independent candidate, fighting his seat on the issue of women's suffrage, sponsored by us. This is really exciting and it takes the Cause very much in the direction that I have dreamed of.

My mother and all my brothers and their wives attended this evening's meeting. I know they don't all agree, but at least they showed up. And my mother is sympathetic. Well, sometimes. She got agitated when she heard Mrs Pankhurst's call to militancy.

I feel hope and enthusiasm again.

8th December 1912

Suffragettes have been attacking letter-boxes, burning letters, setting off false fire alarms. There have been more arrests, including dear Miss Baker, who has barely been out of prison this year. Flora wants to know where I am at every minute of the day. I will not even write in this diary what I have been involved in because I fear she may find it and read it. Not that she ever has intruded on my privacy in the past, but she is worried about my safety.

The government and members of the public are beginning to view Mrs Pankhurst as a dangerous revolutionary. Plain-clothes policemen are attending all our meetings, taking notes of everything that is said. It is all so ridiculous. Why don't they just give women the vote?

16th December 1912

Mr Asquith has told the House today that the Manhood Suffrage Bill will have its second reading after Christmas.

Millicent Fawcett is pressurizing us to halt all aggressive activities until we see whether there will be women's suffrage amendments included in the bill. I bet there won't be. Why would Mr Asquith give us changes this time when he has broken his word countless times in the past?

10th January 1913

I received a letter in the post from Mrs Pankhurst. It has been sent to all members of the WSPU. It states that it is our obligation to stand up for our rights through militant acts:

> ...*If any woman refrains from militant protest against the injury done by the government and the House of Commons to women and to the race, she will share the responsibility of the crime...*

The letter goes on to request an acknowledgement of our support. Obviously, she has mine. But I have hidden the letter at the very bottom of my chest of drawers.

27th January 1913

Asquith's government introduced its Manhood Suffrage Bill today, but when it reached the floor the Speaker of the House of Commons would not permit any changes. He ruled that to include women's suffrage amendments would so alter the nature of the Bill that a whole new one would need to be introduced. So it was decided to drop the Manhood Suffrage Bill for this session!

Emmeline was furious. She says that no one can ever again believe Mr Asquith to be a man of honour. I have never seen her so mad.

28th January 1913

I threw stones in Whitehall today as a protest and broke several windows. I was not arrested but 49 others were.

15th February 1913

A house that was being constructed for David Lloyd George has been seriously damaged in a fire by some of our women. Emmeline has been arrested, although she was nowhere near the scene of the crime. I doubt the authorities believe she is personally guilty of the deed, but she has been charged with incitement to commit a felony.

18th February 1913

Asquith's decision has caused a chain of destructive acts. Hordes of women are going to extremes now to "win the vote, and society is expressing its shock at our "delinquent" behaviour. But what will it take to make the government listen?

Perhaps Emily Wilding Davison was right when she told me that the Cause needs someone to die for it. Not me, though. I am definitely not brave enough.

4th March 1913

The news today is that cricket pavilions, racecourse stands and golf clubhouses have been set on fire. Many women have been arrested, including *me*. I have to confess that now the moment has come, I am petrified. Flora begged to pay my fine, but I wouldn't agree. I will serve my sentence and play my part.

She has promised to notify Mother. If she doesn't hear from me, she will worry.

5th March 1913

Mrs Pankhurst has been sentenced to THREE years' penal servitude for the destruction of the Chancellor of the Exchequer's future home.

I have been imprisoned in Holloway in the Second Division. There are 81 of us in here. Some have been given terms of up to six months. My sentence is two months. I shall protest at my status as a non-political prisoner. I am on hunger strike.

17th March 1913

I am weak today; my writing is shaky. I have little strength, though I am determined to keep a record of every day that passes in this stinking place.

19th March 1913

This morning, when my turn came to be force-fed, I had intended to be resistant and beat off the prison staff, but I am weak and I was shaking with fear, and I failed miserably. Four big wardresses came into my cell, wrapped a towel around me and without further ado pinned me down against the bunk. One of them clamped her hand over my mouth and squeezed it closed. Then a doctor arrived. He was carrying all manner of horrific-looking equipment. He proceeded to insert a rubber tube of approximately two feet in length up my left nostril. It was horrendous. At first I had a tickling sensation and then my eyes began to sting. Then he threaded it further and further until it was fed down my throat. My eyes were weeping. I was gasping for breath and fighting the women, who were too strong for me. A china funnel was then attached to the other end of the piping and a mushy, cabbage-like liquid was poured into it. The doctor took my pulse while one of the wardresses pinched closed my right nostril. Now both were blocked and I couldn't breathe at all. I thought that I would suffocate or choke to death. My eyes were streaming and my arms and shoulders ached from the force of being pinned against my bunk. I fought for breath until the liquid was sucked up into my nose and down my throat, which is the point of this horrid, cruel exercise.

A basin of water was then placed in front of me and the tube was withdrawn and put into the basin. Mucous and phlegm came out with it. I kept spitting as though something was still stuck inside me. My chest throbbed with pain and I felt sick and very dizzy.

I have been at Union meetings where they have discussed the barbarity of this treatment. I remember the letter Marion Dunlop Wallace read out to us all; I have friends who have been through it, but nothing, NOTHING, prepares you for the horror and indignity of experiencing it.

What is even worse is that the tubes they are using are not sterilized. Force-feeding the insane in hospitals is only carried out if it is to save life. Here, it is an act of violence and could very possibly cause serious infection, or if the liquid passes into the lungs it could cause pneumonia.

20th March 1913

I have spent three days, not consecutively, in solitary confinement for hitting one of the wardresses when she forced me against my bunk. Books have been forbidden me. On the days when I have been locked in solitary, I have been allowed no breaks for exercise. Those days are the worst. It is so lonely. Twice I have ended up in tears. One of the other problems is that I am so cut off from the Cause, from the news of what is happening.

I have served a fortnight of my time. Fifteen days: it feels like fifteen years.

13th April 1913

The whisper within the prison is that Emmeline is very sick. She collapses frequently. They are not force-feeding her but she is on hunger strike and has been surviving on nothing but water.

I think the Governors are worried that she might die. Lena, another suffragette in here, says they fear that her death would make a martyr of her. There is talk of releasing her until she recovers her health and then hauling her back in again to complete her sentence. I wept when I heard this, and because I am so tired and weak myself. My legs are growing wobbly.

The only way I can calculate the date is by marking off each day as it passes. As I write, the letters swim about in front of my eyes. I am scared that my notes will be found so I hide them in my underwear. I am writing on scruffy bits of paper intended to be used for hygiene purposes.

I have now served over a month. Some of my hair is beginning to fall out and my teeth feel funny. I shake a lot and am always dizzy. I rarely move from my bunk.

25th April 1913

The government is so determined that Emmeline Pankhurst and others like her should not attempt another hunger strike and thus find themselves released from prison without having served their full sentence, or die inside and become martyrs, that it has introduced a new act. Its official title is The Prisoners' Temporary Discharge of Ill Health Act.

The idea is that if our women go on hunger strike they will no longer be stopped, nor will they be force-fed, but in order that they do not die in prison and so become martyrs, as soon as they grow seriously weak they will be discharged from prison. If they die outside, the law does not give two hoots, but if they survive, the moment they are recovered and have strength, they will be arrested again and obliged to continue their sentence.

It has been nicknamed the Cat-and-Mouse Act. The police are the cats and we are the mice, it seems.

I have ten days left of my sentence to serve. Some days I feel that I won't make it. For the past three days, since they stopped force-feeding me, I have had nothing but water. I feel sick, then retch but there is nothing in my system to throw up.

5th May 1913

Freedom. I thought I would jump for joy but I can barely walk. I am so weak I felt blinded by the light and noise when I shuffled out of those gates today. Flora and Mother were waiting there with Flora's car. They were anxious but thrilled to see me. Both tried to behave as though everything was normal. When Mother embraced me, she wept loudly. They wanted to take me for a meal but I could not have swallowed a mouthful. Instead, we drove back to Bloomsbury in Flora's Fiat and they put me to bed.

What a treat to have Mother with me, at Flora's. I felt safe and happy.

6th May 1913

I have slept for sixteen hours. When I woke Mother was at my side.

"You're a stubborn one you are, Dollie, just like me. But you're brave, too, and I admire you for what you've done."

I think those words mattered to me more than anything.

20th May 1913

My health is improving. I have put on some weight but my moods are dark. I am haunted by the memory of the cries from the neighbouring cells. Women in pain, women giving birth, women being force-fed. Women petrified.

336

4th June 1913

Derby Day. Epsom racecourse. Not only is this horse race one of the most important events in the English calendar, it is also a day of great social importance. The elite of British society attends this meeting, including the King and Queen with a host of guests.

What a far cry it will be from Holloway prison! I am attending because I have learned a secret. There is to be some form of protest, but I don't know what it will be. I am not involved. Flora is driving down with me. I have not told her why I want to be there, but she is happy to indulge me in this outing

I shall write more later.

Later

My God, what a shocking day.

The crowds attending were numerous indeed. And what

finery! I have rarely seen such outfits. It was like a scene dreamed up for a moving-picture show.

Epsom is shaped almost like a horse-shoe. The races are flat sprints. At one of the events, the King entered into competition a horse named Anmer, and the crowds flocked to the railings to watch it perform. Flora and I were positioned close to the finishing line.

The start took the jockeys along a fast straight that led to a long and gradual bend. The bend sharpened at Tattenham Corner, where the horses slowed down before picking up into the home straight to finish in front of the Royal Box.

As they drew towards us, the horses were galloping for their lives, battling it out towards those final furlongs. It was terribly exciting. I was jumping up and down, entirely caught up in the thrilling atmosphere: thudding hooves; fresh, sharp air; crowds shouting for the King's horse or for whichever animal they had placed their bets on. And then, suddenly, a small figure, a woman, appeared on the track. She had slipped beneath the iron railing and was pounding towards the approaching beasts. A flash of material caught my attention. White, green and purple. Our colours! Inside her coat she had sewn the suffragettes' flag. She ran like lightning towards the galloping horses and, as Anmer rounded the very last bend at Tattenham Corner, she grabbed – Lord knows how – the King's horse by its bridle.

"It's one of them women!" "What does she think she's doing?" Questions, voices, catcalls were being hurled from every direction.

"Who is that?" begged Flora. "I can't make out her face."

By then I knew exactly who it was.

Emily Wilding Davison.

"Emily, stop!" I screamed, fearing she would break her back.

The speed of the charging horses sent her flying. She actually somersaulted. It was the most extraordinary and terrifying sight.

I went cold, remembering what she had spoken of in the past.

The crowd roared and shouted. Folk were appalled. The jockey was thrown. He went flying like a bullet through the air. The horse went down, stumbling and neighing, and there on the ground stretched out before the beast lay Emily, my comrade. A heavy silence settled, as though the world was in shock, but then people began to swarm out of the throng, from behind the white-painted rails, on to the racecourse itself. There was much shouting and calling of orders. Confusion and panic took the place of the earlier competition excitement. I looked about for our bearded King George V or his wife, Queen Mary, but, although they were there somewhere, neither came forward. Lord knows what the King was thinking. Of his poor animal, I suppose. Eventually, the horse managed to stagger to its feet, but clearly it was traumatized. The jockey also got up, but not Emily. Her injuries were far too grave.

"Did you know about this?" Flora asked me.

I shook my head.

9th June 1913

Emily died yesterday afternoon. She was operated on last Friday but her condition never really improved. Mary Leigh, Charlie Marsh and several other close suffrage friends visited her bedside. Flora tells me that someone had draped the WSPU colours from the screen around her bed.

She has become the first martyr to our movement, prepared to give her life for women's rights, for what she passionately believed in, but what a horrible shock to us all!

I want to say a word or two about Emily because there are many now who are calling her crazy, or a "crank" or hysterical, particularly the newspapers and the establishment, who take every opportunity to ridicule our cause. Others are accusing her of doing more damage than good, but these remarks, all of them, are unjust.

Emily studied at Oxford University where she gained a first-class honours degree in English. Well, that is to say, she sat the exams, but because she was a woman she was not entitled to graduate or use her degree professionally. Later, she went on to London University, where she took a BA. London University is less stuffy than Oxford and they allowed her the honour.

From this it is clear that she was hardworking and determined. Emily was not a crazy crank or a fanatic, but a passionate woman and a serious-minded, sensitive individual who cared desperately that a woman's place in society should be equal to that of a man. So strong was her commitment that she believed the Cause was worth dying for if, in the dying, she could bring our fight closer to resolution.

21st June 1913

Emily's coffin, draped in our colours, was followed by 2,000 uniformed suffragettes. Charlie Marsh – she and I broke windows together in the Strand – carried a cross. Flora and I walked side by side, holding hands, sisters in silence. My mother accompanied us, too. It was very moving.

The coffin was placed on a train at King's Cross Station, headed for its final resting place in Northumberland. Many women accompanied it, keeping vigil by it. Bizarrely, I glimpsed, among the throng of faces, Celia Loverton. I called and called, but there was no way I could have reached her or caught her attention. Still, it satisfied me enormously to see her there. The word is spreading. Women everywhere are understanding that this is their battle, whoever they are, whatever their background.

Emily was buried near her home in Morpeth. It is intended that her gravestone will be inscribed, "Deeds not Words".

I think many of us are left with dozens of questions and a sense of emptiness. I know that I am.

I shall end this diary now. I began it to be my companion after the loss of Lady Violet. I have found friends and, I believe, my path in life. Now my energies must be directed towards the future: gaining a place at university and afterwards finding work as a journalist so that I can tell our suffrage story, which, by then, I trust will have a triumphant ending.

Emily is dead. Thousands of us have served some time in prisons all over Great Britain, manhandled and despised. For what? Because we believe that we are the equal of men, that we have the right to participate in the building of a just and equal society and because we cannot stand silently looking on while almost 50 per cent of British people live in conditions that are below the breadline, conditions that force them to scratch and scrape a living, in what is nothing short of an abyss.

We act with courage, proud to be women.

And so our fight goes on.

Historical note

Calls for women's rights date back many years. One of the earliest was *Vindication of the Rights of Women* published by Mary Wollstonecraft in 1792. Some individual women called for the vote during the 1830s and 1840s. However, organized campaigning did not get underway until the 1860s.

Women were not allowed in the House of Commons. Instead they relied on sympathetic MPs to present their case. In 1866 a Second Reform Bill was being debated. Emily Davies and Elizabeth Garrett presented a petition to JS Mill, MP for Westminster and a supporter of women's rights. Mill presented the petition to the House of Commons, asking for suitably qualified women to be included in the Bill. MPs voted the demand out by 194 votes to 73. Working-class men in towns gained the vote, but women were excluded.

In 1866 a woman called Lydia Becker formed the Manchester Women's Suffrage Society; other societies were set up in London and Edinburgh. Relying on friends in the House, Lydia Becker and other women presented petitions to Parliament every year. All were rejected.

At this point, many people were opposed to giving

women the vote. The arguments varied. Many people believed a woman's place was in the home and that it was against nature for women to be involved in politics; a man's world. Others believed men were superior to women and therefore politics should be left to them.

In 1884 the right to vote was extended to working-class men in rural areas. Again women were excluded. By this stage they had won the right to work as nurses, teachers, factory workers and could own property, but still they were not entitled to vote.

Women in New Zealand gained the vote in 1893 and a year later the vote was given to women in South Australia. In 1895 the British general election returned a number of MPs sympathetic to women's suffrage.

Encouraged by these events, the women's suffrage campaign gained momentum and the women's fight for the vote became a major political issue. Thousands of women up and down the country rallied to "the Cause", as it became known.

There were two main strands. The first and largest organization was the The National Union of Women's Suffrage Societies (NUWSS). Formed in 1897 under the leadership of Mrs Millicent Fawcett, it brought together all the existing women's suffrage societies. The NUWSS was run on democratic lines and believed in using only peaceful methods to win the vote. By 1914 it had a membership of nearly 60,000 women throughout the country. They were known as suffragists from the word suffrage meaning the right to vote.

The second strand was the Women's Social and Political Union (WSPU). It was formed in 1903 in Manchester by Emmeline Pankhurst and her two daughters, Christabel, a law student, and Sylvia, a socialist and artist. The aim of the WSPU was immediate enfranchisement. From the outset, the WSPU rejected traditional campaigning in favour of militant action. From 1906 its members became known as suffragettes, to distinguish them from the law-abiding suffragists.

As time passed, WSPU tactics became increasingly militant. Between 1906 and 1914 more than 1,000 women were arrested and went to prison. From 1909 many imprisoned suffragettes went on hunger strike. The government introduced force-feeding, a brutal technique, which caused a public outcry and won the suffragettes enormous support. However, not all women agreed with the militant tactics of the WSPU. While the Pankhursts and their followers rushed the Houses of Parliament, the NUWSS continued to petition peacefully and educate the public through pamphlets and books.

Despite their differences the two organizations often worked together, joining forces at huge demonstrations and meetings. By 1910 it looked as if success might be in sight. The newly formed Labour Party supported votes for women, although they were uncertain about how it should be achieved. Some Liberals, too, supported the woman's vote, although their leader, Asquith, and other powerful men in the party, were determinedly opposed. An all-party committee in the House of Commons drew up a conciliation bill, which would have given votes to women householders and wives of male householders but, largely due to the manoeuverings of Prime Minister Asquith, it was defeated.

This infuriated the WSPU. From 1911 suffragettes turned to ever more militant tactics. In 1912 they broke hundreds of windows in London's West End. The leadership was arrested except for Christabel, who fled to France.

Over the following few years, suffragettes carried out a series of arson attacks on houses, railway stations and other buildings. No one was hurt but these tactics alienated the British public.

In 1914, World War I broke out. Emmeline and Christabel called an end to their militant campaign. They threw their energies behind the war effort, working with the government to recruit soldiers and women workers. This did not please all members of the WSPU. The organization split. Some women, including Sylvia Pankhurst, joined the peace movement, others continued to work for suffrage peacefully. By 1917 the WSPU no longer existed. Suffragettes were released from prison and thousands of British women were recruited into the war effort. They worked in all areas from munitions factories to nursing on the Western Front. It was increasingly clear that women could no longer be excluded from voting. In 1918 the Electoral Reform Bill finally gave the vote to all house-holding women aged 30 and over. A second Act allowed women over 21 to become MPs. Seventeen women stood for Parliament, including Christabel Pankhurst but only one was elected and she did not take her seat.

In 1919, during a by-election, Viscountess Nancy Astor became the first female MP in the House of Commons. By 1923 there were eight women in Parliament. In 1928 the vote was extended to women aged 21 and over, on equal terms with men.

Timeline

1832 Reform Act means that the right to vote is extended to include the more prosperous males only.

1833 Slavery is abolished in Britain and its Empire.

1837 Victoria becomes queen, aged 18.

1854 The Crimean War begins, and continues until 1856.

1866 John Stuart Mill presents a women's suffrage petition to Parliament.

1867 London Society for Women's Suffrage is formed. Reform Act grants the vote to more British men. All women remain excluded.

1869 Municipal Corporations (Franchise) Act allows single women property owners the right to vote in local elections. *The Subjection of Women* by John Stuart Mill is published.

1871–1883 Private members' bills for women's suffrage are presented to every year without success.

1876 Alexander Graham Bell patents the telephone.

1882 Married Women's Property Act allows women to keep their own property after marriage (until now, a married woman's possessions were legally owned by her husband).

1882 First Boer War (in South Africa) begins.

1893 The manufacture of motor vehicles begins in the UK.

1896 The Lumières hold the first public demonstration in Britain of their Cinematographie, showing their film entitled *Arrival of a Train.*

1897 National Union of Women's Suffrage Societies (NUWSS) formed, with Millicent Fawcett as president.

1899 Second Boer War begins.

1903 Pankhursts and others launch the Women's Suffrage and Political Union (WSPU) in Manchester. They break away from traditional campaigning methods used by previous societies.

1905 Christabel Pankhurst and Annie Kenney are arrested outside the Free Trade Hall.

1909 Marjorie Wallace Dunlop becomes the first suffragette to go on hunger strike.

1910 Black Friday: police assault women following a rush on the House of Commons.

1913 April: The Prisoner's Temporary Discharge for Ill Health Act, nicknamed the Cat-and-Mouse Act is rushed through Parliament.

1918 The Representation of the People Act gives the vote to all women over 30 who are householders or wives of householders; occupiers of property with an annual rent of £45 or over and graduates of British universities. These changes give more than 8.4 million British women the right to vote.

1928 All women over 21 gain the vote, irrespective of property qualifications.